Idle Gossip

"I know your audacity and conceit exceed all bounds," she whispered in a low, angry voice, her eyes flashing.

"The Hilliard name is now associated with my own. I will not allow you or your sister to sully it by a dalliance with a creature like d'Orly." The words were quietly threatening, and wrapped in ice, but he continued to smile engagingly for the benefit of their audience.

"You are a guardian in name only, my lord," she said, barely managing a smile as they whirled past Lady Jersey. "You chose to ignore us for three years, and I see no reason for you to take a hand in our affairs now."

"Don't you, Miss Hilliard?" His features softened as he gazed into her eyes, and his arm tightened around her.

Charade of Hearts

Carol Michaels

DIAMOND BOOKS, NEW YORK

CHARADE OF HEARTS

A Diamond Book / published by arrangement with
the author

PRINTING HISTORY
Diamond edition / April 1992

ISBN: 1-55773-688-X

Diamond Books are published by The Berkley Publishing Group,
200 Madison Avenue, New York, New York 10016.
The name "DIAMOND" and its logo are trademarks
belonging to Charter Communications, Inc.

PRINTED IN THE UNITED STATES OF AMERICA

10 9 8 7 6 5 4 3 2 1

For Aunt Pauline and Uncle Pat
with love

Charade of
Hearts

Chapter 1

BELLA MEERSHAM HAD not reached her rather advanced years of forty and eight without learning to recognize the danger signs of an explosion about to break over her head. Warily, she eyed her young niece Alexandria Hilliard, whose lovely face was now suffused with a pale blush. Not, as Bella knew, a blush of maidenly modesty, but one which betokened a rare dressing down for some unfortunate—no doubt the writer of the letter Alexandria was waving about.

"How dare he! Of all the insufferable, abominable, rag-mannered—" Alex paused, searching for words, and finding none, flung the offending missive across the table to her aunt.

Bella rescued the letter from a dish of strawberry preserves and inwardly quaked as she watched Alexandria pace angrily about the breakfast room. Just like her dear Papa, Bella thought. The red hair, a trademark of the Hilliards, went hand in glove with an unpredictable temper. Alex was capable of flying into a rage whenever the well-being of her younger brother and sister were threatened, and it behooved those in the vicinity to take cover. Bella made a halfhearted effort to calm her.

"My dear, you are working yourself into a fury, and doubtless it is all a misunderstanding. Besides, it is not good for your complexion, although you look quite becoming this morning. Is that a new gown?"

Her niece was not to be diverted, and angrily snatched the letter back. "I don't wonder you cannot decipher his scrawl. His penmanship is no better than his manners. This . . . this insult is from Lord Arlington. Whatever possessed Papa

1

to name him as guardian to the twins is something I shall never understand. He has no regard for us, that much is apparent. He cares not if Marietta has the chance to contract a suitable alliance. Do you realize it has been three years since Papa died, and not once has Arlington seen fit to call?"

"I gather the Marquess is not agreeable to your plan for visiting London," Bella remarked, sipping her tea and waiting for the storm to pass. She knew from past experience that Alexandria's rages were passionate but of short duration.

"Agreeable? I doubt the gentleman was ever agreeable. He does not even grant me the courtesy of a personal reply, but has had his secretary pen this letter."

"Oh, so it's the secretary who writes so poorly. Odd, that. One would think a secretary must needs have an excellent hand. Well, you cannot fault Lord Arlington for that, dearest. Good help is so difficult to come by these days."

"And," Alex continued, ignoring her aunt, "he writes that it is not *convenient* for his lordship to entertain us at this time, and recommends we continue to reside here at Allenswood. Aunt Bella, it is so unfair. If Arlington were any sort of a proper guardian, he would take measures himself to see that Marietta was presented."

"It's very bad of him, Alexandria, I am sure, but perhaps it is for the best after all. I did not wish to trouble you, but I have heard some rather unsavory rumors concerning the company Arlington chooses to keep. Really, I have not been at all comfortable with your notion of visiting him in Town. I fear he is not a suitable person for you to know, even if dear Anthony did name him as the children's guardian. Besides, my dear, we go on quite well in the country, and I cannot think what London could possibly have to offer that we do not enjoy here."

Her wrath vented, Alex resumed her seat, and made an effort to compose herself. "Allenswood is fine for you, Aunt Bella, and perhaps for me as well, as I am past the marrying age now. But it is hardly fair to keep Jeremy and

Marietta here. She is turned seventeen and deserves a Season in London. I know she'd make an excellent match if only the ton could see her. She is beautiful, isn't she, and with such sweetness, I know she would take. And now that Jeremy's finished school, he should be allowed to see something of Town before he settles down to manage the estate."

"My dear, I wish you would not think of yourself as an old maid. You can hardly be considered an ape-leader at twenty-three. Why, there are any number of gentlemen in the neighbourhood dangling after you. There's young Sefton, who seems to spend an inordinate amount of time writing you sonnets—even if they are quite dreadful—and there's that nice Mr. Marston, who I am certain would offer for you in a minute if you would give him an ounce of encouragement. And, of course, Lord Barstow. Why, he was just telling me last evening that he counts it a privilege to be of service to you."

Alex laughed at her aunt, her customary good humour restored. "Shame on you, Aunt Bella. Andrew Sefton is only a boy, and you know it would be reprehensible in me to encourage him. As for John Marston, while he is probably the kindest gentleman I have ever met, he would bore me to tears within a week."

"Lord Barstow would—"

"Lord Barstow's mama would never approve. She will pick out a prettily behaved schoolroom miss whom she can manage, and Barstow will do precisely as his mama bids, I promise you. But it's not my future which concerns me. I have to think of Marietta, and I am determined that she shall have a Season. If Arlington is so disobliging, why then we shall just have to manage without his assistance."

"Alexandria, promise me you will not do anything rash."

"Not rash, my dearest aunt. I only intend to insure that Marietta has her Season. Arlington may stand as guardian to the children, but he has no control over my actions. I have my legacy from Mama, and I shall use it to take us all to London."

"I knew you were planning something foolish. You

cannot have thought, child. Why, we would have no place to stay, and we wouldn't know anyone. We would be social outcasts. We had as well stay here at Allenswood."

"Nonsense. I shall appeal to Mr. Crimshaw. You must remember him, for he used to handle all Papa's affairs, and I know he will be able to help us. I shall write to him at once and ask him to engage a suitable house for us, and the necessary staff. He has lived in London all his life, and I am certain he shall be able to tell us just how to go on."

"It is not just a matter of finding accommodations, Alex, although that will be difficult enough this late in the year, but it is Society I am thinking of. Without an entree into the right circles—"

"Do not fret, Aunt Bella. I'll write to Lady Fitzhugh as well. She was Mama's dearest friend, and I have no doubt she will be wistful of seeing her old friend's family. Mama always said she was very kind and not at all high in the instep, although she is received everywhere."

Bella retrieved the hartshorn from her reticule as Alex left the room. She felt distinctly queasy. There was no sacrifice Alex would not make for the sake of the twins. If she thought removing to London would benefit Marietta or Jeremy, then they would soon find themselves in London. Bella looked around the cozy morning room regretfully, fearful that her pleasant life was about to take an unpleasant turn.

Her thoughts were shattered as Jeremy and Marietta erupted into the room. Their laughter and noise filled the small room as they exuberantly hugged Bella, and then each other, dancing around and around in their excitement. Bella couldn't help smiling as she watched them. Like Alexandria, they both had the Hilliard hair, but there the resemblance ended. Where Alex was tall, Marietta was petite. Alex's eyes were of a silvery green, sometimes almost gray, but Marietta's eyes were a clear crystal-blue, and set off by long, black lashes. Marietta's hair was a lighter shade of red, highlighted with streaks of gold. It produced a halo effect that was quite misleading.

Jeremy, a head taller than his twin, had the same dark

auburn locks as Alex, and they tumbled over his wide brow in careless disarray. He gave Marietta a final twirl, and they ended their impromptu dance before their aunt. Jeremy bowed deeply, and Marietta sank into a low, graceful curtsey.

"Will we do for London, do you think?" Jeremy asked, with a teasing smile for his aunt.

Bella nodded, and Alex agreed from her post at the doorway. "But mind you, if we're to cut a dash, you'll both have to stand still for fittings for new clothes."

"A dress coat by Scott?" Jeremy pleaded. "Do say yes, Alex. Deverow says he's all the crack."

"But Jeremy," Marietta couldn't resist taunting him, "Lord Barstow swears by Hallsby. I know I have heard him say countless times that a coat by Hallsby is far superior to that of either Scott or Weston."

"Don't listen to her, Alex," Jeremy retorted. "Just because he visited London once two years ago, he thinks he knows everything."

Bella sniffed. "If you mean to conduct yourselves like a pair of heathens, there will be no point in taking you to London. Now be seated, and try for a little conduct, if you please." She favoured each of them with a speaking glance. "And I shall remind you that Lord Barstow is a fine gentleman, very sensitive and the soul of amiability. Instead of poking fun at him, Jeremy, you would do well to pattern yourself after him."

She cast a sly glance at Alexandria, for Bella still cherished hopes of a connection between their houses. Barstow's lands marched with Allenswood, and it would be comfortable to have Alex installed there as the future Lady Barstow.

"We all know Lord Barstow is a paragon," Alex agreed, smiling, quite aware of her aunt's matchmaking. "However, I do feel we will do best to be guided by Mr. Crimshaw in London. He has, after all, lived there all his life, and Papa always said his advice was invaluable."

"But Alex," Marietta said, looking puzzled, "what about Lord Arlington? He is our guardian, and I should think he would be the proper person to advise us and show us about."

"Unfortunately, Lord Arlington has informed me that it is not *convenient* for him to entertain us at present, and, in fact, has recommended we remain here."

"Lord, that's torn it," muttered Jeremy.

"I see no reason for concern," Alex replied with measured calm. "We have managed extremely well for three years without any assistance whatsoever from the Marquess, and if Lady Fitzhugh will stand our friend, we shall not have need of his help now."

Marietta giggled. "Will it not be strange, Alex, if we chance to meet him in London? Why, we would not recognize our guardian or he us!" Her dimples peeped out as she laughed at the confusion such a scene would evolve. She continued to pour out tea for them, totally unconscious of how delightful she appeared. The sun coming in the window highlighted her hair, her eyes sparkled, and her smile was infectious.

"Indeed, it would be most awkward," Alex answered, thinking again that this lovely child must have a Season. "I intend to call on him once we're settled. There will be nothing he can do then except to acknowledge us. Perhaps he may even prove to be of some use."

Bella thought that notion a trifle optimistic. She had heard scores of *on-dits* concerning the redoubtable Lord Arlington, even living retired as they did. He was one of London's most sought-after bachelors, and seemed immune to the lures thrown out to him by matchmaking mamas, preferring instead to while away his evenings with actresses and ballerinas. He appeared to have nothing but scorn for Society's reigning belles, and his arrogance and outrageous behavior would have been condemned in a man of lesser rank and wealth. It was not a connection she wished her niece to pursue. Anthony Hilliard, for whatever misguided reasons, had named him the children's guardian, however, and until now, Alex would not hear a word against the man.

"Excuse me, Miss Hilliard," Susan, the front parlour

maid, interrupted, dropping a curtsey. "Lord Barstow is wishful of a word with you."

"Very well, Susan. Please show him into the drawing room, and tell him Miss Meersham and I will join him directly." Alex, who had been about to deny her presence to their visitor, had caught the frown on her aunt's face. Better a prose with Barstow now than a scold from Aunt Bella later. With a quelling look for her sister's impish grin, Alex rose and followed her aunt from the room.

Jonathan Quimby, Viscount Barstow, was, as Bella lost no opportunity to point out, a fine figure of a man. He stood six foot tall, with dark hair pomaded into what he considered a modish style. His broad shoulders may have owned some of their breadth to padding, and his roman nose might be a shade too prominent for classical good looks, but Bella believed him to be exceedingly handsome.

He was dressed for riding, in a dark green coat of excellent cut worn over a short waistcoat, beige breeches, and glossy brown top boots. Bella, casting an experienced eye over his sartorial elegance, greeted him with a marked degree of warmth to cover Alex's cooler reception.

"My dear Miss Meersham," he said, bowing stiffly. "You are in looks this morning. And, Miss Hilliard, your loveliness quite takes one's breath away."

Not noticeably, thought Alex, and then chided herself for being uncharitable. She knew he meant well. Smiling, she enquired, "And to what do we owe the pleasure of such an early call? I fear you find us quite at sixes and sevens, sir."

"I know you will forgive my impetuous visit when I confide the reason. Mother is giving a small rout next month, and I rode posthaste to deliver your invitation personally. It would be a most lacklustre affair were you unable to grace it with your presence. And of course, yours also, Miss Meersham."

"How very kind of you," Bella said. "But I fear we must decline. We shall, no doubt, be in London next month."

"What? Why, how is this?" he said, turning to Alex with an accusing look. "You mentioned nothing of any such plans last evening."

Alex could have cheerfully boxed her aunt's ears for disclosing their plans, but she replied calmly, "Surely, my lord, you know it has long been my intention to provide Marietta with a Season. Now that she has turned seventeen, I feel it is time."

Barstow, for once, appeared at a loss for words. "It just seems so sudden," he murmured after a moment. "Have you considered this quite thoroughly? You know a Season in London requires a great deal of advance preparation, and it is rather late in the year to begin making arrangements. Have you leased a house as yet?"

"Our arrangements are not complete, at present," Alex hedged, unwilling to admit that Arlington had refused to sponsor his wards. "We shall, of course, have assistance from Papa's man of business."

"Believe me, Miss Hilliard, I speak from experience when I tell you that London is a vast and confusing metropolis. Why, I got quite lost there on one or two occasions when first I visited. I shudder to think of delicately reared females, such as yourself and Miss Meersham, adrift in London with no gentleman to offer you his protection."

"Thank you, my lord, for your concern. However, Jeremy will be accompanying us, and you must know that the Marquess of Arlington stands as guardian to both Jeremy and Marietta," Alex replied, with a warning look at her aunt.

"Jeremy? Arlington? Ah, Miss Hilliard, you cannot have considered. Jeremy is only a boy, and unschooled in Town ways. And," he laughed harshly, "as for Arlington—well, if he ever bestirred himself on behalf of any *respectable* lady, it is more than I ever heard. No, I cannot be easy in my mind with your plan."

"Really, Lord Barstow—"

"I know, you will say that I worry overmuch. But you, my dear Miss Hilliard, have never been in London. I know whereof I speak, I assure you. If only I could accompany you, be on hand to lend you the benefit of my advice, how much easier in my mind I should be."

"It is extremely kind of you to concern yourself, but we will have Papa's man of business to guide us, and Mama's dear friend, Lady Fitzhugh, as well, so—"

He had not heard a word she said, and interrupted without apology. "Perhaps something might yet be arranged. I've been intending to return to London for some time, although I rather thought that next year when—but that is of no importance. It might as well be this year as next. I cannot promise you anything, not definitely, but I believe I will take my leave now and speak to Mother at once. I will not hold out to you empty promises, but I feel you may be hopeful that something can be arranged. Yes, indeed."

"My lord," Alex cried, far more alarmed than hopeful. "I assure you that it is not at all necessary to rearrange your plans. I'm deeply appreciative of the kindness you do us, but I beg you not to put yourself to so much trouble. Mama had many friends in London, and I am sure we shall manage quite well."

"Let us not be hasty, child," Bella said, rising and taking Barstow's arm. "I find his lordship's idea an excellent one, if his mama may be brought to agree. We should be so much more comfortable with a gentleman we know so well to escort us and show us all the sights."

Alex watched helplessly as Bella showed Lord Barstow out, their heads bent together deep in plans. Visions of Barstow dogging her footsteps in London assailed her. And he *would* try to manage Jeremy, she thought. It was amazing how he always managed to say just the one thing to put her brother on edge.

Well, there was little sense in worrying over what could not be undone. And it was not likely, she consoled herself, that Amelia Quimby would allow her only son to visit London at the same time as the Hilliards. Not if she knew Lady Barstow. It was ironical, she thought, that Lady Barstow should spend so much of her time trying to prevent an alliance that had little hope of ever coming about. Much as Bella might wish it, Alex would never accept Jonathan Quimby in marriage.

Bella had lectured her on more than one occasion for

what she termed Alex's foolishness. Whistling a fortune down the wind, and closing her eyes to such an agreeable connection. Until recently, Alex had managed to merely laugh at her aunt's obvious maneuvering. But the thought of Jeremy and Marietta making their debut in London brought home to her that Jeremy would soon be taking a wife. A new wife and a new mistress for Allenswood. She had managed the estate successfully for the past three years, and she owned it would not be easy for her to hand over the reins to another. It would certainly be better for everyone if she were to marry.

Bella thought Lord Barstow the perfect solution, but try as she would, Alex found it difficult to even like their pompous neighbour. He was not well read, of but moderate intelligence, and totally lacking in a sense of humour. He frequently questioned her when she found something amusing, for he seldom understood her own sense of the absurd. But what vexed her most was his annoying habit of presuming to lecture Jeremy and Marietta.

His homilies had little effect on Marietta—other than setting her in whoops—but with Jeremy it was different. He deeply resented what he considered Barstow's presumption in censuring his conduct. It seemed to Alex that whenever his brother was with the older man, he changed from a laughing, good-natured young man into a sullen, ill-mannered boy. And that, above all else, clinched the matter in her mind. She would not wed merely to please her relatives, yet neither would she consider a man they held in aversion.

Sighing, Alex recalled her parents and how happily they had been wedded. She could still remember the way her mama's face would light up when Papa entered the room. And for many minutes her parents were quite capable of forgetting anyone else was present. They were so devoted. Alexandria thought regretfully that if she could not have that kind of union, she would much prefer remaining a spinster.

Her melancholy thoughts were interrupted as Marietta

came into the library, three morning dresses draped over her arm.

"Alex, do you think these would be suitable for London if Madame Dupre were to add new ribbons and lace?" She watched anxiously as her sister inspected the gowns. Aunt Bella had told her that Alex would be footing the cost of her Season, not, as she had supposed, the trust fund set up for her and Jeremy. She couldn't understand Lord Arlington's refusal to finance the London visit, for he had never before refused them anything of a reasonable nature. Marietta had quietly decided to find a way of visiting the Marquess in London, and explaining to him that Alex could ill-afford the expense of a Season for them all. She was certain that once he understood the matter, he would be most agreeable. In the meantime, she didn't wish Alex to be put to any unnecessary expense.

Alexandria, however, was shaking her head as she fingered the material. "I do not think it would be worthwhile, but we shall see what Madame Dupre has to say. You might be able to wear them until our new gowns are made up. Come and look at this fashion journal, and you will see how sadly out of date we are."

When Bella returned from paying her morning calls, she found her nieces still in the library, their heads bent together over the fashion plates. Marietta at once implored Bella to help her persuade Alex to order a celestial-blue crepe gown. It was shown with an opera front, open over a pale blue satin slip.

"Would she not look magnificent in this, with Mama's sapphires to set it off? But she will not even consider it. Alex only wants to look at gowns for me. Aunt Bella, tell her she must have new gowns as well."

Bella nodded her agreement, but her mind was elsewhere, and she begged their attention. "I've the most exciting news, my dears. I've just come from Lady Barstow, and she tells me she means to open Barstow House for the Season. We shall not be quite without friends after all, and you know Lady Barstow moves in the first circles. Is it not wonderful? I'm certain we must have Lord Barstow to thank. He must be very taken with you, Alexandria, to follow us to London."

"Certainly, it will be agreeable to have acquaintances there," Alex answered with unruffled calm. "But I am confident Lady Fitzhugh will introduce us to all her friends, and we shall not be obliged to hang on Lord Barstow's coat sleeves.

"He would not consider—"

"Aunt Bella, I know you mean well, but if you love me, stop your matchmaking, for we are not at all suited."

"Are you certain, my love? I don't wish to upset you, but I sometimes think you are blind to his most excellent qualities, and he, poor man, is so devoted to you."

"I do know how good he is, but I think there must be more than that for a happy marriage. No doubt I shall remain a spinster, but I assure you that is a state I much prefer over marriage with someone I would forever be coming to points with. You would do much better to concentrate your efforts on Marietta's marriage. Think on it, Aunt Bella, for that is why we go to London."

Marietta smiled, her eyes dreamy. "Perhaps I shall meet a gentleman like Papa. Do you remember, Alex, how Mama used to tell us she fell in love with him the very first time she saw him?"

"Yes, at Lady Tattinger's ball. She said there were dozens and dozens of beautiful young ladies there, but Papa never looked at anyone else."

Bella's eyes grew misty as she recalled her sister's debut. "Your mama created a sensation that year. It wasn't just your papa who thought she was beautiful—everyone did. When she entered a ballroom, she made all the other chits look like schoolroom misses, and she but a girl of seventeen herself. Ah, but she had an air about her. She was the toast of the Town, and they all said she was an incomparable. Your mama could have married a duke, you know, had she wished, but I do not believe she ever considered another besides Anthony. Your papa swept her off her feet."

"Mama said she stood up with him twice that first night, and would have danced every dance with him except

Grandmama would not allow it," Marietta said, her eyes large with envy.

"It would have been most improper," Bella said, truly shocked to even think of such a thing. "Do remember, should we be fortunate enough to procure vouchers for Almack's, that you must be on your best behaviour. You mustn't ever even think of standing up twice with the same gentleman, and on no account, dance the waltz until one of the Patronesses gives you her approval. To do so would sink you beneath reproach, and your Season would be ruined. And why I'm running on about Almack's, I cannot think, when we may not even be able to procure vouchers."

"I am certain that if Lady Fitzhugh finds us acceptable, she'll be able to help us there. Mama always said Lady Fitzhugh knew everyone who was anyone. Unless she thinks we're country dowds, I'm sure she will do everything in her power to launch Marietta, for Mama's sake."

"Country dowds, indeed," sniffed Bella. "I am certain, Alexandria, that the Hilliards and the Meershams must be found acceptable in any company they choose to seek. I have no cause to blush for your manners. At least, I won't if you'll only remember to keep a civil tongue in your head and refrain from using that vulgar cant your brother teaches you."

"But it's so descriptive," Alex said, laughing. "No, no, don't alarm yourself, Aunt Bella. I'm only teasing. I promise to mind my tongue. You know I would not do anything to endanger Marietta's debut."

"I know you would not intentionally do so, but you do have a deplorable tendency to speak without thinking. No doubt it is the Hilliard temper. I fear it leads you to act impulsively at times, without giving proper thought to where your actions may lead."

Alexandria was honest enough to own that there was much truth in her aunt's words. Sometimes, it seemed as though words poured from her mouth on their own volition, and though she always regretted it, it was difficult to control her temper. She promised to do her best to mend her ways, and then diverted Bella's attention to the fashion journals, and the ladies spent the rest of the afternoon in that agreeable manner.

Peace reigned at Allenswood for the next two weeks. Alexandria, feverishly wishing for a reply from Lady Fitzhugh, was careful to present only a cheerful demeanour before her sister and aunt. She didn't wish them to suspect how worried she was. Not that Marietta would have noticed. The girl passed her days in a trance-like state, imagining her come out in London. Bella, too, had her share of dreams. She cherished the notion of chaperoning, not one, but two, young ladies who would follow in their mother's footsteps to become the new toasts of the Town.

Jeremy, unconcerned with the planning for London, had ridden with his friend Andrew Sefton to a nearby town. The two young men, as planned, spent a week there, the highlight of which was a boxing match that had been widely advertised. It was not until the day of his return that chaos descended on the peaceful house.

The ladies were closeted with Madame Dupre, who had been persuaded to lend her personal assistance in refurbishing their wardrobes. The small drawing room was cluttered with muslins, crepes, satins, laces, and hats of every size and description, when Jeremy strode in, angrily kicking aside a length of muslin.

"What right does Barstow have to censure my conduct?" he demanded of his elder sister, ignoring the others. "He is neither related to me, nor my guardian, and I am warning you, Alex, I will not stand for it."

Alexandria, kneeling before Marietta to mark a hemline, was so startled she pricked her finger with a pin. She turned to face her brother, who stood in the doorway, furiously snapping his riding crop against his boots.

"Whatever has Lord Barstow done to put you in such a taking that you forget your manners?" she said sharply.

Jeremy flushed and belatedly made a bow to Madame Dupre, begging her pardon. He apologized sulkily to his aunt and sister as well, and then asked Alex if she would allow him a word in private. She promised she would attend him shortly in the library. Bella made as if to accompany her, but Alex waved her back.

"Pray, don't disturb yourself, Aunt Bella. I gather he's in a rage over some·well-intentioned, if ill-judged, advice from our neighbour. You continue here, and I shall return as quickly as I can."

When Alexandria opened the door to the library, Jeremy was striding back and forth in considerable agitation. Seeing his sister, he apologized again for bursting in on her. "But, by heavens, the fellow's a coxcomb, and there's no enduring him!"

"I will agree that Lord Barstow frequently takes too much upon himself, but you must own that generally his advice is sound, and it's always well meant." Seeing the chagrin on his face, she relented, adding with a smile, "It's only that he presents it in such an odious manner that makes one long to hit him."

"I knew you would understand, Alex. Sefton and I had a time—it was beyond anything great—and I even won a tidy bundle backing the black. By Jove, what a fight it was. You should've seen it." Recollecting that he was addressing his sister, Jeremy laughed, and continued, "Well, you know what I mean. Anyway, after the mill, Sefton and I went over to Chandler's for a drink, and who walks in but Barstow. And without so much as a by-your-leave, he joins us. I give you my word, Alex, even then I was prepared to do the civil, and even offered to stand him a drink."

"That was well done of you," she murmured.

"Yes, it was, but he didn't appreciate it. *He* starts lecturing me on the evils of gambling. And in front of Sefton, too. Told me I could get into deep water and all sorts of balderdash about how green I was. *He* said I mustn't be a charge on you, and *he* would undertake to guide me when we go up to London."

"I'm surprised you didn't land him a facer," his sister said sympathetically, and then, alarmed, "You didn't, did you, Jeremy?"

"Lord, no!" he assured her. "But I did tell him that neither you nor I stood in need of his guidance."

"And what did he say to that?"

"He said that his dearest wish is that one day he will take the place of the brother I never had." He paused to see what effect this had on Alex, and with the air of one bracing himself to hear the worst added, "You wouldn't marry him, would you?"

Alexandria tried not to laugh at his woebegone expression, and impulsively hugged him. "You may rest easy on that head, love. Barstow holds no appeal for me. However, it is excessively awkward for you to be forever pulling caps with him when we are such close neighbours. Do try for a little conduct, Jeremy, and try to remember that his intentions are good."

"Fudge! What about *his* lack of conduct? It's not very civil of him to always be lecturing me. He doesn't have the right."

She sighed. "I know, and I promise I shall talk to him about it. Now run along and change. The Vicar and the Crombys are dining with us this evening."

Alex watched him leave, but did not hasten back to the drawing room. She needed a few minutes alone to compose herself before joining the others. It was becoming increasingly difficult to maintain her cheerful facade. It wasn't just the worry over Jeremy's growing aversion to Barstow. What on earth would she do if Lady Fitzhugh and Mr. Crimshaw did not answer her letters?

Marietta had her heart set on a Season now, and even Jeremy was looking forward to London. She could not bear to disappoint them. She cursed her wicked tongue, knowing she should have said nothing until her arrangements were complete. If only Arlington had not behaved so reprehensibly, she thought, blinking back tears. If he were any kind of proper guardian, *he* would provide his ward with a come out. Taking a deep breath, Alex lifted her chin. Her sister deserved to have a Season, and she had rashly promised it to her. Come what might, she would find a way—she must find a way—to provide her one.

Chapter 2

TWO DISMAL DAYS of constant rain followed, which perfectly matched Alexandria's gloomy feelings. Almost ready to cancel her plans, she rose despondently on Friday only to find the sun shining brilliantly once more. Hoping it was an omen, she hurried downstairs to the breakfast room. Bella was there before her, busily sorting the correspondence that Susan had left on the silver salver. Postponing the moment for as long as possible, Alex poured her tea before glancing at the stack of letters Bella placed beside her plate.

Trying to appear unconcerned, Alex sifted through the mail. Her stomach muscles tightened as she noted one letter addressed to her from Crimshaw and, directly beneath it, an elegant envelope bearing Lady Fitzhugh's insignia. With trembling fingers, she opened the one from Crimshaw first. If he had not been able to secure lodgings on such short notice, Lady Fitzhugh's reply would be of little importance. Glancing briefly at her aunt, who seemed immersed in her own correspondence, Alex quickly scanned the lines. A moment later she let out a most unlady-like whoop.

"Aunt Bella, Crimshaw has replied at last, and he has not only gotten us a wonderful town house, but an excellent staff as well."

"I am very glad, my dear, but surely that is no reason to screech like a hoyden."

"I am sorry, it is only that I feared he might be unable to find us anything on such short notice. And he confirms how very fortunate we are, because the Devereaux of Sussex were to have the house, but a death in the family changed

17

their plans at the last moment. And he has engaged their butler, housekeeper, and chef for us, too."

"Well, if the Devereaux were to have it, then we may be assured that it is situated in a good part of Town. I recall the family quite well. I wonder who could have died?"

"Lord Hatherfill, the Duke's uncle, and I am vastly obliged to him for popping off so conveniently."

"Alexandria!"

Bubbling with laughter, Alex rose and came round the table to kiss her aunt. "Forgive me, dearest. I know I am a perfect beast for teasing you so. It is only that I am so relieved."

Her aunt patted her hand, reminding her again that she must reform her ways if they were going to London.

Alex returned to her seat, promising blithely, "I shall be the soul of discretion and behave so well you will not recognize me. Now, let us see what Lady Fitzhugh writes." She opened the second letter, and sat for several minutes, her brow wrinkled in concentration. Lady Fitzhugh had written in haste apparently, so great was her excitement at being reunited with the Hilliards. At least that was what Alex thought she meant. She struggled to decipher the crossed and recrossed lines.

"I cannot make it all out, but there is a part about a Lady Jersey, and then she writes we must call on her immediately we arrive in London. Oh, how very kind of her."

"Kind, indeed, if she intends to present you to Lady Jersey. Sally Jersey is one of the Patronesses at Almack's, and her seal of approval is all you need to be admitted to the first circles."

"Aunt Bella, isn't it wonderful? Everything is working out splendidly. I'm so excited my heart is beating double-time. I just knew the sun shining this morning was a good omen."

Bella smiled at her niece's excitement and confessed that she, too, was beginning to look forward to their trip. It did not look to be the disaster she had been fearing.

"Well, my dear, if we are to be in London by April first, as you wish, I'd best set Mary and Susan to packing the linens. When you write Lady Fitzhugh, please say all that is proper from me. I wonder if she has changed. She was rather flamboyant when your mama and I knew her, although always most agreeable. I shall look forward to renewing our acquaintance."

It seemed there were a thousand and one details to attend to, and the days flew by. Alex was stunned at the myriad packing apparently necessary for a protracted stay in London. Aunt Bella had insisted on packing all the bedding and linen, for they were to spend two nights on the road, and one could not, she explained, depend on the sheets being properly aired. Also the silver service and the best china had to be cleaned and boxed, for there was no telling what the house in Ventnor Square might contain.

It was with a quiver of mirth that Alex viewed the mountain of luggage occupying the front hall on the morning of their departure, and she wondered if there was a similar mountain at the Barstow Manor House. Lord Barstow had informed her that his mother would leave for London on the morning of the 29th of March, and Alex had immediately set forward their own date of departure to the 28th, much to Bella's dismay.

Her aunt cited arguments for departing with Lord Barstow, ranging from their safety and comfort to the pleasure to be derived from traveling with congenial company. Alex laughed at her notion that they stood in any danger, pointing out that John Coachman, two outriders, Jeremy, and their groom Tenby would certainly provide adequate protection.

"And, dearest aunt of mine," she teased, "you are indulging in daydreams if you think we would derive any pleasure from listening to Lord Barstow lecture Jeremy and Marietta for three entire days. Indeed, we would be fortunate to survive such a trip."

The weather favoured her decision, and the morning of their departure dawned clear and sunny. After endless confusion in packing and repacking, the ladies were finally seated in their old but still elegant town coach. Jeremy chose to ride for the first leg of the trip, and his restless

chestnut pranced around the carriage in a fret to be off.
Tenby was still loading the *foregon* and second coach, with
conflicting directions from Mary and Susan. Both girls were
agog with excitement over their visit to London and, as a
consequence, were more hindrance than help.

Alex, impatient herself, left Tenby in charge, and gave
John Coachman the nod to start. The carriage rolled forward
at a dignified pace, which Old John felt befitted the station
of the Misses. Having been with the family above thirty
years, he was immune to Alex's pleas that he step up the
pace, merely turning a deaf ear. She resigned herself to the
slow speed, fully doubting that they would reach Town in
only three days.

The excitement and anticipation of setting forth soon
wore off, and although they broke the tedium of the journey
frequently with rest stops, Alex felt stiff and out of sorts
when they finally reached London late in the afternoon of
the first.

Bella was able to point out some of the more notable
sights as they passed through Town, but it had been years
since she was in London, and she was amazed at the
changes in the metropolis and by the vast number of
carriages and pedestrians in the streets. Even had she been
an expert on London, it is doubtful she would have been
able to keep apace with the dozens of questions Marietta
flung at her.

Alex smiled at her younger sister, who had let down the
window and was regarding the fashionable street with large,
dazzled eyes. She turned to glance out her own window as
their carriage slowed to a halt, narrowly avoiding an
overturned dray cart. Two gentlemen had just stepped out
the doorway of one of the narrow buildings lining the street,
and paused there, idly conversing. Alex's attention was
drawn to the taller of the pair, and she knew immediately
that she was seeing her first "non-peril." Impeccably tai-
lored, his broad shoulders did justice to his blue kerseymere
coat, and the lace at this throat and cuffs looked impossibly
white and crisp. He was unusually handsome, she thought,
watching him smile at his companion. He turned his head

slightly, possibly aware of her scrutiny, and her good impression of him was at once spoiled. The look of haughty disdain in his brown eyes brought a blush to her cheeks, and she hurriedly turned away, praying their carriage would not be long delayed.

Her wish was granted, and they moved off promptly. She listened to Marietta's chatter and her aunt's soft voice answering the child's questions and slowly recovered her composure. There had been no reason for the gentleman to stare so rudely, she thought. Handsome is as handsome does, Aunt Bella would say, and she blithely dismissed the gentleman as an arrogant, vain creature whose censure need not concern her.

Moments later they arrived in Hanover Square, and the heavy carriage at last halted on the cobblestone street. Alex, glad of Jeremy's assistance as he handed her down from the carriage, paused to look about. It was an elegant square, built around a small park enclosed by a low railing. All of the houses appeared large and of the first quality. Crimshaw had done well, indeed.

The three ladies stood surveying the house on the south side of the square that would be their home for the next few months, and voted themselves pleased. They were still admiring the frontage when the wide double doors swung open and a young footman rushed out to assist them. The butler stood just within the large, marbled foyer, waiting to welcome them.

Dobbs, as he was called, soon had them comfortably settled in the yellow drawing room and an appetizing tea set before them. Alex glanced around with marked approval. Although it was not really cold, the air still held a dampness, and the fire in the stone hearth was a welcome sight. She gazed at it, mesmerized as its flickering lights picked out the amber thread woven in the window tapestries and cast a warm glow over the room.

Sipping her perfectly brewed tea and nibbling a biscuit, Alex would have been content to remain in her chair indefinitely. She knew, however, that the housekeeper, Mrs. Delahan, was anxiously awaiting an interview and

Monsieur Andre, the French chef, wished to discuss the dinner menu.

She reluctantly informed Dobbs that as soon as she put off her traveling dress, she would see Mrs. Delahan. Turning to her aunt, she asked, "Would you be an angel and order dinner for us? And have it set back, for I'm afraid it will be some time before we see Jeremy again. He was so eager to see something more of Town—I only hope he does not lose his way."

"I should not worry your head over him, dear. He has our direction and has only to make enquiries, but where has Marietta wandered off to?"

"She said she was going to explore the house. I don't know where she finds the energy, for I vow I am exhausted. If you see her, ask her to come up and change. Then we can all be comfortable."

Marietta had paused only long enough to cast off her hat and pelisse before asking Dobbs if the house contained a library. His countenance did not betray his curiosity, but he wondered that such a taking little miss would immediately seek out the library. She did not, he thought, look at all bookish, but then one never could tell. He opened the paneled doors for her, and she thanked him prettily.

It didn't take Marietta long to find the volume she was seeking and she lifted down the heavy tome. The engraved cover proclaimed the book to be the *Index to the House of Lords* and she anxiously thumbed through it till she found the entry she was looking for. She then quickly copied the direction for Lord Arlington's London town house and tucked the slip of paper in her reticule.

If she could convince Alex to allow her to go shopping tomorrow with only Susan to accompany her, she would hire a carriage and call on Lord Arlington. She was certain that once matters were properly presented to him, he wouldn't refuse to allow the trust to underwrite her come out. If the *La Belle Assemblée* was accurate, she would have need of innumerable gowns and ensembles to present a respectable figure, and she was determined not to allow Alex to bear the cost of that. After all, she reasoned, Alex was getting quite old, and it did not look as if she would ever marry, so she would have need of her own fortune. Feeling rather noble, Marietta hurried off to find her bedchamber and change her gown before her sister should come looking for her.

Alex found her an hour later seated demurely in the drawing room, attired in a charming sprig muslin with a high waist and tiny puffed sleeves. She looked very sweet and innocent, but had Alex been less tired, she might have noted the brilliance in Marietta's eyes and recognized that her tongue was running on greased wheels—a sure sign that her sister was up to mischief.

Bella cast a suspicious look at Marietta, but decided the girl's high spirits could be marked down to the excitement of her being in London, and she merely remarked that if her niece meant to run on in such a manner when she appeared in Society, she'd soon find herself described as a bubble-head.

Jeremy entered, in high spirits himself, and apologized for his lateness, having, as Alex had guessed, lost his way. "It's not like anything I had imagined," he confided. "There are so many streets, and they are crowded with all sorts of people, and jammed full of carriages and horses, and you won't believe the amount of noise and bustle it all makes. But just by sheer luck, I found myself in front of Cribb's Parlour, and who should come strolling out but Harry Collingsworth. You must recall him, Alex, for we were at school together, though I barely recognized him. He looks like a regular Town beau now."

Dobbs' entrance to announce dinner effectively stopped the flow of information Jeremy was so anxious to impart. Still, he greeted the announcement with enthusiasm, confiding to Alex as he took her in that he was as hungry as a bear.

Jeremy enlivened dinner with a descriptive account of all the sights he'd seen, but to the ladies' disappointment, he was unable to describe the style of dress of any of the ladies he'd seen. He could, however, recall in great detail, and did, the appearance of several dandies, and in particular, his

friend Harry, whose major accomplishment seemed to be
the ability to tie his neckcloth in the dashing style known as
the *Mathematical*. And, Jeremy told them, his friend had
most generously offered to teach him this valuable art.

"I am glad you have found a friend so readily, Jeremy,
but do keep in mind that you shall be needed to act as our
escort," Alex said, and could not help smiling at his
crestfallen air. "I don't doubt, however, it will be long
before several gentlemen are vying for that privilege."

"When they see Marietta, they will be beating down the
door," he agreed cheerfully, with a teasing look for his
sister.

Bella judged it appropriate to change the subject before
they turned her niece's head, and suggested they discuss
their plans for the morning. It was agreed that the first order
of business must be to call on Lady Fitzhugh, which treat
Jeremy hastily declined, although he pledged his word he
would return early.

He excused himself shortly after dinner, confiding that
Harry had invited him to join a party of his particular
cronies for an evening at Covent Garden Theatre, and he
hastened off to change his clothes for more suitable evening
attire. He left the ladies planning an early evening, tired
from their long journey, and anxious for the morning and
their first venture forth in London.

It appeared they had the blessings of the gods, for the
morning dawned bright and sunny, with only a hint of soft
April breeze. Bella, after assuring herself that she looked
every inch the proper chaperone, scurried down the hall to
check on her nieces. It was of the first importance that they
present an impressive appearance when they called on Lady
Fitzhugh.

After tapping lightly on Alex's door and bidden to enter,
she found her young charge attired in one of her new
gowns, faithfully copied by Madame Dupre from the
fashion journals. Alex pirouetted before her, and was
declared to be the epitome of elegance. Her half dress was
of a deep green, veiled by a tunic of pale green muslin. She

had chosen a stylish hat adorned with green ribbons of the same shade as the tunic, and it set off her auburn locks perfectly. Alex curtsied at the compliments Bella paid her, and together the ladies went to inspect Marietta.

When she saw her sister, Alex felt vindicated in her judgment to bring the child to London. Marietta looked enchanting in a pretty china-blue walking dress adorned with blue and white ribbons, which played up the blue in her eyes. Her light hair was brushed back, hanging in long curls. A matching chip straw hat lay on the bed, and Alex picked it up. She placed it carefully over Marietta's curls and tied the ribbons artfully beneath her chin. Bella pronounced her charming, bid her mind her manners, and the ladies, well pleased, set off on their first morning call.

Lady Fitzhugh's residence was only a short drive from their own in Hanover Square, and Bella barely had time to caution Alex to mind her tongue, and to charge Marietta not to be putting herself forward, before the chaise rolled to a stop.

It was an imposing residence, and they were shown into a spacious drawing room. With one accord, the ladies stopped and simply stared. The room was decorated in every possible shade of green and pink. From a cloud of rose cushions slowly arose an elderly matron of astonishing proportions. Her vast figure was draped in a robe of forest green, and her head was wrapped in a bright pink turban, secured with a vulgarly large diamond brooch. Lively brown eyes danced in the wrinkled face, and before Alex could take it all in, she found herself in a smothering embrace against the lady's more than ample chest.

"My dearest Alexandria! I declare I would know you anywhere, for you are the image of your dear mama. Let me look at you, my girl." Alex was abruptly released, and she hastily dropped a curtsey, but Lady Fitzhugh had already turned away to quiz Bella.

"Ah, Miss Meersham, how delightful to see you again, but, my dear, you have grown quite old. It must be from living in the country for so long. A stay in London will put new life in you, mark my words. And this must be little

Marietta." She paused, unfolded a lorgnette produced from
the folds of her voluminous robe, put it to her eye, and
inspected the girl from head to toe. "You will do, my girl."
She nodded, and lowered the lorgnette, indicating her
guests should be seated.

Alex, regaining a measure of composure, thanked her
warmly for her kind letter and for receiving them. She could
not resist adding, "You are not at all what I expected."

"I daresay. You will find, my girl, that when you reach
a certain age and have enough of the ready, you can please
yourself, and say or do as you will. It makes life a great deal
more interesting, and although they might call me an
eccentric, the ton still comes when I beckon. My parties are
the biggest squeeze in London."

Lady Fitzhugh paused long enough to instruct her butler
to provide suitable refreshments, and then directed her
attention to Bella. "I have planned a small dinner party for
this evening so the girls can meet some eligible gentlemen.
Won't do for them to attend their first ball without knowing
anyone. Now then, can they dance?"

It was only the first of many questions Lady Fitzhugh
fired at Bella. Alex found herself relegated to schoolroom
status as her aunt and Lady Fitzhugh discussed both her and
Marietta as though they were not present. It was impossible
to take offense, since Lady Fitzhugh had obviously exerted
herself considerably on their behalf and intended to sponsor
their debut.

Alex attempted to interrupt, trying to inform her bene-
factress that it was Marietta who would be making her
debut. She was politely, though firmly, rebuffed, and had
little to do except sip her tea and chat with her sister. When
Aunt Bella finally recalled her presence, it was only to
indicate that the interview was over. As the ladies rose to
take their leave, Alex and Marietta were, each in turn,
enveloped in a warm hug from Lady Fitzhugh, instructed to
be in looks for the evening, and ushered out.

Alex made an effort to bring her aunt to her senses during
the drive home, reminding her that she was no schoolroom

miss and that it was Marietta who was coming out. Bella, for once, ignored her wishes.

"Really, Alexandria, can you not see that Lady Fitzhugh is enjoying herself planning a few small entertainments for you both? It would be churlish of you to deprive her of that pleasure, especially as she is doing so out of regard for your dear mother."

Bella allowed her no opportunity for further argument, but took her aside the minute they reached the house, and insisted on inspecting their wardrobes for suitable gowns for the evening. Marietta, who had been waiting for just such an opportunity, sought out Susan and told the maid she was needed to accompany her on an errand.

Susan, well accustomed to Marietta's high flights, was not so easily persuaded. "What kind of rig are you running now, miss? Does Miss Alex know what you're up to?"

"No, Alex does not know, and I cannot tell her, or she will try to stop me. It's for her own good that I have to do this. Now, come along, and I shall explain everything as we go." She didn't wait to see if her maid followed, but with a glance over the banister to make sure the coast was clear, hurried down the stairs. She was out the door in a flash, and much relieved to find Susan right behind her.

The girls were able to hire a hackney coach without any problem, and once settled, Marietta gave her maid a rather garbled version of the necessity of visiting Lord Arlington. Her explanation was frequently interrupted by "ohs" and "ahs" as the carriage rolled through the fashionable district, though it was unclear how much Susan understood. Both girls were in awe at the tremendous traffic in the streets and the finery of the ladies strolling along. It was some minutes before they even realized their carriage had halted.

Marietta gazed at the imposing residence before her, and felt her stomach tightening. What had seemed an excellent plan, no longer appeared quite so reasonable. She wiped the palms of her hands on her gown, and taking a deep breath, motioned Susan to follow her. Screwing up her courage, Marietta marched bravely up to the door and boldly lifted the brass knocker. The door was immediately opened by the butler, who so far forgot himself that he momentarily allowed his astonishment to show. However, he quickly schooled his features into the impassive mask that all good butlers are able to assume. Marietta politely asked him to inform Lord Arlington that Miss Hilliard wished to have a word with him.

Hodges was at a loss. In seventeen years of service to Phillip Lyndale, the fifth Marquess of Arlington, he had never before been faced with a young lady of quality behaving with such impropriety as to call on his lordship with only a maid to accompany her. Other ladies had called, yes, but they were of a different sort, and Hodges knew to a nicety how to deal with them. He was tempted to deny his master, but the angelic look in the young lady's eyes caused him to relent sufficiently to show her and her maid into a small drawing room. Informing her that he would just see if his lordship was at home, he bowed out.

Hodges knew the Marquess was in the library with his secretary, Mr. Carstairs, and after a hesitant knock, looked in. Lord Arlington was standing before the fireplace, his arm on the mantel, in a languid pose that did not deceive those who knew him well. His tight-fitting coat did little to conceal powerful muscles and a broad set of shoulders. His height was such that few gentlemen cared to cross him, and while his countenance was not displeasing, the brown eyes could look at one so cynically that he wasn't easily approached, and servants hastened to do his bidding.

Hodges bowed apologetically. "Begging your pardon, my lord, but there's a young lady wishful of seeing you."

The noble brows arched. "A young lady, Hodges? You denied me, of course?"

"No, sir. I put her in the small drawing room."

"Indeed?"

"Yes, sir. She's quality, sir. A Miss Hilliard."

"I see. Very well, Hodges. Please offer Miss . . . er, Hilliard some refreshment. I shall see her directly."

When Hodges had withdrawn, Arlington turned to Carstairs. "Hilliard is, I believe, the name of my ward. Was there not some communication from her recently?"

Carstairs grinned. "You know there was, Phillip. You never forget a detail. It was a very forthright letter from the lady, proposing she visit you here with her younger brother and sister. You instructed me to return a reply that it was not convenient at this time."

"That is as I thought, but perhaps you were not clear?"

"Apparently not," Carstairs laughed. He had long since lost his fear of the haughty Marquess. He knew Arlington to be totally fair to those he employed, loyal to the few men he counted as friends, and possessed of a keen sense of humour.

"Please await my return, Robert. You may have much to answer for." Picking an imaginary particle of dust from his sleeve, Arlington strolled leisurely from the room. Expecting to see some Friday-faced woman, brash and pushy, he was agreeably surprised to behold Marietta. She was seated demurely on the sofa, her maid standing protectively behind her.

She rose at his entrance, turning her enormous blue eyes on him, and impulsively rushed forward, her hands outstretched. "Lord Arlington, I'm so pleased to finally meet you, and you are exactly as I had imagined. I am your ward, you know, Marietta Hilliard."

He had little choice but to take her tiny hand in his and escort her back to the soda. Arlington was renowned for his ability to depress encroaching females with a mere glance, but he was not a heartless man, and Marietta rather reminded him of a helpless, playful kitten. It was with unusual kindness, therefore, that he rebuked her.

"While I am honoured, Miss Marietta, to make your acquaintance, I believe it would have been better to await a more proper introduction. It's not at all the thing for a gently bred young lady to call upon a bachelor. If you are indeed my ward, your actions scarce do me credit."

"I know," she replied, unabashed. "But you are my guardian, after all, and it was the only thing I could do, because I wished to see you privately. And when I have explained it all to you, I am certain you will understand perfectly."

"I had thought you to be in the country. How is it that you are in London?"

"That is what I wished to explain! My sister, Alexandria, felt that it was time I made my come out, and she brought me to Town, and my twin brother, too. We are leasing the house in Hanover Square that the Devereaux were to have, only someone died and we got it instead. So you needn't worry that we shall inconvenience you, for I promise we shall not, not in the least. Lady Fitzhugh is going to sponsor us, you know. Only I do not think it fair that Alex should have to pay for my debut, which is what she intends to do. She is not married, sir, and shall need her independence, especially if Jeremy marries, which I should think likely. And that is why I had to see you." Marietta paused, and with the air of one who had made everything perfectly clear, gazed triumphantly at the Marquess.

Arlington, accustomed to girls of Marietta's age blushing and stammering replies to his questions, was astonished by the tiny whirlwind before him. "If it's a matter of your trust fund," he said finally, "your sister is aware that she has only to forward your bills to me. There is no reason for her to bear the expense. I fear you have not understood the matter correctly."

"Oh, no, it is you who do not understand. Alex told me you wrote her an odious letter telling her not to come to London, and so now she's determined to arrange our affairs without any assistance from you. So you see, sir, she will not send you my bills. Or Jeremy's, either."

His left brow rose half an inch. "I am not in the custom of writing odious letters. I merely instructed my secretary to return a civil reply to your sister."

"Yes, and that's another thing. Alex took offense because you did not write her yourself. Though I expect that was only because you refused permission to allow us to visit you."

Arlington struggled not to laugh at this ingenious explanation. The child had no notion of how outrageous she was, but he found her a refreshing change, and idly wondered what kind of dragon the older sister was. Nothing of his thoughts showed, however, and he advised her courteously, "You make take a message to your sister, child, and tell her your trust will continue to pay all your expenses, and those of . . . er . . . Jeremy as well."

"I fear that will not do, sir. She would not listen. I thought that if I could just talk to you, and explain how it is, well then, you would not mind so very much—" She broke off her words, suddenly shy at requesting such a favour.

"And just what is it that I am not to mind?" he prodded.

"Calling on us, sir. And, maybe, telling Alex that she was right to bring us to London?" Another miss might have been daunted by the stern expression on Arlington's face. Marietta, however, peeped up at him, and caught the laughter in his eyes. "You will, won't you?" she crowed. "I promise you that afterward we shall not trouble you in the least."

"Let me see if I have this correct. I am to call on your sister, apologize for my odious letter, assure her she was right to bring you all to London, and beg her to allow the trust to foot your bills?"

The sarcastic manner in which he uttered the words was lost on Marietta. She jumped up, and taking his hand in hers cried, "I knew you would understand. You are the kindest and best of guardians. Now, when can you come? We are already promised to Lady Fitzhugh this evening, I am afraid."

"Obviously, I shall have no peace until this matter is settled. Will tomorrow do? I'll pay a morning call on your sister."

Marietta voiced her thanks enthusiastically, and was on the verge of taking her leave, when one more thought occurred to her. "You will not think it necessary to mention to Alex that I was here? I fear she would not like it above half."

Arlington, after assuring her of his compliance, instructed a footman to procure a carriage for her. He saw her and her maid safely bestowed, and then leisurely returned to the library. Robert looked up at his entrance and enquired how he had fared with the young lady.

The Marquess lit a cigar, and blew a cloud of smoke. "Did I not instruct you, Robert, to return a *civil* reply to Miss Hilliard? Her younger sister, who happens to be my ward, informs me that you wrote a most odious letter. It was my ward who called, by the way, Miss Marietta."

"Phillip! She never said—"

"Yes, a *most* odious letter, and now I must do penance by calling on the dragon of a sister tomorrow, begging her pardon, and imploring her to allow the trust fund set up for my wards to foot the bill for their stay in London." Arlington lounged in his chair, booted legs stretched out before him, and gave every appearance of a man in a daze.

Robert stared at him. That the most arrogant of peers had taken a set down from a schoolroom miss, and apparently in good humour, was enough to astonish him. That he further meant to bestir himself at the chit's behest was a thought to boggle the mind.

"Do you mean to tell me that you are actually going to pay a morning call? I don't believe it."

"I would take you with me, my friend, but I fear you would inadvertently give away my ward. I have sworn the dragon sister shall not know of her visit."

"I cannot wait to see this paragon who already has you at her beck and call. I never thought I'd see the day when you would succumb to the lures cast out by a schoolroom miss."

"Nor shall you. You mistake the matter, Robert. My ward is only a child, albeit an engaging one. I go because she is my ward."

"Then I am at a loss. You never did a thing for your niece, in spite of your sister's admonitions, so why are you putting yourself out for this ward of yours?"

"Unlike my ward, my niece is in capable hands. I might curse the day Anthony Hilliard named me guardian, but I cannot escape the obligation, and obviously Miss Hilliard is inept at managing the girl. Only look how she came here today. I shall have to take steps to ensure that she behaves herself, as it will soon be known that she is under my protection. Do not frown, Robert. However much you may deplore my affairs, you must own that I have never brought a breath of scandal to the family name. Nor will I allow this engaging minx to do so."

"I am relieved. Still, if Miss Hilliard was obstinate enough to come to London on her own, what makes you think she will take kindly to your hands on the reins?"

"Why, Robert, you disappoint me. Am I growing so old you doubt my ability to persuade a lady to accede to my wishes?"

"Lord knows enough of them have set their caps at you, but this is a different sort of thing. The sister's no London-bred miss, and from the tone of her letter, she doesn't recognize your many . . . er . . . virtues."

"You will soon learn, my friend, that all women are the same. A little attention, a little flattery, and I shall have her eating out of the palm of my hand. Especially as she is an older woman who has been left on the shelf. No, the she-dragon will obey me, I promise you."

Carstairs watched as Arlington took a pinch of snuff, looking supremely confident of his ability to handle the elder Miss Hilliard. He didn't voice his opinion that the lady in question might not fall so complacently in line as Phillip believed. He only wished he might be present to see the confrontation.

Chapter 3

THE LADIES AT Hanover Square enjoyed a late breakfast the next morning, amiably discussing the success of the small dinner given by Lady Fitzhugh and the impromptu dance that had followed.

"Though how she could call it *small* when we had twenty-four sit down to dinner, and five courses, has me in a puzzle," Bella said, smiling at her nieces, who showed little sign of fatigue even after dancing half the night away. She thought she had seldom seen Alexandria in better looks. Her morning dress, with its apron front and stomacher, suited her trim figure. The green ribbons lacing the front matched the satin ribbon holding back her curls.

"I confess I am much surprised to find you both at breakfast, for I do not believe either of you sat out one dance last night."

"No, and it is scarcely surprising since there were more gentlemen than ladies present. Lady Fitzhugh rather stacked the cards in our favour, I think," Alex said. "And Marietta made several conquests. Young Gillingham almost knocked me over in his rush to stand up with her before Lieutenant Hastings could cut him out."

Marietta's cheeks turned pale pink with pleasure, and her dimples appeared as she laughingly recalled her success. "Did not Lieutenant Hastings look absolutely smashing in his regimentals? Miss Comstock practically swooned after he danced with her, but she told me he does not meet with her mama's approval."

Bella had spent the evening seated beside Lady Fitzhugh, receiving full particulars on each of the gentlemen her

34

nieces were introduced to. Hastings, she recollected, was a
younger son possessed of only a modest property. "Lady
Comstock will look higher for Sara than your Lieutenant,"
she told Marietta. "She married her lord for position, and
she will expect the same of her daughter. She let fall that she
counts Lady Barstow a close friend and is looking forward
to seeing her again. I should not be at all surprised if she is
considering Lord Barstow as a possible son-in-law."

If she hoped to dismay Alex with this bit of gossip, she
was doomed to disappointment. Alex calmly continued to
butter a croissant and sweetly enquired what her aunt had
learned of Gillingham.

"Viscount. Lovely estates, 30,000 a year. Most eligible."

Alex laughed, while Marietta goggled at their aunt. "Did
Lady Fitzhugh give you a history of *all* the gentlemen?" she
asked, awed.

"She did. You are most fortunate, my dears, that she was
so vastly fond of your mama. It is for her sake that she is
willing to exert herself on your behalf and put you in the
way of meeting the most eligible bachelors in London."

"But Mama never cared for rank or fortune. She only
wanted us to be as happy as she was with Papa."

"That may be true, Marietta, but I know of no reason
why one cannot be happy with a gentleman of substance. I
daresay it's much easier. Your papa may not have held a
title, but he had a considerable fortune, and none of you
ever had to live in poverty. Had your mama done so, I make
no doubt, it would have changed her viewpoint."

Alex was about to contest this when Dobbs entered and
presented her with a calling card. Some of the colour
drained from her face, and she announced in a stricken
voice that Lord Arlington was calling. Nervously, she
instructed Dobbs to show him into the yellow drawing
room.

Bella rose with alacrity. "I was going to speak to you
about Arlington. Lady Fitzhugh told me he is a leader
among the ton, and it can only be to our credit to stand on
terms with him. She was going to try to arrange something,
but I hardly think she could have done so this quickly."

Taken aback, Alex stared at her in disbelief. "It seems only yesterday that you were telling me of his unsavory reputation, and how you believed he was not a suitable person for me to know."

"Really, Alexandria, it does you no credit to throw my words back at me. Obviously, I was misled by idle gossip, which should be a lesson to us all. Lady Fitzhugh assures me he is a high stickler, a Corinthian, and he is even related to royalty on his mother's side."

Alex thought of several improper retorts, but bit her tongue. She suggested instead that they not keep his lordship waiting. Marietta, taking advantage of their brief dispute, had hurried ahead, and it was she who performed the introductions.

Lord Arlington executed a neat bow over Alex's hand and pronounced himself charmed to meet her.

Alexandria murmured something that passed for politeness and drew back, appalled to recognize the gentleman she'd seen in the street the day before. She was further discomforted by his air of amusement and feared he had recognized her as the provincial chit that had stared so boldly at him from her carriage window. She had no doubt that he was laughing at her and longed to give him a proper set down.

The Marquess was, in fact, trying hard to hide his amusement, but not for the reason Alex had imagined. When the ladies had first entered, he'd presumed Bella to be the dragon-lady his ward had described as being past her prayers. That it was, instead, the vision of loveliness standing before him appealed to his sense of the ridiculous. If Marietta could describe her sister as being on the shelf, he would hate to know what she thought of him.

While Bella welcomed him effusively, Alex had a chance to study him. She had never seen a more handsome man. She made note of the broad shoulders, the well-fitting coat, moderately starched shirt points, and the neckcloth tied to a nicety. She looked in vain for signs of the dignified fop she had expected. There was, in fact, nothing about him that she could fault unless it was his air of vast superiority.

A blush suffused her cheeks as she encountered his eyes and realized he was observing her, not with the disdain of the day before, but with a touch of quiet humour. For a brief moment, she felt as though he could read her thoughts. Quickly, she indicated they should all be seated, and politely enquired how he came to know of their visit.

"There is very little that goes on in London that I am not aware of, Miss Hilliard. London rivals a small village for the rapidity with which news travels—good or bad."

It vexed her that he should think her an unsophisticated green girl, she answered him more sharply than she intended. "And to which category do you ascribe our arrival, sir?"

Bella looked startled by her impertinence, but Lord Arlington smiled lazily and replied smoothly, "Why good, Miss Hilliard. The arrival of three such charming ladies can only enliven the Season."

Bella, a little flustered by the unexpected compliment, started to thank him, but Alex broke in, taunting him.

"I wonder, if you believe that, why you were so set against our visiting London?"

"Ah, that is why I have called so promptly. I must beg your forgiveness for my deplorable temper. I fear the day your letter arrived I was . . . out of sorts. I instructed my secretary to answer you without, I regret to say, giving proper thought to your request. And, may I add, ladies, that having now met you, I find my hasty temper even more regrettable."

Marietta smiled her approval at his pretty fabrication, while Bella hastened to reassure him that there was nothing at all to forgive. Alex quelled a strong impulse to smile at him, reminding herself that he had neglected them for three years and if matters had been left to him, they would still be rusticating at Allenswood.

Arlington, while making idle conversation with Bella and his ward, took note of the elder Miss Hilliard's stiff posture and the determined tilt of her chin. Not on the shelf, he thought, but no schoolroom miss to be easily won over, either. He would like to see those eyes when they were not so full of distrust. Indeed, her eyes seemed to change with the light, and he could not quite decide if they were green or silvery gray. He returned a light answer to one of Bella's questions and then directed his attention to Alex.

"I hope you will allow me to escort all of you to the theatre on Friday. I have in mind just a small party, but I am certain my ward would enjoy it excessively."

"Oh, do say yes, Alex." Marietta was beside her chair in an instant, an imploring look on her pretty face. "I should like it above all things."

Alex, about to accept, glanced at the Marquess. He wore the supremely confident air of a man sure of his charm, and his smile seemed to mock her. She did not doubt he was seldom refused.

Nettled, she replied, "I am sure we're much obliged to you, sir, but I cannot help feeling that having come to London against your wishes, it would be a shocking imposition to place you in the position of escorting us. I am certain it is much against your inclination."

He watched, bemused, as the green eyes flashed and the tiny chin lifted. "I assure you, Miss Hilliard, I never allow myself to be imposed upon. In this instance, I am much inclined to see my ward properly introduced to London Society. It is, after all, one of my duties as her guardian." He uttered the words with the languid air common to all London gentlemen, and with the condescension natural to a peer toadied to by most of the ton.

"A pity you did not recall your duty sooner!" she snapped in reply, stung by his patronizing tone.

"Alexandria!" Bella cried, aghast, and then begged Lord Arlington to excuse her niece. "I fear she is overly tired after our long journey and the late hour we returned home last evening."

Alex, all too aware of the impropriety of her behaviour, wished devoutly that she might disappear. Her unruly tongue had betrayed her again, and however much she might wish to wipe the arrogant grin from Lord Arlington's face, she knew there was no excuse for her bad manners.

She fully intended to beg his pardon, but before she

could, Dobbs entered and announced the arrival of Lord
Barstow. With the long ease of familiarity, Barstow stepped
in behind him, greeting the ladies warmly. Surprised to see
the Marquess there, he nodded and murmured a cool hello,
his disapproval patently obvious.

"How do you do," Arlington returned, pleasantly
enough. "I heard you were in Town. Someone mentioned
you bought Marlow's greys. A pity."

"Yes, it was unfortunate for you that I got to Marlow
first. I heard you were interested in purchasing them."

"No—not once I had the opportunity to inspect them.
Breakdowns. All show and no substance. I own I am
surprised your groom did not warn you against buying
them."

Barstow swelled with hostility. His groom *had* advised
against the purchase. What rankled was that the only reason
he had insisted on buying the pair was the knowledge that
Arlington coveted them. He blustered, "I doubt the ladies
find such conversation of interest, sir. If you will excuse
me." He bowed to Bella, enquiring how she was finding
London, and in a tactless aside, quizzed Marietta, asking if
she was behaving.

Where Jeremy would have flown up in the boughs at his
avuncular manner, Marietta only laughed. With a conspir-
atorial look at Arlington, she nodded and answered demurely, "I trust so, sir. My guardian does not seem to find
my manners lacking."

Arlington rose, and smiling at Marietta remarked, "Indeed, I find my ward's manners completely delightful. I am
looking forward to Friday. Shall I call for you at eight?"

Alex, mindful that she already owed the Marquess an
apology, said nothing, allowing Bella to accept the invitation on their behalf. She was more than a little amused by
Arlington's conversation with Lord Barstow, but would not
own it. Instead, she told herself it was only another
indication of the man's arrogance, and coolly turned her
back on him, asking Barstow how his mother did. She only
half-listened to his rambling reply as she tried to hear what
Bella was saying to the Marquess.

Both conversations were halted abruptly as Jeremy burst into the room, demanding to know who owned the bang-up chestnuts outside.

The Marquess, after being properly introduced to his other ward by Bella, acknowledged the team in question was undoubtedly his own. In his careless way, he had noted the way Barstow had frowned at the boy's manners and the look of dislike in Jeremy's eyes as they greeted one another. Prompted by an unworthy desire to irk Barstow, he immediately asked if Jeremy would care to try his chestnuts' paces. Nothing more was needed to win his instant approval by the lad, and they left with only a nod to Barstow.

That their neighbour was annoyed was obvious, and Bella immediately set about soothing him. Although Marietta excused herself on the flimsiest pretext, Alex felt obliged to remain and give Barstow her undivided attention. And she tried. But it was difficult to keep her mind on his monologue, regaling them as he was on the rigours of the journey he and his mama had endured. Her wayward mind kept returning to thoughts of Arlington, and she tried to puzzle out what it was about the Marquess that had prompted her to such uncivil conduct. With a start, she realized Barstow was addressing her.

"It had been my intention," he was saying, "to invite you to the Opera on Friday, but I gather Arlington has been before me. I must own I was rather surprised to find him here."

"Were you? Surely, it is nothing remarkable. He is guardian to the twins."

"Ah, but his reputation is such that one would have no expectation of him behaving in a proper manner." He turned to Bella and added rather jocularly, "I only hope he does not intend to make our Alexandria the object of his attentions."

Bella answered him with less than her usual patience. "Really, Lord Barstow, I have been assured by Lady Fitzhugh that the Marquess is quite respectable, and indeed, he has been most kind. As for his making Alex the object of his attentions, you are far wide of the mark. They did not hit it off at all."

"I am indeed glad to hear that, but cannot own myself surprised. Alexandria is very nice in her tastes, as I've been privileged to know. The rough manner some Town beaus choose to adopt would not be at all acceptable to someone of her fine sensibilities."

"Would you please stop speaking about me as though I were not here?" Alex said, and with her innate sense of fairness added, "As for Arlington, I certainly cannot accuse him of rough manners. Top-lofty perhaps, although it really was very kind of him to allow Jeremy to drive his team."

"Hmmph. I only hope you will not have cause to regret his attention to the boy. The Marquess is a gamester and, I am told, up to every rig in Town. Precisely the sort of person an impressionable lad like Jeremy would choose to emulate, which might very well prove fatal."

"Jeremy is neither as impressionable nor as green as you seem to believe. My lord, I know you mean well, but I must beg you not to take it upon yourself to censure him. Especially while we are in London. He does not concede your right to do so, you know, and, in fact, it makes him highly resentful."

"That only proves my point. A steadier boy would not take good advice amiss. Of course, I realize his being hot at hand stems from the unfortunate loss of your papa, so I don't take offense when he displays a bit of temper. I hope I am too good a friend for that."

Alex sighed. Barstow's opinion of his own consequence and self-righteousness would not be penetrated by any words she could utter. She adroitly turned the conversation, and they chatted almost amiably about the delights London had to offer. It was with no little relief that she finally heard Barstow announcing his departure.

"But you must not think I'm deserting you, for I intend to be a frequent caller," he teased, with a broad smile for Alex. It was several more minutes before he actually left, causing Bella to remark that he had never seemed so prosy in the country.

Alex reminded her that they were due in Curzon Street for their fittings with Madame Theresa, an outstanding modiste who was presently enjoying the patronage of the ton. Bella scurried to get ready, and Alex asked Susan if she had seen Marietta.

"She was in the kitchens last I saw her. There's a new litter of kittens there, and Miss Marietta was playing with them."

Alex found her still there, curled up in a large rocking chair, a snowy white kitten asleep on her lap. She was engaged in a lively debate with the cook and Mrs. Delahan on the merits of country life. That she had won over the kitchen staff was evident by the smear of cherry tart on her chin and a similar smear on the kitten's whiskers.

She saw Alex and flashed her a grin. "Has he gone? Is it safe to come out now?"

"Yes, brat, but he promised to be a frequent caller, and you cannot hide out in the kitchen forever. And if you do not hurry up and change your dress, you'll miss the fittings with the modiste."

When the ladies arrived at the fashionable salon, they were awed by the elegance of the interior. Marietta, before venturing any farther into those hallowed precincts, extracted a promise from Alex that the bills would be sent to Lord Arlington.

An observant assistant, overhearing part of their conversation, at once conveyed the information to Madame Theresa, who hurried out to wait on these new clients herself. Arlington was a favourite of hers. A rarity in the ton, he paid his bills promptly and without haggling. Curiously, she assessed the ladies. It was obvious that they weren't members of the *demimonde* for whom the Marquess normally paid bills. Interesting, this. She assigned the young girl and the older woman to an assistant. She, Madame Theresa, would have the dressing of Miss Hilliard.

The red hair, the tall, slender figure, those green eyes— *Mon Dieu*! It would be a pleasure to dress this one, she thought. The modiste chatted confidently with Alex while draping her form with a length of a beautiful willow-green china crepe. She would, she explained, cut the bosom low, just so, and the waist high.

The crepe was removed, to be replaced by a silvery satin. Not for Miss Hilliard the whites and pale pastels of the young girls. She measured, pinned, made notations, and all the while listened. Madame was a success because she made it her business to know what went on in the ton. She determined that Miss Hilliard, with that face and figure, and dressed in her creations, would create a sensation. When she learned Arlington was escorting her to the theatre the following night, she immediately promised to have the satin frock ready, even if she had to work all night.

"The Marquess will be *très enchanté*."

Alex, belatedly aware that the modiste was supposing a romantic involvement between her and Arlington where none existed, tried her best to disabuse her of the notion. She diligently explained the Marquess was escorting them to the theatre only because her younger sister was his ward. This the modiste would not allow. She smiled knowingly.

"The Marquess has no sense of duty. If he takes you to the play, it is only because it pleases him to do so, *n'est-ce pas*?"

Bella and Marietta joined her, the latter in raptures over the materials she had selected for numerous walking dresses, carriage dresses, morning dresses, gowns and capes. As the ladies prepared to leave, Madame kindly gave them the name of a milliner she highly recommended. Alex, thanking her for her assistance, did not see Lady Jersey enter the salon behind her. Had she glanced back, she would have seen the modiste hasten to Lady Jersey's side, anxious to impart the latest *on-dit*—the handsome Marquess, Lord Arlington, had at last a respectable romance.

When the family returned to Hanover Square, pleased with their efforts, they discovered a number of visitors had called in their absence. Dobbs handed Alex a stack of calling cards, and there were two posies for Marietta as well as one for Alex.

Marietta excitedly read the cards attached. One was from

Lieutenant Hastings and the other from Lord Gillingham. She blushed rosily and begged Alex to read her own card.

With nervous fingers, Alex undid the card and read the very properly phrased and stilted message from Lord Barstow. Chiding herself for the ridiculous feeling of disappointment, she made her excuses and hurried to her bedchamber to change for dinner.

They were promised, once again, to Lady Fitzhugh. Her ladyship had more people she wished them to meet. Alexandria felt that if they continued to dine at Lady Fitzhugh's, they must surely meet every eligible bachelor in London. Her mama's old friend was indefatigable in her efforts.

During the short drive to her house, Jeremy could do little but rhapsodize over Lord Arlington. He was, according to Jeremy, a great gun. His guardian had taken him to Weston's and Hoby's, and kindly recommended him to both his tailor and his bootmaker, with the result that Jeremy was being completely outfitted. Alex thought he was looking extremely handsome in a light blue coat of Bath superfine, with moderately starched shirtpoints. If the modesty of his attire was due to Arlington's influence, she would not quarrel with her brother should he choose to continue to emulate the Marquess.

Dinner was a more elaborate affair than the Hilliards were accustomed to attend. Marietta was seated far down the table, between Gillingham and a foppishly dressed gentleman whom Alex did not recognize. Jeremy appeared happily content with a pretty girl on either side, and Alex found herself seated between Lord Quarrels, who evinced a desire to entertain her with all the latest gossip about their fellow guests, and an elderly, distinguished man, introduced to her as Lord Norwich.

Alex had heard of Lord Norwich. He had a reputation for being a devastatingly brilliant speaker in the House of Lords, and he proved no less effective as a dinner partner. She could have spoken with him for hours, but politeness demanded she give some of her attention to Lord Quarrels. Searching for a topic of mutual interest, she turned to him and enquired if he knew the young ladies seated next to her brother.

"The dark-haired chit is Miss Calvert," Quarrels said, delighted to oblige his beautiful dinner partner. "An immense fortune there, but the daughter of a Cit. Her parents live retired, somewhere in the North, I believe. Miss Calvert is here with her aunt, Lady Edenbough. The story goes her mama married for love, and her parents consented to the match for the money. Their estates apparently were mortgaged to the hilt before Calvert stepped in. The blonde chit seated on your brother's right is Miss Harrington. This is her first Season, and she, no doubt, is seeking a rich husband. She's only a modest portion herself, but is extremely well-connected."

He paused to sip his wine, and with the glass shielding his face, whispered, "I say, have you done something to offend Sally Jersey? She keeps staring at you as though there was a spot on your nose. Which, I assure you, there is not. It's most enchanting, your nose, I mean."

Alex, aware of having been under scrutiny, stole a glance at the beautifully attired lady seated down the table. Their eyes met. Lady Jersey's were rife with speculation, and Alex, embarrassed, quickly looked down.

"I do not see how I could possibly have offended her. We have only been in Town a few days, and I met Lady Jersey for the first time just before dinner."

Sally Jersey turned to her own dinner partner, continuing the sort of idle conversation at which she was so adept. It left her mind free to continue puzzling over what it was about Miss Hilliard that could have caught the fancy of a hardened bachelor like Arlington. She discounted the beauty of the girl. Not that she wasn't attractive, but far more beautiful women had set their caps at the Marquess without success. Her sole purpose in attending the dinner was to solve this riddle, and perhaps, as a favour to Maria Fitzhugh, provide vouchers for the Hilliards to Almack's.

Lady Jersey knew it would be a feather in her cap to be the one who introduced Miss Hilliard to those sacred portals if Arlington was indeed taken with the girl. She and her pretty sister would do much to enliven the dullness of the assemblies. Of late, Lady Jersey had found them quite boring, but the Hilliards might well provide some amusement. In Town only a few days, and the petite Miss Marietta had already captivated a number of bucks. The brother was fine-looking, too. He was certain to cause a number of hearts to flutter.

Lady Fitzhugh rose, and the ladies, following her lead, left the gentlemen to their cigars and port. They retired to a large, gilded apartment, and Sally Jersey deftly managed to be seated next to Lady Fitzhugh and Bella Meersham. She adroitly began questioning Bella about her nieces. Bella, primed by Lady Fitzhugh, immediately remarked how very kind it was of Lord Arlington to immediately call on them and to devote so much of his time to his wards.

"And what of Miss Hilliard?" Lady Jersey asked, unabashed. "I understand she is not his ward. Is he kind to her as well?"

Bella was saved from answering as Alex and Marietta joined her. Lady Fitzhugh told them that Bella had been singing their praises as musicians and begged them to give the company a song.

The Hilliard sisters were able to oblige with composure, for the family had spent many musical evenings at home. Alex accompanied Marietta, playing the pianoforte while her sister sang. She did not believe she possessed more than an adequate talent, but Alex was more than a little proud of Marietta. She thought her sister had a true, sweet voice that was certain to delight.

The gentlemen joined the ladies in the salon while the Hilliards were still singing, and enthusiastically called out requests for more, but Alex thought it only polite to give the other young ladies a chance to perform, and very prettily pleaded fatigue.

Miss Harrington shyly took her place, and later, Miss Calvert. Both girls sang well, and Alex was inclined to think her brother taken with Miss Calvert. Jeremy volunteered to turn the pages of her music for her, and was still by her side, deep in conversation, when Bella indicated it was time for them to depart.

They dutifully took leave of their hostess, thanking Lady Fitzhugh for a wonderful evening. She seemed extremely pleased with them, and whispered in Bella's ear as they were leaving. It was not until they were seated in the carriage that the others learned her news.

"Jeremy," she said, "please be certain to reserve Wednesday evening next. You shall be needed to escort your sisters to Almack's."

She was delighted with the excitement her announcement caused. Marietta, in the midst of a yawn, looked at her in open-mouth astonishment before giving a whoop of glee. Jeremy didn't understand what all the fuss was about, but he was content as long as his sisters were happy. It was left to Alex, the most practical of the trio, to demand the details.

Bella was happy to explain. "Lady Jersey, as you know, is one of the Patronesses, and she was impressed with all of you. While you girls were playing, she told us she would send the vouchers. Lady Fitzhugh told me, just as we were leaving, that her curiosity was piqued. I could not believe it, but it seems the latest *on-dit* is that Lord Arlington has developed a tendre for you, Alex."

"Nonsense. You must have misunderstood her. Why, nothing could be farther from the truth. You know we almost came to points when he called on us."

"I know, my love, and I suspect that modiste we visited had something to do with setting the story about. Apparently Lady Jersey got her information from her, but it really does not matter. The important thing is that everyone will be anxious to meet you. We could not have planned it better. Indeed, Lady Fitzhugh congratulated me on our strategy."

"I think it's monstrous. Do you want people to accept us merely because of some ridiculous rumour? And suppose it comes to Lord Arlington's ears? He is bound to think we are shockingly vulgar, engaging in such a deception. Oh, Aunt Bella, I am mortified to think of it, and I cannot believe you would condone such a thing."

"You are refining too much on this, Alexandria. After

all, we did nothing to spread such a rumour. People will gossip, and you know it's impossible to still wagging tongues. *You* cannot be held responsible for what people say."

"Oh, don't you see, Aunt Bella? If Lady Fitzhugh thinks we are responsible for this rumour, then others will, too."

Marietta was puzzled. "Why are you so rattled, Alex? Lord Arlington does like us. He would not be taking us to the theatre otherwise."

"Don't be foolish. Arlington is escorting us because you are his ward—not because he has any romantical interest in me. Nothing could be farther from his mind."

"I think he likes you well enough," Marietta disagreed. "You have to watch his eyes. I noticed his mouth says one thing and his eyes say another. Did you not notice, Alex? He has the most engaging laughing eyes."

"I did, and I do not care to be laughed at, thank you." With that curt announcement, and realizing the carriage had halted, Alex waited only for the steps to be let down before she was out and hurrying to the door. She was anxious the others shouldn't see her tears. The footman opening the door was startled to see her sweep past him without a word.

Alex, dismissing her maid, threw herself on her bed and allowed the pent-up tears to flow. She was sick with apprehension that Lord Arlington, hearing the rumour that he was taken with her, would set it at her door. She could not bear to have him think she was so encroaching or would do anything so disgustingly vulgar. However much she might deny it to the others, she had wanted Arlington to think well of her.

In the darkness of her room, Alex admitted to herself that the Marquess was the only man she had ever met who came close to resembling the hero of her dreams. It was foolish, she knew. Arlington might possess extraordinary looks, but his behaviour was a far cry from the man of her dreams. He was arrogant, disdainful, self-centered, and in the course of ordinary events, she doubted he would look twice at her. And now . . . now he would undoubtedly look at her but with a glance of scathing contempt designed to depress her pretensions. He would either think she was setting her cap at him or that she was a mercenary baggage using their slight acquaintance to further her own rise in the ton. Either way, she was mortified. However could she ever face him again?

Chapter 4

ALEX MAY HAVE spent a restless night, but Marietta awoke the next morning full of anticipation and eager to start the day. She had spent a most agreeable night, dreaming of the stir she would create at the theatre. In full expectation of receiving morning callers, Marietta sat patiently while Susan coaxed her curls into a new, more modish style, twisting the long hair into a knot on top of her head and allowing several carefully arranged curls to fall on the sides and at the neck in ringlets.

Stepping back, Susan admired her handiwork with all the lavish praise her young mistress could wish, telling her she looked a fair princess. Reverently, she assisted Marietta into a walking dress of a soft amber hue, embroidered with a rope of French braid. Assured she looked most becoming, Marietta descended to the morning room, where Alex and Aunt Bella were still having breakfast.

Though gratified by the compliments she received on her new hairstyle and ensemble, Marietta was not so puffed up in her own conceit that she failed to notice the dark shadows under her sister's eyes, and enquired solicitously as to her health. Alex confessed to spending a restless night, but passed it off lightly, blaming it on the unaccustomed noise and bustle of London streets. She averred she missed the peace and quiet of Allenswood.

Bella unwittingly abetted her, remarking on how peaceful the chirping of crickets and frogs could be, particularly when one was used to hearing their noise.

"Not that frogs chirp; they croak, I believe. But that's such a vulgar-sounding word. You will not credit it, my

50

dears, I am sure, but when I first visited Allenswood, it was several nights before I became accustomed to their noise. There was one cricket I especially recollect. He was extremely loud, and I used to think he always sought me out most particularly."

"How do you know it was a 'he,' Aunt?" Marietta asked, intrigued.

"Oh, it must have been, don't you think? He was loud, extremely noisy, and stayed up half the night."

Alex, thankful for Bella's diverting chatter, momentarily recalled the nightmare that had caused such havoc with her sleep. Lord Arlington had figured prominently, publicly denouncing her as a miserable, scheming wretch who had ruthlessly taken advantage of their connection to further her own ends. The Marquess had been attired solely in black, and loomed a terrifying ogre. She tried valiantly to dismiss the disturbing images from her mind and returned her attention to Aunt Bella.

Her aunt's discourse was interrupted, however, and Marietta was proven correct in her expectation of callers. Dobbs entered and announced the arrival of Lady Comstock and Miss Comstock, and the ladies hastened to the drawing room.

While Lady Comstock exchanged pleasantries with Bella and Alex, Sara chatted amiably with Marietta. She, too, had received vouchers for Almack's, and confessed her nervousness. She envied her new friend the support of her brother, and shyly asked if Mr. Hilliard waltzed.

Marietta, who had inherited her mama's romantic disposition, immediately promised that should they receive approval to perform the waltz, she, Sara, would have Jeremy for a partner. Miss Comstock blushed and admitted she would not know how to go on if a gentleman as elegant and handsome as Mr. Hilliard should ask her to stand up with him.

Marietta instantly devised a plan to visit Hookam's Circulating Library and asked Sara to accompany her. Obtaining Lady Comstock's and Alex's approval, she begged her friend to wait, and ran off to plague her brother into providing them escort. She found Jeremy still in his chambers, endeavoring to tie a neckcloth vaguely reminiscent of the style Lord Arlington favoured. Appealed to, she assured him he looked perfection, and then hurriedly explained her errand.

"Now, why the devil should I visit a library? Had enough of that sort of thing at Eton."

"We've only to stay a minute. Aunt charged me to select a book for her. The thing is, Jeremy, Sara is nervous about her debut, and since she admires you, I thought it would help to set her at ease if you would lend us your escort. She's the shyest thing, having lived quite retired and only going about with her mama. She has no brothers, you see, and she thinks you excessively handsome."

Jeremy, recalling Miss Comstock as a devilish pretty girl, was flattered but unconvinced. "You must have maggots in your head if you think taking her to a library will help. More like, it would give her the megrims."

"No, stupid! It's your escort. Sara only needs to spend some time in your company to discover that there's not the least reason to be nervous of you. And after the library, we can all go to Gunter's for an ice. Sara says it is the most divine place."

"Doing it too brown, Mari. Why should the chit be nervous of me? Only met her once."

"I know, and it's too ridiculous, but Sara thinks you elegant. She confided in me that she'd be terrified to stand up with you. I daresay it comes of not having any brothers. Please, Jeremy." She perceived that he was weakening and added, with an air of innocence, "You must know that her mama is pitching her at Lord Barstow."

The thought of prosy, pompous Barstow with a pretty little thing like Miss Comstock was all that was needed to persuade Jeremy. He immediately yielded, adding only that he would *not* enter the library but would walk his horses while they completed their errand.

The trio set off in the carriage Arlington had placed at their disposal, and it wasn't long before Sara was laughing at the lighthearted banter that passes so frequently between brother and sister but is foreign to an only child. They were on easy terms by the time they reached Hookam's, and to Jeremy's demand that they not keep him waiting an age, Sara even returned a saucy reply.

"Be assured we won't, sir. I much prefer to keep my head in bonnets, not in some dusty old books, thank you."

The riposte pleased him so much he was still chuckling when Gillingham hailed him. "Turning into an eccentric are you, Hilliard? Laughing to yourself in the middle of Bond Street! I say, what have you done with your sister? I called in Hanover Square and Miss Meersham told me she was with you," he said, peering about as though Jeremy had secreted her somewhere in the carriage.

"If you are referring to Marietta, she and Miss Comstock are in the library. Should be out soon. Promised not to keep my horses standing an age."

"Your sister's not bookish, is she? I must say she doesn't look like a bluestocking."

"Ha! Not Marietta. No, they are only discharging an errand for our aunt, and then we're off to Gunter's. Would you care to join us?"

"Done," agreed Gillingham, much relieved to discover no flaw in the enchanting Miss Marietta. "Though I shall be seeing you this evening as well. Lord Arlington invited me to join his party for the theatre." He saw no reason to confide in his new friend that the Marquess had let fall a broad hint that he wouldn't take it amiss if the Viscount chose to pay court to his ward. No doubt it was in an effort to bring them together that Arlington had invited him. However, since he was already in raptures over Marietta, he could find no fault with the scheme, was pleased to see the Marquess entertaining again, and altogether felt the evening promised to be most agreeable.

The only member of the proposed party who was not experiencing any degree of anticipation was Alexandria. She had even considered crying off from the excursion, pleading a headache, but on consideration she decided that would not only be cowardly, but would certainly add to the gossip already brewing.

That gossip was brewing she had no doubt. The Comstocks were not the only morning visitors they had received. One lady after another was admitted by Dobbs to the house in Hanover Square, and each lady made it a point to enquire about the Marquess, until Alex thought she would surely scream if his name was introduced one more time.

Her patience was sorely tested when one young lady, Miss Wrexford, in Town for her second Season, questioned her boldly. Taking advantage of her mama's preoccupation with Bella, Miss Wrexford had whispered slyly, "Do tell me how you first came to meet the Marquess. I tried to do so last year but never had the opportunity!"

Alex stared at her in no little astonishment. "Lord Arlington called shortly after we arrived in Town. He is guardian to my younger brother and sister."

"Oh, I know that is what you are putting about, but you may trust *me* with the real story. Is it true he has been visiting you in the country for years? I vow it is prodigiously romantic."

"No, it is certainly not true," Alex said, striving hard to check her temper. "I made the acquaintance of Lord Arlington for the first time this week when he called here, and frankly I fail to see why that should occasion so much comment."

Miss Wrexford studied her. There was nothing in Miss Hilliard's appearance to account for the sudden infatuation of a gentleman like Lord Arlington, who was reputed to be a connoisseur of beauty. Nor was she a lively conversationalist. Miss Wrexford decided, with some disappointment, the entire tale must be a hum and turned her attention back to her mama, more than ready to take her leave.

Alex's relief at their departure minutes later was shortlived. Miss Wrexford was succeeded by other, equally curious, visitors. Their probing questions were posed more delicately perhaps, but the nature of the calls remained the same. Alex thought their curiosity much out of proportion to the situation. To judge from the astonishment of the ladies passing through their salon, one would think the Marquess had never before escorted a respectable party to the theatre. Was his reputation as a rake so well established, then, that this one simple excursion would set all the cats to meowing? Even given the rumour of his supposed attachment to her, their curiosity seemed out of bounds. Alexandria endured it as long as she could, and then finally escaped.

She took Susan with her, and on the pretext of needing a new fan to match her satin gown, she explored the shops in Bond Street. The extent of the merchandise offered was overwhelming to one used to the small provincial shops in the village, and for a brief time, Alex was able to forget her problems. She purchased several ribbons for Marietta, a pair of long evening gloves for herself, and was examining a new ivory fan when Lady Bideford approached her.

Alex had been introduced to the older woman at one of Lady Fitzhugh's dinners and retained an impression of a rather good-natured, kind-hearted matron. She greeted her warmly, and they chatted for a few moments about the fan Alex wished to purchase. Alexandria was relaxed, but she stiffened visibly when Lady Bideford mentioned Lord Arlington.

"You will forgive me, I hope, Miss Hilliard, for my presumption, but I have of course heard that Arlington is escorting you to the theatre this evening. La, I doubt there is anyone in London who is not aware of it, and it will occasion much talk," the older woman said, her double chins quivering as she laughed.

"So it has," Alex agreed curtly.

"Oh dear, how unfortunate," Lady Bideford said, the laughter leaving her eyes abruptly as she noted Alex's distress. "Well, I do not wish to add to the gossip mill, but I pray you will not allow yourself to believe all you hear. Much of what is said about Arlington is mere idle speculation. While he is not a saint by any means, he is often painted blacker than is warranted. You must trust that I know whereof I speak. The Marquess does a great deal of good, my dear, but without any fanfare."

"Thank you, Lady Bideford. I believe you mean well, but what Lord Arlington chooses to do or not do is hardly any concern of mine. The Marquess stands as guardian to my younger brother and sister, and I fear the attention he has bestowed on them has been . . . misjudged."

"Have it as you will, my dear," the woman said, nodding her head knowingly. "Now, let me give you one more piece of advice. If you are seeking a fan, you would do much better at a little bazaar I know of." She lowered her voice so the clerk waiting patiently would not overhear and added, "Wickford's is dreadfully overpriced."

Alex dutifully accepted the directions offered and watched Lady Bideford sail from the shop. At least the woman had meant well, however misguided her intentions. She paid for her purchases and had just stepped outside the shop with Susan when her steps were halted again.

She heard her name called and glanced up, groaning inwardly when she recognized Mrs. Ponsonby waving urgently at her. It was too late to pretend she had not heard the woman's strident voice.

Mrs. Ponsonby hailed her again, hurriedly stepping down from her carriage. An overweight and overdressed matron of advanced years, she obviously still considered herself a beauty and dressed in an extremely youthful style that only emphasized her age. She puffed up to Alex, extending her hand.

"How delightful to see you again, Miss Hilliard," she said, regaining her breath. "I heard you are attending the theatre this evening with the Marquess. Now, I know you are new to Town and not yet up to the mark, so you will pardon me if I just give you a bit of a warning."

Alexandria was too well bred to snub the woman directly, though she had taken her into dislike the instant Lady Fitzhugh had introduced them. She managed to smile politely, certain there was nothing she could say to dissuade the woman in any event.

"There's a nasty bit of rumour going round," Mrs. Ponsonby said, her pudgy face pressed close to Alex. "Not that I give it any credence, but you should know, my dear, that people are saying you have set your cap for Lord Arlington."

"Really, Mrs. Ponsonby, I—" Alex began, drawing back from the pungent odor of the lady's breath.

"Quite all right, my dear. No need to deny it to me. Why, anyone with a grain of sense could see you are much too nice in your tastes to be impressed with a rakehell like Arlington, but I think it is perfectly dreadful of that man to use you to mask his affair with that brazen little actress!"

"I beg your pardon?"

"Well, my dear, of course you would not know, but, believe me, it is common knowledge in Town that Arlington has Cecily Fanchon under his protection, and if he is taking you to Drury Lane tonight, then you may be sure it is only that he may see her. Oh dear, perhaps I should not be speaking so frankly to you, you not being married and all, but really I could not allow you to remain ignorant of the man's perfidy. Just because he is a Marquess, he thinks he is exempt from civilized conduct. Well, let me tell you—"

"Really, Mrs. Ponsonby, I must—"

"Goes round Town with that haughty air of his, as though he's too good for the rest of us, when all the time he is carrying on with actresses and such. My dear Thomas, God rest his soul, may not have had a title to his name, but he was a proper gentleman for all that, and I've nothing to hide my head over. Not like *him*. Snubbing people as though he were some sort of saint, when all the time—"

"Excuse me, ma'am," Alex interrupted more firmly, "but I see our carriage is waiting." She motioned to Susan, and deliberately turning her back on Mrs. Ponsonby, crossed to where John Coachman was waiting for them. The footman let down the steps and she slipped quickly inside. With Susan settled opposite, the coach rolled forward and Alex glanced out the window. Mrs. Ponsonby was still standing in front of Wickford's, hands on her hips and glaring venomously at her.

Alexandria sighed. Her introduction to the ton was not proving the simple matter she had imagined. She sat, looking out the window, but not seeing anything. She knew she had incurred the wrath of Mrs. Ponsonby, no small matter given the woman's vicious tongue. No wonder

Arlington had snubbed her. A half smile lurked at the corners of her mouth as she imagined what the ill-bred widow might say of her. Probably that she was so desperate to ensnare the Marquess, she was willing to turn a blind eye to his dalliance with an actress.

Was there any truth in her words? Given Lady Bideford's warning, Alex wondered, and then chided herself for caring one way or another. It cannot possibly matter, she thought, but with such little effect she was quite relieved when the carriage finally halted in the square.

Alex directed Susan to stow her purchases in her bedchamber and went in search of her aunt. She found Bella in the salon and was thankful no visitors were present. She slipped into the wing chair and gave her aunt a brief recital of her afternoon's excursion, omitting much of the details of Mrs. Ponsonby's conversation. But the woman's words haunted her, and over a cup of tea, she asked casually, "Did Lord Arlington mention the name of the theatre we are to visit?"

"Why, I believe it was Drury Lane," Bella said absently.

Chapter 5

ALEXANDRIA DESCENDED THE staircase that evening with her head held proudly, though her thoughts were still in turmoil. On the one hand, she dreaded facing the Marquess and seeing the condemnation in his eyes if he had heard the rumours linking her name to his. On the other, she was more than a little annoyed to think he would dare to take them to the theatre where his bit of muslin was appearing. Only her distrust of Mrs. Ponsonby, and her own firsthand knowledge that rumours spread without any basis in truth, kept her quiet on the subject.

She was the last to come down, and she saw the others standing in the hall below. Her knees trembled slightly, but they were hidden by the folds of her luxurious satin gown. The bodice hugged her figure, molding her breasts before flaring out and ending in a demi-train. If assurance was needed that she was in looks, it was written on the face of Gillingham.

"I feel much inclined to bow before such regal beauty, Miss Hilliard," he declared, bending a knee gallantly.

"Thank you, sir." Alex smiled, turning to him gratefully and managing, for the moment, to avoid facing the Marquess, unaware that Lord Arlington was watching her, a gleam of appreciation in his eyes.

When at last Alex summoned the courage to face him, she managed to greet him with a measure of composure that belied her inner feelings. Irreverently, she gave thanks that he was not attired in black, like the ogre of her dreams. Indeed, he looked quite resplendent in a long-tailed blue dress coat, with brilliant white lace at his wrists.

"Lord Gillingham leaves me with little to add, Miss Hilliard, other than that his taste is improving. You do look lovely, and will certainly do me credit."

"Which must, of course, be an object with me, my lord," she replied with a challenging look.

He smiled that calm, vastly superior smile of his, and merely returned a civil reply before remarking it was time they left. He chose to give Bella his arm, leaving Jeremy to escort Alex and Lord Gillingham to squire Marietta.

The drive to the theatre was a short one, and Lord Arlington entertained his guests with a lively description of the comedy they would see that evening. Alex heard him mention the Theatre Royal in Drury Lane and was sorely tempted to ask him if they would see Miss Fanchon performing that evening, but even as she considered it, their carriage rolled to a stop in Catherine Street and the steps were let down.

The Marquess lead them through the entrance and up a magnificent stairway to the rotunda. His private box was situated to the left of the stage and contained enough comfortable chairs to seat the entire party. As she took her seat, Alex was conscious of the unusual attention they were attracting. Several persons who had exchanged nods and smiles with the Marquess seemed to be staring at the sisters. Marietta preened, confident as only youth can be that people were admiring their elegant party, but Alex was embarrassed. She could not help but imagine that everyone was gossiping about her and the Marquess.

She sat very straight in her seat, carefully looking neither left nor right, thinking of the desperate stratagem she had devised to counter the rumours. Apparently Arlington had not heard the rumours, and if she could act swiftly enough, perhaps no one would ever dare to enlighten him. It was a reprehensible plan, but if it could be seen by the ton that her attention was engaged elsewhere, no one would credit the gossip. She was determined to flirt outrageously with the first eligible gentleman she encountered. She might, perhaps, be stigmatized as fast, but she found even that to be preferable to what the Marquess might otherwise think of her.

Alex allowed her eyes to stray to the left, covertly watching Lord Arlington. She had to own that he did look magnificent in evening attire. He put her in mind of the rakes she'd pictured when reading one of her mama's novels. They always were portrayed as devastatingly handsome men. The Marquess seemed perfectly cast as one of those dashing types who wins the heart and, frequently, the virtue of the heroine. She sternly reminded herself that only occurred in nonsensical fiction. In real life, rakes were more villainous than heroic. She stole another look at Arlington. He appeared immersed in the play, but she could not believe he was unaware of her. She was achingly aware of his presence.

John Kettering's voice boomed loudly from the stage, and although she had often wished to see *The Merry Gentlemen* performed, she found she was unable to keep her mind on the farce. She began to look searchingly at the occupants of the other boxes, seeking a likely gentleman with whom she might set up a flirtation. There was scattered applause and a few raucous howls at the conclusion of the first act, and with a start, Alex realized the Marquess was asking how she was enjoying the play.

"Mr. Kettering is marvelous. It is small wonder the house is packed," she replied, repeating what she'd heard others saying.

His eyebrows rose. "You relieve me, Miss Hilliard. Almost, you persuade me. I had feared you were not at all entertained, and your thoughts were wandering."

The brown eyes quizzed her, and once again she had the uncomfortable notion he could read her mind. The door to their box opened, and Barstow entered with Miss Comstock on his arm. Sara was in raptures over the play, and while she chatted with much enthusiasm to Marietta, Lord Barstow nodded to Arlington and then bowed low over Alex's hand.

"I confess I found it difficult to keep my eyes on the stage with such a vision as you presented on your arrival! Ah, tonight the star is not on the stage but in this box."

Alex, who had scant patience with such fulsome compliments, might have turned his words aside had not Arlington make a sort of choking sound. Disdaining to look at him, and mindful of her strategy, she rewarded Barstow with a sweet smile.

"I am much obliged and indeed flattered that you even observed us, sir, when you are attended by such charming company as Miss Comstock." She tapped him playfully on the arm with her fan and looked up at him through her lashes.

"Miss Comstock, though lovely, is still unformed. She has not yet attained your grace, if I may be permitted to say so. Indeed, most ladies pale in comparison to your brilliance," he replied, much encouraged.

There was no reply she could properly return, and Alex lowered her eyes, playing idly with her new fan.

"Miss Comstock and her mama were invited by Mother, and I must say I am thankful her desire to visit with Marietta has provided me with an opportunity to see you," Barstow continued. "I intended to look in on you today, you know, but Mother kept me rather busy with her commissions. Perhaps, however, you'd care for a drive in the park tomorrow? It is quite lovely just now."

"How kind of you to think of it, sir. It is, of all things, what I should most enjoy." And, she thought with a pang, if he bores me silly, it will only be what I deserve.

Barstow seemed to visibly swell with satisfaction, and it was with a great deal of reluctance that he turned to answer a question from Miss Meersham. Alex felt Arlington's eyes on her and braced herself to meet what she felt could only be derision for such a contemptible person as herself.

"You will be moped to death, you know," he whispered quietly, his eyes full of humour. "And if you're not careful, you'll have the fellow proposing in the middle of Hyde Park."

"Really, Lord Arlington," she breathed, his words bringing a blush to her cheeks.

"You must see, Miss Hilliard, that you've set him up wonderfully. Bat your eyes at him again and he will swell up enough to pop his buttons. And to grant him a drive with you— Now, I wonder why you did so? Oh, no, spare me. I know it's no business of mine. I only meant to warn you. Unless, of course, you really mean to have him?"

Alexandria refused to answer such nonsense and carefully kept her eyes down.

"No, I don't believe so," the Marquess said after studying her profile for a moment. "And poor Barstow is so full of self-esteem that your refusal will likely puncture him. He will deflate like one of those hot air balloons. Probably go into a decline, and his death will be laid at your door. No, my dear, it would be far better were you not to encourage the fellow."

"I take leave to tell you, sir, that I find your remarks reprehensible," she whispered, while trying hard not to smile at his foolishness. "Lord Barstow is an old friend of the family. That he should drive me through the park is surely unexceptional."

"Oh, quite. Except when you smile in that melting way at him. That would soften the heart of the most hardened rake."

"How can you say so, sir? It has had no effect on you," Alex said without thinking, and then blushed. It was only that she had been thinking of rakes and Arlington.

"Are you implying that I am a rake, Miss Hilliard?"

"Indeed not, my lord. It would be most improper of me to *imply* any such thing."

"A hit," he acknowledged, laughing, and she couldn't help laughing with him, until she recalled her problem. To be seen laughing and chatting amiably with Arlington was what she least desired. Hastily, she turned to her sister and Miss Comstock, complimenting the latter on her attractive gown.

Jeremy seconded her approval, and Sara blushed rosily, cast into confusion. Barstow smiled patronizingly and was on the verge of escorting her back to their own box when the door opened again. A gentleman entered—a man so outra-

geously handsome that Alex thought he must be one of the
actors. She was disabused of that notion by his careless
greeting to the Marquess. Arlington looked less than
pleased to see him, and grudgingly made him known to the
rest of the party. He introduced the stranger, rather curtly, as
the Chevalier d'Orly. The abruptness of his manner may
have caused his guests some unease, but it had little effect
on d'Orly.

The Chevalier was an incredibly attractive man, with
lively blue eyes, glossy locks of blond hair, cut and curled
stylishly, and an air of elegance that bespoke of admittance
to the first circles. His coat was simply cut but looked
expensive, and his linen was of the finest lace. His address
was distinguished and, at least from the ladies' point of
view, enhanced by a slight foreign accent.

Barstow merely nodded in response and hastened Miss
Comstock from the box as though he feared contamination.
The Chevalier bowed gracefully to Miss Meersham and
engaged her in amusing, trifling conversation. Alex, watching, compared him to Arlington. The Marquess, she decided, had a more manly look about him, while d'Orly
appeared almost effeminate. But with his excellent manners
and continental air, he was sure to be a favourite with the
ladies. He, she decided, might do very well for her plan.
Accordingly, when d'Orly turned his attention to her, Alex
gave him her most dazzling smile and enquired how long he
would be in town.

"I confess I had planned only a short visit, but now that
I have seen the beauty London offers, I may extend my
stay."

Arlington interrupted rudely. "Your visit must be cut
short, at least for now, Chevalier. The second act is
beginning."

D'Orly accepted the dismissal with grace and smoothly
bowed himself out, but not before giving Alexandria such a
look of longing that she had little doubt the Chevalier would
find an opportunity to further their acquaintance.

Bella remarked on his charm to the Marquess, receiving
only silence in reply. She decided a morning call to Lady

Fitzhugh was in order. If anyone had knowledge of d'Orly, it would be that lady. Alex had looked quite taken with the Frenchman, and Bella owned she thought him very presentable. However, Alex's inheritance made her a target for unscrupulous fortune hunters, and it would be well to know more of the Chevalier. It was a sad fact of life, Bella thought, that fortune hunters were invariably gentlemen of grace and charm. She would enquire discreetly into his background and expectations.

The noise and confusion in the theatre died down as most of the audience gave their attention to the actors. Alex dutifully directed her attention to the stage, a half smile playing on her lips as she considered the Chevalier.

The Marquess, observing her, wondered what devilment was afoot. His brief acquaintance with Alexandria had convinced him that she had more than moderate intelligence— too much to be taken in by a slippery character like d'Orly. The Chevalier, as he chose to call himself, was known to Arlington as a fellow member of various gaming clubs, and although he was received by some of the less discerning members of the ton, it was well known he was hanging out for a rich wife. And there was that unfortunate affair with Lord Wendover's daughter. Arlington toyed with the notion of dropping a hint in Miss Hilliard's ear, but ultimately rejected the idea. She had clearly demonstrated her resentment of any action she perceived as interference in her affairs. He suspected a word from him would result in her encouraging the fellow merely to be contrary.

He glanced at the haughty profile Alex offered him. Well, at least she was not fawning over him. In fact, she had treated both d'Orly and Barstow far more warmly than himself, and that was enough to arouse his curiosity. He was not, he hoped, overly conceited, but the thought that a young lady of breeding would prefer the attentions of either of those gentlemen to his own was difficult to credit. He returned his attention to the stage, though his thoughts remained centered on Alex as he tried to puzzle out possible reasons for her behaviour.

Alex, too, was staring at the stage, but observing little of what was transpiring. It was only towards the end of the scene that her attention was captured. One of the actresses was commanded to make a curtain call by several dandies sitting in the pit. She reappeared, and Alex studied her. Petite, but possessed of a perfectly proportioned figure, she had long black hair which cascaded in curls to frame an elfin face. That she enjoyed a tremendous popularity was obvious as she received a standing ovation and the stage was pelted with flowers. As she rose from a deep bow, she kissed her fingers to the audience and cast her dark eyes upwards. Alex had the distinct impression that the girl was staring directly into their box. She turned to Arlington in time to see him smile and nod towards the actress.

It was unreasonable, but she felt a sinking feeling in her stomach and more than a small measure of disappointment. It appeared Mrs. Ponsonby had been correct after all. Alex tilted her chin up, determined to take no notice of the actress or of Arlington's interest in the girl. She wasn't offered the opportunity in any event. The Marquess, with a brief bow, begged leave to be excused, and left the box.

Marietta, equally observant but much less reticent, immediately turned to Gillingham. "Is that dark-haired actress one of Lord Arlington's paramours?"

Bella promptly rapped Marietta's knuckles with her fan. "Wherever do you learn such language, child? And what Lord Gillingham thinks of you, I shudder to think, using vulgar cant."

"But Aunt Bella, you said Lord Arlington kept company with—"

Another sharp rap kept her from completing her thought, but there was little doubt of what she had meant to say. The Viscount strove manfully to keep from laughing aloud, and Jeremy only made matters worse as he tried to come to his sister's rescue.

"Marietta is such an innocent, Gillingham. She chatters and has no more idea than a babe of what she's saying. She has, unfortunately, heard rumours of Arlington's . . . er . . . patronage of the arts, and . . . well, she . . ."

This delicacy of manner in describing the Marquess' clandestine affairs proved too much for both Gillingham and Alex. She choked with laughter, while he covered his with a fit of coughing. Jeremy, seeing the absurdity of the situation, gave it up with a rueful grin and tried to turn the conversation.

His aunt supported him, suggesting they stroll in the corridor, and pinched Marietta. She was speedily escorted from the box, with Jeremy taking one arm and Bella the other. Alex knew her sister would receive a severe scold, and thought it unjust since she was only repeating what they had both heard Aunt Bella say. Alex and the Viscount eyed each other solemnly before both again succumbed to unchecked laughter.

"I pray you'll forgive us, Lord Gillingham," Alex said, regaining her composure. "Marietta is, as Jeremy said, an innocent, and I fear Aunt Bella was indiscreet in repeating gossip in her presence. Even living retired as we did, we heard that Arlington has had several actresses under his protection."

"Oh, no! Not several," the young man said, laughing. "Only one at a time, I do assure you. Do not, I beg you, disturb yourself. Only a fool would suppose Miss Marietta has any notion of what that entails. I've never been so diverted."

Alex smiled her appreciation of his understanding and told him, "I know we have not been as strict with her as we should have been. Since our parents died, we all tend to rather spoil her. I must warn you, she has the most distressing habit of speaking of whatever is on her mind regardless of who may be present. I can only be thankful that the Marquess left the box when he did."

"True, but I wonder how he would have answered her? Marietta was speaking the truth, you know. Cecily Fanchon is his latest . . . how should I say . . . fancy? She's all the rage just now, but Arlington remains her favourite. Last month he presented her with a new high-perch phaeton and a matched pair, which she drives most afternoons through Hyde Park. It was the talk of the ton until your arrival."

"My arrival? What can that have to say to anything?" she asked, desperately seeking to distract him from this talk of Miss Fanchon. She had no desire to hear any more details regarding that!

"If tales of Arlington's exploits have reached you in the country, then surely you must be aware that Arlington is hardly in the habit of calling on respectable ladies? There is a fresh rumour afoot that he is much attracted to you, and his escorting you here this evening is so far out of character it was bound to cause comment."

"Nonsense. Marietta is his ward. It cannot be thought exceptional that he makes a push to see her well established."

"If you believe that, then you are not well acquainted with the Marquess. Why, his sister was in Town last Season with her two girls—Arlington's nieces, you know. And not once did he call on them. My mother, who knows the family well, told me Lady Colburn was most put out. She tried to get Arlington to give a ball for the older girl, but he wouldn't have it. He does not attend balls or routs or anything of that nature. Not even Almack's."

"How very strange. And does the ton speculate on the reasons for his dislike of such harmless diversions?"

"Not now. Everyone who knows him sort of expects it. It's only since your arrival that the old rumours have started up again."

"I loathe rumours and gossip-mongers, but I suppose I'd best know what people are saying."

"My mother says it dates back to when he was just a boy, without any expectations. He wasn't always in line for the title, you know. Well, the story goes that he fell deeply in love with a young lady who was the toast of the Season. She seemed to return his regard—until she learned that he had only a modest portion. Then she scorned his attentions and tried to engage the affections of a wealthy young baronet."

"It is hard to imagine Lord Arlington in such a situation."

"He was only about Jeremy's age then, and the lady was his first love. Mama said it changed him completely. Then, only a month later, his uncle and cousin were both lost at sea, and Arlington succeeded to the title. The young lady who had scorned him jilted her baronet and threw herself at Arlington. Whatever occurred between them isn't known. All anyone knows for certain is that Arlington left Town and did not return for several months. He courted one of the ingenues then, and since has only been seen with actresses and ballerinas.

"How extraordinary," she murmured, not knowing what else to say.

He nodded in agreement. "I've heard it said that someone dared to ask him why he prefers their company to that of more respectable young ladies, and Arlington is said to have replied that although actresses make their living at make-believe, they are invariably more honest in their affections."

"I begin to understand," Alex said softly, her heart touched. She could imagine how Jeremy would have been hurt in such a situation.

"That's why I was so pleased when he suggested this party. Not that I wouldn't have been pleased to escort Miss Marietta anywhere," he added hastily. "But Arlington befriended me several years ago when I first came up to town. Helped me out of a devilish scrape, in fact. No man ever had a better friend, I can assure you. And as his friend, I'm truly pleased that he's entering Society again. I think we have you to thank for that."

While Gillingham was discussing Arlington's affairs with Alex, the Marquess was conversing with Cecily Fanchon in her private dressing room. The young actress was seated at her vanity, repairing her make-up for the final act. As her hands worked deftly, her eyes watched Arlington in the mirror. It had been some time since the Marquess had called on her, and disturbing rumours had reached her ears. Cecily had been delighted to see him in his usual box—until she'd noticed the attractive redhead seated beside him.

"I could not help but note that you are not with your usual cronies tonight, Phillip. Did my eyes deceive me, or were there really two charming young ladies in your box?"

Arlington didn't respond at once, and she saw him withdraw an enameled jewel case from his coat. Her heart beating rapidly, she watched him approach until he stood directly behind her, one hand lazily caressing her shoulder, while the other extended the box to her.

"A trinket, my fair Fanchon, to adorn one of your graceful arms."

Without a word she accepted the gift, her eyes still locked on his in the mirror. There was no answering warmth in the brown eyes, and, disconcerted, she looked down at the box she held. Cecily sensed this was not just another trinket, but rather one of the Marquess' infamous parting gifts. With trembling fingers she undid the clasp. A gasp escaped her lips as she beheld the brilliant bracelet of diamonds nestled there, and again her eyes flew to his.

"I am afraid, Phillip. I fear you mean this to say good-bye." Dropping the box on the vanity, she stood, whirling to face him. Tiny hands reached for his shoulders, but he captured them in his.

"What a clever girl you are, Cecily. I find I shall be occupied with . . . family affairs. The bracelet is to console you for my absence."

"As if a bracelet could take your place! Tell me, dearest Phillip, these family affairs— They will be of short duration, perhaps?"

"I would not depend on it, little one. But it cannot signify when so many gentlemen wait outside your door. You've only to smile at one of them . . . Middleton, perhaps?"

Her eyes widened. Surely, he could not know of her affair with Middleton when she had been at such pains to be discreet. He smiled at her, a cold, mocking smile that told her he did indeed know. Releasing her hands, he retrieved the bracelet and slipped it on her wrist. Bowing gracefully, he kissed it into place.

"Let us say adieu amicably. I shall forgive your indiscretions, and you shall forgive my intolerance."

"Your intolerance?"

He smiled, almost apologetically. "You see, dear Cecily, I have no tolerance for deception."

He was in the hall before she could reply. Feeling free of an irksome burden, Arlington returned to his box in excellent spirits. He encountered Bella in the hall with Jeremy and Marietta, and gave Bella his arm. They barely had time to regain their seats before the third act was under way.

Alexandria tried to appear as though she were entranced by the play, but she was wishing she could be home, alone with her thoughts. Gillingham had given her much to ponder, and she found it difficult to think coherently with Arlington's distracting presence beside her.

The curtain rang down on the final act, producing a thundering ovation for Kettering. Bella motioned for Jeremy to give her his arm before Arlington had the opportunity to do so, leaving him to escort Alex. As they exited the box, Arlington expertly maneuvered her through the crowded corridor. She tried to express her appreciation for the treat he had provided, but he waved her thanks aside.

"All gratitude must be on my side, Miss Hilliard. The privilege of escorting you and my ward has made me the envy of every buck in London. No doubt, I will be plagued tomorrow with demands for introductions."

"Certainly a fate to which you must aspire."

"Not precisely," he smiled. "Still, to be the envy of one's fellow men is, on occasion, most gratifying."

"Then, I am sure you have been gratified frequently, if only half the tales I've heard are true."

"What? Do not tell me rumours of my exploits have reached as far as Allenswood. I cannot credit it."

"Obviously you have never lived in the country, my lord. Every word and action you take are occasion for remark. And, as it is known that you are the twins' guardian, certain people feel obliged to keep us informed of your . . . activities."

His mobile brows flew upwards. "You alarm me, Miss Hilliard."

She laughed. "Rest assured that we pay little heed to such tales. Our faith is in Papa's judgement, and if he thought you a suitable guardian, it matters not what others might say."

"Your father was a fine gentleman," he replied in a more sober tone. "I was distressed to hear of his passing."

An impish smile on her lips, Alex could not resist teasing him. "And surprised, I would wager, to find yourself named as guardian."

"You understate the matter, my dear. Shocked would be the more appropriate term. However, I am beginning to find it a pleasant obligation, so you will not find me complaining."

"Why, how noble of you, sir—after neglecting us for the last three years!"

"Not noble, perhaps, but at least honest. Now confess, Miss Hilliard, would it have raised me in your esteem had I ridden posthaste to Allenswood and undertaken to advise you at every turn?"

"If you insist on honesty, then I admit I probably would have wished you to the devil. I have a great dislike for unsolicited advice."

"Yet, you stand on terms with Lord Barstow," he mused, pretending to be puzzled. "Prosy fellow. Just the type to feel that you would benefit from his wisdom."

As Barstow was bearing down on them, with Sara Comstock on his arm, Alex was unable to return an answer, and shot him a reproachful look. Although his face was solemn, she easily read the laughter in his eyes.

Sara was in raptures over the play and the skill of John Kettering. "Did you not think it was marvelous? Sometimes I forgot it was only a play, and although I did not always understand what was going on, Lord Barstow was kind enough to explain it all to me."

Alex dared not look at Arlington, but she heard him saying smoothly, "I am certain he did so quite capably, and perhaps he was able to give you a history of the architecture of the theatre as well?"

"Oh, yes, he told us about it as we entered," Sara answered innocently. Turning to Marietta, she asked if she knew the building had been destroyed by fire and rebuilt only a few years past. Marietta, who had little, if any, interest in such matters, quickly found a more diverting topic, and Jeremy and Gillingham joined them. Alex conversed politely with Lady Comstock and Lady Barstow while Arlington listened with the appearance of due courtesy.

When they reached the steps and found their carriages waiting, Barstow delayed them while he reminded Alex that he would call for her the following afternoon, much to his mother's dismay.

"Oh, Peter. I had hoped for your escort. You know I wished to do some shopping," she said, with a look of much sorrow.

Lady Comstock, whose kindly nature did not lead her to attribute less charitable motives to others, immediately offered to call for her and provide her with company. Lady Barstow agreed reluctantly, and the arrangements were set. Sara, who had no wish to accompany them, begged to be allowed to visit Marietta instead, and gaining consent, was able to bid them good evening quite happily.

Lord Barstow could not be brought to such a speedy departure. He felt compelled to admonish the ladies against standing about in the night air. "It's just on evenings such as this that one is most likely to catch an inflammation of the lungs. One is beguiled by the warmth into standing about conversing—"

"Just so, Barstow," Arlington interrupted. "Let us not keep the ladies standing here. Good night." And without further ceremony, he handed Bella into his carriage. When they were all comfortably settled, Marietta told him she had not before clearly understood the benefits of having a guardian.

"No one has ever been able to get him to leave so quickly before," she confided, full of admiration.

Bella, unwilling to give up her previous good opinion of Barstow, chastened her mildly. "Really, Marietta, it's unkind of you to make sport of Lord Barstow when he is so . . . chivalrous."

"You may call it chivalrous," Jeremy said, "but I call it dashed stupid. First, he tells us how dangerous it is to stand about, and then he keeps us standing there."

Alex refused to comment, but looked up to see a pair of

quizzing brown eyes watching her, and could not refrain from a small smile. It was obvious Arlington had risen another notch in her brother's esteem, and she, too, found herself responding to his easy charm. He did not detain them when they reached the square, much to Marietta's disappointment. She would have liked a private word with Gillingham. But the gentlemen escorted them to the door, and with barely time for a word or two, took their leave.

Bella and Marietta wished to discuss the evening in full detail, but Alex felt strangely reticent. She pleaded a slight headache and retired to her room. Mary was allowed to brush out her hair, and assist her into a nightdress, before Alex dismissed her. Although the hour was late, she found she could not sleep, and her thoughts kept returning to Lord Arlington.

She owned she might have misjudged the man, and half-wished she could start over with him. How would he react when he heard the rumour of his supposed tendre for her? Would he think, as did Lady Fitzhugh, that she had cleverly circulated that bit of gossip? She turned restlessly, unable to bear the idea that he might think her a scheming female—no more worthy of his regard than the female who had jilted him.

If only she had not babbled so mindlessly to Madam Theresa. It was the modiste, she was sure, who had started the rumour. She and Lady Jersey. Sally Jersey seemed just the sort to harangue the Marquess about her. Alex could imagine her telling him in that silky voice, "Why I had it straight from the modiste, and she got it from Miss Hilliard herself." She felt her face flushing in the dark as she pictured the scene. Surely, it would be better to pretend an attraction for the Chevalier. He, after all, was an accomplished flirt, and little harm could come from that. She consoled herself with the thought that after a little time, she could be seen to lose interest in the Frenchman.

Mary was surprised to find her mistress still asleep when she drew the curtains the following morning. Sunlight flooded the room, and Alex, after opening her eyes, promptly shut them again. Mary told her it was going on ten o'clock and the others were already breakfasting in the morning room. She allowed Alex a few minutes to sip her chocolate before returning to assist her into a pretty green and white dressing gown. Alex applied cool water to her face, which helped a little, but she still looked pale and very tired when she went down to join the others.

She found Marietta in high spirits, planning an afternoon expedition to Westminster Abbey and the Tower of London. Jeremy, it seemed, had obligingly offered her his escort. Marietta taunted her sister, "It's too bad you are promised to Barstow, else you could join us, Alex. Jeremy promised to take us to Gunter's for an ice afterwards."

The reminder of her afternoon engagement did little to raise her spirits, but she tried to appear cheerful, and teased her brother. "Since when have you developed an interest in historical sights? Do I have Miss Comstock to thank for giving your mind a new direction?"

Jeremy reddened and stood abruptly, knocking over his chair. "I don't know what the world's coming to if I can't offer my sister escort without a deuced lot of fanfare!" He left the room without apology, and the three ladies sat stunned. Alex, who had spoken only in jest, decided Miss Comstock was a force to be reckoned with, and then smiled with real amusement at her aunt.

"Poor Lady B. Her plans have gone all awry. Here is Barstow promised to drive me to the park, while the young lady his mama selected for him seems to prefer our Jeremy. Would it not be ironic, Aunt Bella, were Jeremy to cut out Barstow?"

"I do not find the thought amusing, Alexandria. Do you really believe Jeremy's feelings are engaged?"

"In truth, I haven't given it much thought. But what else would induce him to volunteer for a historical expedition? I cannot remember that he ever evinced a desire to see anything other than a mill or horse race."

"Well, I can tell you that Sara thinks him quite handsome," Marietta said. "And I don't believe she even considers Lord Barstow as a suitor. For my part, I think he's a great deal too old for her. She and Jeremy would deal much better together, and I do know Jeremy has promised to stand up with her at Almack's."

"I can only advise you not to tease him over the matter," Alex said. "It's early days yet."

Dobbs's entrance put an end to their tête-à-tête. He presented Alex with a small parcel. "It has just been delivered by hand, miss. There was neither card nor message with it."

Alex stared at the elegantly wrapped box until prompted by Marietta to undo the ribbons. Lifting the cover, she found a delicate gold hat pin with a lustrous pearl head. Carefully, she removed it and extracted the card beneath, to read the note silently.

For windy excursions in the park, a hat pin is a most useful implement, excellent not only for securing hats, but for deflating hot air balloons. The card was simply signed with a flourishing A.

"What does it say, Alex? Who is it from?" Marietta was demanding, while Bella watched her curiously.

"It's from Lord Arlington. Merely a hat pin, in case it's windy in the park today." She tried to speak casually, and laid the box aside, hoping to divert her family. Bella, however, pounced on the box and read the card aloud.

"How very odd. What does he mean about deflating balloons? Is there to be a balloon ascension in the park? But surely, a hat pin wouldn't deflate one of those? And even if it would, who in the world would wish to do so?"

"It's nothing, Aunt Bella. A trifle only. You must excuse me now, for I promised Mrs. Delahan I'd see her this morning." Without waiting for a reply, Alex pocketed the tiny box and card, and fled the room.

Chapter 6

MISS COMSTOCK ARRIVED at the house in Hanover Square that afternoon just minutes before Lord Barstow was announced. Sara giggled as Jeremy groaned, and Alex frowned a warning at them both. The younger party was anxious to set out, and after greetings were exchanged, edged toward the door. Barstow could not allow them to leave, however, without first cautioning Jeremy on the dangers of driving in London.

"These Town avenues are not to be compared with our quiet country roads, you know. One must always be alert if one is to avoid a mishap."

"I shall take care," Jeremy promised.

"Have you procured a copy of the *Picturesque Guide to London*? It's invaluable, I assure you, for anyone wishing to visit our historical monuments. What a pity you did not think to consult with me, for I could have given you the loan of a copy. The information contained within is really most remarkable."

Lord Barstow continued to instruct Jeremy in this helpful manner, while Marietta stood regarding him much as one would a specimen under glass. Alex guessed she was considering him in the guise of a potential suitor for Sara, and finding him lacking. Fearful of what her impetuous sister might feel compelled to say, Alex urged them to be off, reminding them that the hour was already well advanced.

"Remember now, Jeremy, don't spring your horses," Barstow called after them.

Alex saw her brother's face darken, but he left without

retort, and she turned to Barstow, exasperated. "That really was not necessary. Jeremy is a capable whip, and you only succeeded in putting up his back."

"Oh, he may ride a trifle testy, but I have no doubt he will heed my advice. Besides, my dear, I could not reconcile it with my conscience were I to say nothing and he later suffered an accident. I only regret that I did not know of his intention to visit the Tower. Its history is quite fascinating."

Alex's conscience had troubled her over using Lord Barstow for her own ends, and to quiet it, she had told herself she would be an attentive companion to that gentleman, and he would enjoy spending a pleasant afternoon in her company. However good her resolve, it wavered rapidly as she suffered through a long recital of the Tower's infamous and bloody history, from the horrors endured by Lady Jane Grey to the impressive behaviour of Princess Elizabeth at Traitor's Gate. It was only at the entrance to the park that she was able to turn the conversation.

She exclaimed over the number of carriages driven by the most fashionable gentlemen, and espying Lord Quarrels, waved gaily. His carriage passed in the opposite direction, and he doffed his hat to her. Lord Barstow explained the deficiencies of the cabriolet Quarrels was driving as compared to the advantages his own barouche offered. Alex barely heard him, her interest fixed as she saw Lady Jersey driving with Lady Cowper in a stylish curricle, and the latter smiled kindly as she nodded to her.

The pace was necessarily slow, and they had not progressed very far when she observed Lieutenant Hastings. He was standing alongside one of the paths with two other gentlemen, and sported his military colours. Alex thought he looked impressive in scarlet regimentals, and impulsively begged Barstow to pull over.

The Lieutenant was delighted to see her, and after introductions were exchanged, he enquired after Marietta. They chatted amiably for a few minutes, and as he and his friends took their leave, the Chevalier d'Orly cantered up on a showy black stallion. Smiling warmly at Alex, he barely acknowledged Barstow, and received only a frosty nod in return.

D'Orly executed a courtly bow from horseback. "My prayers have been answered. Surely it was destiny that directed me to ride in this direction, that we might meet again so soon. I had not anticipated that pleasure until tomorrow evening."

"Tomorrow?" she queried, puzzled.

"But, yes. I have just come from Lady Comstock, who is planning a small party for her daughter. She is such kindness, and does me the honour of extending an invitation. She confides in me she is to invite all the Hilliards, also. My acceptance was then of a certainty. You will attend, will you not?" The blue eyes looked up at her beseechingly, and the Chevalier seemed to hold his breath awaiting her answer.

"How can I accept an invitation I have not received?" she asked, laughing. As he started to gesture excitedly, she reassured him. "Do not be alarmed, sir. My brother and sister are with Miss Comstock even as we speak, and they will escort her home later. Should Lady Comstock extend an invitation, you may be sure they shall accept on behalf of our family. Will there be dancing, do you think?"

"*Assurément.* You will stand up with me, yes? A waltz to show off your beauty and grace."

"A quadrille or country dance, sir. I'm not allowed, as yet, to perform the waltz. One must have the approval of the Patronesses of Almack's before one waltzes in public."

"They must be brought to grant this approval, then. To deny me the opportunity of waltzing with you would be too cruel." D'Orly would have continued save his horse chose that moment to take offense at a passing carriage. The stallion reared up on its hind legs, demanding the Chevalier's full attention.

Alex, once assured the horse would not bolt, could not help but admire the attractive tableau man and stallion presented. D'Orly's blondness contrasted sharply with the black, satiny coat of the horse he called Diablo.

Lord Barstow was pointedly less enthused. He had his

hands full controlling his own team, which reacted nervously to the black's temperamental display. He snapped the whip, setting them off at a canter, and put as much distance as possible between them and the Chevalier. Alex glanced back to see d'Orly, his horse well under control, wave a cheerful farewell.

Barstow, his team steadied, slowed them to a walk. "Impertinent fellow. He has no business riding that horse in the park if he cannot control it. Those foreigners are all alike. No sense of propriety. And asking you to waltz. The idea. Why, I wonder you did not give him a setdown."

"No, did you? I should think he waltzes very well."

Barstow glared at her. "I take leave to tell you, Alexandria, that such levity is not becoming. I can only pray that it won't lead you into making yourself the subject of further gossip by encouraging that coxcomb. I have it on excellent authority that his reputation is scandalous, and it would scarce do you credit to be seen with him."

"If Lady Comstock has admitted the Chevalier to her home, I can hardly be censured for behaving civilly to him," Alex replied stiffly.

"Civilly? Ha! I may be thought a conservative, but setting up a flirtation in the middle of Hyde Park is not my notion of civil behaviour. I call it brazen—"

"Brazen! Why of all the pompous—" She broke off, and taking a deep breath, replied in measured tones, "Please be so good as to return me to my home at once."

Realizing that he had gone too far, Lord Barstow offered an apology of sorts. "I didn't mean that *you* are brazen. It is only that you are unfamiliar with Town ways and might unintentionally step beyond the line of what is pleasing, and while I know your intentions must be above reproach, I fear others would judge you more harshly. I may have spoken a trifle harshly, my dear, but you must know that your welfare is always my first concern."

"You take too much upon yourself, sir. I have not given you leave to concern yourself with my affairs," Alex said in a low voice, staring straight ahead.

Barstow was nonplussed. His mother had warned him,

frequently, that Miss Hilliard would not defer to his superior judgement, and as usual, Mother was right. He turned his horses, but reluctant to foreswear his habitual adoration of her, especially as she looked so fetching with the gold feathers curling over her red hair, he made one last attempt to bring her to a sense of her injustice.

"I know Miss Meersham would agree with me had she witnessed d'Orly's conduct. It is obvious to any person of discernment that the Chevalier is little more than a fortune-hunting—"

"There you are out, sir. Aunt Bella thinks d'Orly very personable, and she chatted with him at length last evening. And if you think that my fortune is the only reason that a gentleman would pay me compliments, well . . . well, it is unkind of you to say so!"

"I can see that you are determined to misunderstand me. Let us say no more until we are calmer." He proceeded to say a great deal more, remarking more than once that a period of cool reflection would no doubt be beneficial, and he would repose his trust in her usual good sense.

Alex did her best to curb her temper, but her nerves were on edge, and it was an effort of will not to flee the carriage and walk home. She adjusted her hat and, feeling the hatpin, had a most uncharitable impulse to use it on Lord Barstow. Imagining his shocked countenance did much to relieve her feelings, and she was able to take her leave of him with at least a semblance of cordiality.

Bella had returned from her call on Lady Fitzhugh, and Dobbs informed Alex that her aunt was in the yellow salon. Alex greeted her as cheerfully as possible given her frame of mind. Removing her hat and gloves, she enquired politely how Lady Fitzhugh was faring.

"Quite well," Bella replied, pouring out a cup of tea for her niece. "It is an extraordinary thing, but although Flora rarely leaves her home, she knows everything that goes on in the ton. She told me several persons have commented on the favourable impression both you and Marietta made at the theatre, and it must be true if one is to judge by the number of invitations that arrived today. Lady Comstock

had her man hand-deliver a card to a small rout she is giving
for her Sara tomorrow night. Do you think she is aware of
Jeremy's regard and means to encourage him?"

"Hardly. He has been acquainted with her for less than a
week," Alex said a trifle tartly.

"Sometimes that is all that is necessary," Bella said, her
mind intent on other matters. "Recollect your mama made
up her mind in only one night. I discussed the matter with
Flora, and *she* feels it would be an unexceptional match.
Jeremy may not possess a title, but he does have birth and
breeding, as well as a very nice income. I am certain anyone
would consider Allenswood a desirable property."

"How delightful that you have it settled between you.
Now all you have to do is to inform Jeremy and Sara."

"Whatever ails you, Alexandria?" Bella asked, glancing
at her in surprise. "It is not like you to be so waspish. Why,
anyone would think to hear you speak that I mean to do
Jeremy a mischief instead of very properly expressing a
natural concern that my nephew should be happily settled."

Instantly contrite, Alex reached over and squeezed her
aunt's hand. "Please forgive me. I seem to be turning into
the worst sort of shrew since coming to London. I confess
the thought of losing Jeremy so soon is distressing. I
thought I had reconciled myself to losing Marietta, but it did
not seem quite so imminent while we were still in the
country. And now, to think of losing Jeremy, too—well, we
shall have to make some plans."

Putting her thoughts into actual words made them seem
more real, and Alex felt a tightness in her throat. She
paused, sipping her tea, before adding, "I have had it in
mind for some time to lease a small house, and I hope you
will come bear me company, Aunt Bella."

"Who is rushing their fences now? Goodness, child, I do
not think we need consider that as yet. You caused quite a
stir last night, and I should own myself surprised if you do
not receive several offers yourself."

"I hope I do not overly disappoint you when I tell you
that Lord Barstow is not likely to be among them. We rather
quarreled in the park this afternoon, which is partially

why I am out of temper. I conversed for a few minutes with the Chevalier d'Orly, and our dear neighbour instantly accused me of setting up a flirtation with him. He warned me my reputation would suffer if I encourage the Frenchman. Did you ever hear anything so ridiculous?"

Bella was dismayed. Lady Fitzhugh had told her all about the charming Chevalier, warning her to discourage him from dangling after Alex. How that might be accomplished, neither she nor Flora knew. She nibbled on a biscuit, choosing her words carefully before replying hesitantly, "That you would allow anyone to set up a flirtation with you is certainly nonsense. As for the Chevalier, he's an amusing rogue, but not, I think, to be taken seriously."

"I wish you could have seen him, Aunt Bella. He has such a flair for dramatics. He was dressed in the lightest of colours, and riding a showy black stallion. A pretty picture. I am certain d'Orly will add a great deal of excitement to the Season."

"It would appear so. However, it is doubtful *we* shall see much of him. I understand that after his contretemps with Miss Wendover, he was snubbed by several members of the ton."

"Lady Comstock does not know it, then. She has invited him to her party for Sara, and we shall see him there tomorrow evening. Now tell me, who is Miss Wendover and what occurred?" Alex coaxed, handing her cup to Bella for a refill.

"She's the only daughter of Lord Augustus Wendover, and stands to inherit a modest fortune. The *on-dit* is that d'Orly pursued her when she first came to Town. There were rumours of clandestine meetings and that an elopement was nipped in the bud. Her father has removed her to Bath, where she is now guarded by two elderly aunts."

"Well, I hope you don't mean to cut the Chevalier merely on the basis of some rumours. I have learned one thing in London, and that is how unfairly gossip is started and spread—without a bit of truth in it. Only look how the news was spread of Lord Arlington's supposed *tendre* for me. Just because I was naive enough to mention to that modiste that

the Marquess was taking us to the theatre. Even Lady
Fitzhugh believes I deliberately started that rumour to
attract attention."

Bella deemed it prudent to say no more. She knew how
determined Alex could be if the girl believed someone was
being treated unfairly. Another word, and her niece would
become d'Orly's chief champion. She turned the conversation to the invitations they had received, and directed Alex's
attention to the stack of cards on the table.

Alex sorted through them, reading several aloud. The
invitations ranged from breakfast to alfresco parties, routs,
masquerades, and balls. They were engaged in a lively
discussion of the relative merits of the breakfast as opposed
to the picnic when Jeremy and Marietta returned.

Appealed to, Marietta quickly voted for the picnic, and
then, flushed with excitement, asked if Lady Comstock had
sent them an invitation. Once assured of that, the twins took
turns exclaiming over the sites they had seen, particularly
the Tower of London.

"I'm quite familiar with its history, thank you," Alex
interrupted with a smile. "Lord Barstow told me every
detail, I promise you."

Marietta giggled, and Jeremy, in unusually high good
humour, told her, "You must be sure to tell old Barstow that
I brought the girls home safely."

"I am certain he will be much relieved, for he seems to
think you cow-handed. However, it is rather doubtful that
he will be calling any time in the near future," she replied,
and explained their disagreement.

Marietta laughed gleefully. "He called you brazen? I
cannot believe he possessed so much courage." But Jeremy
was defensive on Alex's behalf, and she had to restrain him
from his instant desire to call Barstow to book for his insult.

"No insult was intended, and to be fair, the fault was as
much mine as his. Forget Lord Barstow and tell me instead
about Lady Comstock's rout." Alex watched Jeremy closely
as the talk turned to young Sara Comstock. He did not look
like a man infatuated, nor did he seem wishful of talking
about Sara, as men in love were reputed to do. He appeared

much more interested in his plans for the evening, at least as far as Alex could tell.

Lord Gillingham was going to call for him later, Jeremy explained, and they were going to White's, an exclusive gaming club.

Alex bit her tongue to keep from uttering the warning on her lips. White's was known throughout England, for many a fortune had been won or lost there on the turn of a card or the throw of the dice. She fought the urge to caution Jeremy against the dangers of high play, managing instead to wish him a pleasant evening.

The following morning she was not so certain she had been wise. Jeremy, normally an early riser, slept late. He woke with an excruciating headache and looked rather drawn when he entered the breakfast room. In reply to Dobbs's cheerful good morning, he remarked his head felt as though an entire platoon was using it for target practice.

Alex observed his grimace as he removed the cover from a dish of kippers, and she saw him wince as he took his seat opposite her. She knew he'd not returned home until early morning, and judged him to have been in his cups—the only explanation for the serenade beneath her window that had awakened her. She left him in peace for the moment, turning her attention to Marietta. His twin was anxious to know if she would be allowed to visit the Exeter Change with Sara.

"Please, Alex. Lady Comstock will send her carriage, and Sara's maid will go with us. Do say yes. Sara says we may get all manner of bargains on ribbons and stockings, even kid gloves. It's the most wonderful place and even has a menagerie on display. Sara said there is even a hippopotamus that Lord Byron has said looks just like Lord Liverpool!"

Neither she nor Bella had any objection to the scheme, and Marietta happily ran off to dispatch a footman to the Comstocks with a note for Sara. Bella, rising, announced she was calling on Flora, and to Alex's offer to accompany her, returned a vague reply that she would only find it dull as they would be discussing old acquaintances.

Alex and Jeremy were still at the table when Bella reappeared, and they both stared at her. Their aunt's morning dress was of primrose silk, a shade that in itself would have excited attention, but it was the hat that caused Alex to gaze in disbelief. The straw hat was a veritable bed of flowers, among which violets and daffodils vied for attention. As Bella talked, the flowers quivered, almost as if swaying in the breeze. Jeremy stared, fascinated. Alex choked on a morsel of toast, in awe of the vision before her.

Bella, noting their astonishment, twirled around to show off her new ensemble. Remarking how much younger one felt when dressed in cheery colours, she bid them good morning.

"Those colours combined together are enough to blind a man," Jeremy said as soon as she had left. "That hat made me distinctly queasy."

"Perhaps if you had imbibed less freely last night, your constitution would not be so sensitive this morning."

Jeremy flushed guiltily. "Did I disturb you when I came home?"

"Disturb me? Why, no," Alex replied calmly, buttering a fresh slice of toast. "How could I think it anything but pleasant to be awakened near dawn by my brother singing a rousing rendition of 'I Knew a Fair Maiden' beneath my window?"

"I hoped I had only dreamt that! I am sorry, Alex. I own I had a trifle too much to drink, but I did not think I was so bosky as to sing to my sister."

"I assure you it was not the serenade I objected to, but only the hour. I am surprised the watch did not take you up."

"Not a chance. Lord Arlington says they are a useless lot. He says most of the watchmen are so aged and decrepit they could not catch an old lady hobbling down the street. He thinks the watchmen are a national disgrace."

"Well, you should be thankful for it. Was Arlington at

White's, then?" she asked, pretending a casualness she did not feel.

"Hmmm," Jeremy said, around a mouthful of toast. "I played whist with him and some others, but I wasn't so bosky then. He lost several hands to me, so you need not think your brother is entirely inept."

"I don't, Jeremy," Alex said, reaching across a hand to him, but her mind was troubled and a moment later he had to repeat his question.

"I said, do you think Aunt Bella heard me singing last night?"

"I'm very sure she did not, or she would have mentioned it this morning. Fortunately for you, her rooms are on the far side of the house. But I do hope you don't mean to make this a habit."

Jeremy pledged his word against a recurrence, and promised he meant to spend a quiet afternoon. His only plan was to call at his tailor's to pick up his evening dress coat, which he wished to wear that night to the Comstocks. Alex let him go, wondering if she should have said more. She knew a young man must be allowed a certain amount of freedom, but she had not counted on him visiting gambling houses and coming home in his cups. And what disturbed her the most was that his guardian had allowed him to play cards at his table. Had Jeremy lost to the Marquess, it would have been a very awkward situation. With a sigh, she retired to the library to work on her accounts.

She was still in the library two hours later when Dobbs announced Elizabeth Lyndale Milton, the Viscountess Colburn, was calling. Surprised, she tidied her hair, and adjusted the apron on her morning dress, before entering the yellow drawing room where her visitor waited.

Lady Colburn had her back to the door, studying one of the framed prints. Alex had ample opportunity to observe her. She was not as tall as her brother, but had in common with him dark hair and a slender build. She looked very sophisticated in a royal-blue pelisse trimmed with ermine. A tiny matching hat perched jauntily on her curls.

"Good afternoon, Lady Colburn," Alex said, making her presence known. "How very kind of you to call."

"Miss Hilliard? I hope you will forgive me for just dropping by, but I confess my curiosity compelled me to see for myself the lady capable of commanding my brother's attentions. My brother, you know, is Lord Arlington."

"Yes, of course. He has mentioned you. Will you be seated?" Alex said, gesturing to the sofa. "As for commanding Arlington's attentions, I fear you give me too much credit. Perhaps you are unaware that Arlington stands as guardian to my younger brother and sister? I believe it is only out of concern for their welfare that the Marquess was good enough to lend us his escort."

"Ha!" Lady Colburn stared coldly at the girl before her. "My brother, as I have good reason to know, does not recognize that he has a duty to anyone excepting himself. I assure you, Phillip does exactly as he pleases. I envy him that at times. He truly does not have the slightest regard for what others may think of him."

"If duty did not prompt him, then I can only say he must be captivated by my younger sister. Marietta is a minx, and has managed to charm the most hardened of males since her cradle days. And she thinks very highly of her guardian."

"It would be a first. Phillip has never had any use for schoolroom misses. I doubt he could even tell you the names of his own nieces, both of whom are charming girls. Why, when Deidre, my oldest, had her come out last Season, he refused to have anything to do with her. I was never so vexed with him."

Embarrassed by Lady Colburn's persistence in frankly discussing her brother's character, Alex tried to turn the conversation. She politely asked if the younger Miss Milton would be making her debut this Season, and would they have the pleasure of seeing her at Almack's.

"Yes, that's why we are in Town. We have received vouchers, of course, but Deborah is in a quake over her first public ball. Is your Marietta a bundle of nerves, too?"

"Oh, no. I don't believe Marietta has ever been nervous. But then, she has her twin to lend her support. A brother can make all the difference. Did you not find it so when you were younger?"

Lady Colburn settled herself more comfortably on the sofa, and her face seemed to soften. "Phillip was different then. He was an indulgent brother, if somewhat strict in his notions. We were fairly close, once. It wasn't until he came into the title that he became so unapproachable. Why, I hardly saw him for almost two years, and then it was only by chance that we would meet. I am sorry to say that he has become almost a stranger. I would give much to have the old Phillip back again." She eyed Alex speculatively. "Perhaps you will have a salutary effect on him."

"I should not wager on it," Alex warned her. "We were practically at dagger heads when we first met. I have a great dislike for persons inclined to order one about," she continued, determined to make it clear that she had no interest in the Marquess.

"Did he do so? How very curious."

Alex flushed under Lady Colburn's scrutiny, and was afraid she was giving the wrong impression. She was saved from further embarrassment by her aunt's return. After making the ladies known to one another, Alex could almost see the wheels turning behind Bella's eyes. Fearful that her aunt would be only too willing to engage in a long and intimate discussion of the Marquess, she was much relieved to hear Lady Colburn declare that she must take her leave. Alex saw her out, with promises to renew their acquaintance at Almack's, and managed to avoid Bella's questioning with the pretext of needing to check on her gown for Lady Comstock's rout.

The gown in question, a pale blue robe of shimmering silk, was in perfect condition. Alex decided to wear a fluted pelerine of a deeper blue, which would help disguise the extremely low decolletage that was the fashion. Her judgement was vindicated by the admiring looks of her family when she descended to the drawing room that evening.

Alex laughed at their compliments, covering a momentary qualm at seeing the twins looking so grown up.

Marietta had beguiled Susan into putting up her hair, and
even the decorous neckline and tiny puffed sleeves of her
gown did not lessen the effect of an elegant young lady.
Jeremy, handsome in a long-tailed evening coat, satin knee
breeches, silk stockings, and brilliantly buckled shoes, bore
little resemblance to her scapegrace younger brother. He
looked every inch the gentleman about town as he bowed
over her hand. Her pride in them brought a stinging
sensation to her eyes, and only Bella's entrance in an
outrageous creation of emerald-green crepe restored her
balance.

Both the neckline and the hem of Bella's gown were
edged in feathers dyed various shades of green and blue.
Jeremy jokingly told her she looked like a bird of paradise.
Bella, who had always dressed rather conservatively, was
allowing herself more freedom in London, and plainly
enjoying the effect she created. She waved her fan at
Jeremy, and then urged them all to hurry, for they were
already fashionably late.

The house in Cavendish Square was brightly lit, with
candles in every window to welcome the arriving guests.
Numerous carriages lined the circular drive, causing Bella
to comment on the crush. "I had thought this was to be a
small, private party."

"It was," Marietta said. "But Sara was allowed to invite
all her particular friends, and Lady Comstock invited all her
friends, so it's likely to be a squeeze." She did not appear
at all daunted by the prospect, and was craning her neck to
see out their carriage window. "Alex, did you know Lord
Barstow would be here? Look, he's just going in with his
mama."

Alexandria declined to look, and advised her sister to try
for a little more conduct unless she wished to be thought a
green girl, just up from the country, who could not help
staring at the nobility. Her words had little effect on the
irrepressible Marietta, who continued to note the various
personages arriving. Alex let the matter drop, as their
carriage was next in line.

Once inside, and through the receiving room, there was

little opportunity for further conversation. The ballroom
was a delight. The vast expanse of marble floor was already
thronged with people. Huge chandeliers held a multitude of
candles, and masses of fresh flowers stood against the
walls. Alex watched, pleased for her sister, as Marietta was
instantly surrounded by a bevy of young gentlemen, all
clamouring for a dance. She saw both Lord Gillingham and
Lieutenant Hastings in the crowd, but it was Gillingham
who drew the honour of leading Marietta out for the first
set.

Lieutenant Hastings watched Marietta depart with patent
disappointment. Finding himself beside Alex, he politely
solicited her hand, but with such a marked lack of enthusiasm, she had to smile. She declined his offer kindly,
explaining that her role was that of a chaperone and she did
not intend to dance. As the Lieutenant left her, Lord
Barstow saw his opportunity and hesitantly approached her.

"Ah, Alexandria, how lovely you look. Dare I approach?
I've been in an agony of remorse since our encounter. Will
you cry friends if I most humbly beseech your pardon?"

"Most certainly, my lord," Alex said, giving him her
hand. "There is no need for an apology. I ask only that you
restrain yourself from censuring my conduct."

"I know I have not yet earned that privilege, but does not
the concern of a friend weigh with you?"

It was unfortunate that Lady Barstow, sighting her son in
conversation with Miss Hilliard, chose that moment to
approach them.

"How charming you look in blue, Miss Hilliard. A
delightful gown. I am quite certain Lord Arlington will
agree with me," she said, with a tittering laugh.

"I do not take your meaning, ma'am," Alex returned
coolly, while Barstow looked in puzzlement from one to the
other of the ladies.

"Come, come, child, you are among friends. Why, it's
all over Town that Arlington is enamoured of you. I really
must congratulate you—it's an amazing stroke of fortune."

Alex stood stiffly and spoke in a low voice, fearful others
would hear them. "You are mistaken, Lady Barstow. The

Marquess has merely shown a passing kindness for his wards, and his actions have been misconstrued."

"Of course, my dear," the older woman murmured, tapping her playfully on the arm with her fan. "I understand your reluctance to say anything prematurely, and you may rely on my discretion."

Infuriated with Lady Barstow's obtuseness, Alex would have walked away, but the Chevalier d'Orly appeared and blocked her path. He looked more romantic and handsome than ever with his blond hair brushed over his brow. He had chosen a well-cut and tight-fitting black tail coat which set off his slim build to advantage. Bowing gracefully before Alex, he solicited her hand for the set forming.

Ignoring the indignant look from Barstow, and the haughty stare of his mother, Alex promptly replied that she would be delighted, and defiantly allowed d'Orly to lead her out. Mindful of watching eyes, she went down the aisle with grace, and when once again facing her partner, gave him her most enchanting smile. The Chevalier eyed her appreciatively. As the movement of the set brought them to together, he whispered softly, "You dance exquisitely, my lovely one. I fear it will be my undoing. Already, you have captured this poor heart of mine. I am your humble servant—command me as you will!"

This oft-practiced and impassioned speech was lost on Alexandria. She neither blushed nor lowered her eyes, but only returned a prosaic, "I beg your pardon?"

The Chevalier, feeling that perhaps Miss Hilliard had not heard his avowal, bided his time until the steps brought them together again. Clasping her hand, he stared soulfully into her eyes. Alex, gazing into his large brown eyes, was put forcefully in mind of a cherished cocker spaniel she had once owned. Just so had the little dog looked at her, his woebegone expression indicative of his feelings at being left behind. A more perceptive gentleman might have read the amusement in her eyes, but d'Orly attributed her soft smile to warm approval, and begged leave to escort her to the balcony for a breath of fresh air.

"Indeed not, Chevalier. It would be most improper. I

should not have even allowed myself to be enticed into dancing, for I am here as chaperone to my sister."

"Bah! You are far too young to be a chaperone, and much too beautiful. It is you who should be chaperoned. Is there no father or uncle to, how do you say, watch over you?"

Alex gently withdrew her hand and turned towards the ballroom as she answered him. "I assure you I am quite capable of watching out for myself as well as my family. I have done so ever since our parents died. But I would appreciate it if you could manage to get me a glass of lemonade. It is rather stuffy in here."

He hastened to do her bidding, elated at discovering no older male stood between him and the rich Miss Hilliard's fortune. He had almost succeeded in eloping with the Wendover girl when her father had interfered, placing her out of his reach. This time there would be no papa to wreck his plans.

The Chevalier returned to find Alex in one of the small alcoves, seated beside her sister on a gilded settee. Their court included Hastings, Gillingham, Barstow, their brother, and two young dandies with whom he was unacquainted. D'Orly glanced contemptuously at the gentleman, convinced there was no competition here. He deftly managed to usurp Barstow's place and presented Miss Hilliard with her lemonade.

Alex expressed her gratitude, giving play with her fan, ignoring the wrathful looks Barstow was directing at her. The Chevalier pleaded for the privilege of another dance, and after searching her card, she allowed him a quadrille. Barstow stiffened and angrily turned away, while Alex pretended to be too engrossed with d'Orly's pretty compliments to even notice.

Jeremy eyed his sister and wondered what rig she was running. He knew her well enough to know she didn't normally listen with patience to the sort of pap the Frenchman was dishing up. He also knew she would brook no interference in her affairs on his part, and decided the wisest thing to do was withdraw.

Marietta was equally surprised at her sister's warm

reception of the handsome Chevalier, but she was more inclined to believe that Alex had developed a tendre for d'Orly. She watched the byplay between them, fascinated, and it was with reluctance that she gave her hand to the Lieutenant for the next set.

Marietta's tiny feet, encased in a pretty pair of Denmark slippers, performed the steps automatically. As conversation was not expected during the continuous movement of the set, her mind was free to dwell on Alex and the obvious encouragement she was giving the Chevalier. Although Alex had received several suitors at home, neither she nor anyone else had ever taken them seriously. It never occurred to Marietta that Alex might wed—not until the evening at the theatre. She had noticed Arlington's arrested look as he had unobtrusively watched her sister.

With all the simplicity and confidence of a seventeen-year-old, Marietta set out to arrange matters to suit her convenience. She had decided Arlington would make an ideal brother-in-law. He was kind, generous, and even handsome—if one had a penchant for older men. He was the perfect husband for Alex, she decided, but how it might be contrived, she didn't know. She only knew that the Chevalier d'Orly did not fit in with her plans. He might look like *Adonis*, she thought, but for some unaccountable reason, she mistrusted the Chevalier's good looks.

The set concluded, Marietta accepted the Lieutenant's arm and strolled back to where Alex waited. She was dismayed to find d'Orly still dancing attendance on her sister, but as Gillingham was waiting to claim her own hand for the quadrille, she had no opportunity to draw him off, nor the least notion of how she might do so. She watched as Alex took her place beside d'Orly in the same set, a tiny frown creasing her brow.

Lord Gillingham recalled her attention. "I might almost be jealous of the way you keep staring at the Chevalier. Is my conversation so little entertaining that your mind wanders?"

"I am certain you could not be so absurd as to be jealous of the Frenchman. Besides, he has not shown the least interest in me," she returned, neatly executing a *grand ronde*.

"He would be interested in any lady as long as she had a fortune to recommend her."

"Do you mean he's a fortune hunter?" Appalled, Marietta craned her neck to see over Gilly's shoulder, studying d'Orly with frank curiosity.

"Rumour has it that he must marry well, and soon. His creditors are growing impatient," Gillingham added, not adverse to discrediting the Chevalier in her eyes.

Unwittingly, he had given Marietta the seed of an idea, and it began to germinate in her mind. If d'Orly continued to press his suit with Alex, and he was giving every indication of doing so, then perhaps he would be interested to learn that her own fortune was even larger than her sister's. It was pure fabrication, of course, but with a little encouragement, she thought she might be able to draw him off, and then Alex would see what a nodcock he was. Marietta briefly considered confiding in Gillingham, but decided her young beau might not quite approve.

The subject of all this cogitation was, indeed, giving an excellent rendition of a young man deep in the throes of love. When Alexandria was not dancing, d'Orly was beside her, lavishing her with compliments. When she stood up with another, he could be observed lounging against the wall, jealously smoldering in his eyes as he watched her. Alex did nothing to discourage him, and people were beginning to notice. She silently congratulated herself. She knew she could count on Lady Barstow to spread the news of her infatuation with the Frenchman. By tomorrow, it would be all over Town. Smiling upon the young man, she wondered how long she would have to maintain the deception. She found his conversation and those languishing airs of his most tedious.

The Chevalier had to repeat his request to be allowed to call on her in the morning, and he felt a touch of uneasiness at her lack of attention. His avowal that the hours before he saw her again would be meaningless rather lost something of its passion with repetition. But her smiling assent, and her assurances that she would be delighted to receive him, did much to restore his faith in his powers of seduction. He judged it an opportune time to take his leave.

The Chevalier bowed over Alex's hand. "Forgive me, but I must depart, for I can no longer bear to see you dancing with others. I go to be alone with my thoughts, and to dwell on your perfection. I shall be counting the moments until we meet again." With one last soulful look, he clicked his heels together and was gone.

Chapter 7

ALEXANDRIA AWOKE THE next morning feeling as bleak as the day promised to be. The skies were overcast and one could almost feel the dampness in the air. It did not deter her aunt from calling on Lady Fitzhugh, however, or Marietta from wishing to visit with Sara Comstock. Alex saw them both off with a feeling of relief. She needed some time alone to puzzle out her feelings.

Taking her tea with her, Alex retired to the small salon and sat in the large wing chair near the window. The raindrops splashing against the panes of glass mirrored her feelings. She knew Aunt Bella was concerned about her and had looked askance the evening before when Alex had openly encouraged the Chevalier.

Well, what else was she to do? Too many ladies had let drop sly hints about her, almost accusing her of setting her cap for the Marquess. Alex blushed, recalling a certain Mrs. Drummond's remarks when they had been introduced at Lady Comstock's. The stylish matron had gazed at her appraisingly and said softly, "Ah, you are the newest one to set her heart on our dear Marquess. You look to be a nice child, so do allow me to give you a word of warning, my dear. Fix your interest elsewhere, for you are not likely to succeed in bringing Arlington to heel, not that I blame you for trying."

Alex had merely stared at her. What could one, after all, say to such a remark? But Mrs. Drummond had not been nonplussed. She'd warned Alex that she wasn't the first to think of reforming the Marquess, nor would she be the last. Alex shook her head, thinking again of the lady's refusal to

97

believe her protests that she had no interest in Lord
Arlington. Mrs. Drummond had smiled knowingly, looking
almost sympathetic, before Lady Comstock had drawn her
away.

Well, she could only hope that after her blatant display of
interest in the Chevalier such talk would die off. At least her
own family was convinced of her sudden interest in d'Orly,
even if they did not quite approve of the Frenchman. Alex
sighed, tracing a lonely raindrop as it rolled slowly down
the window. It reminded her of a tear, and must be the
reason she unaccountably felt like crying. She swallowed
hard, consoling herself with the thought that whatever her
own problems, at least Marietta was having a wonderful
Season—and that, surely, made up for everything else.
Jeremy, too, was enjoying the visit to Town. Too much,
perhaps?

Alex knew he had gone out again after they had returned
home. To White's, probably. She prayed he was not
becoming addicted to gambling and wondered again if she
should have spoken to him about it. The news that he had
played cards with Arlington disturbed her more than she
wanted to admit, and she fully intended to have a word with
the Marquess about that. He had no business playing against
his ward. And if he had won against Jeremy, the gossips
would have made much of it. Yes, she thought, she would
certainly speak to Lord Arlington about his conduct.

Dobbs tapped gently on the door and Alex looked up,
summoning a smile. It would not do to allow the servants
to see her languishing. News traveled rapidly in London
below stairs. Lady Fitzhugh had told her that her own
servants were the best source of gossip. They knew everything!

She glanced at the card the butler proffered. The Chevalier d'Orly was calling! Alex, with a supreme effort of
willpower, produced a look of pleased delight and asked
Dobbs to show the gentleman to the drawing room. She
would join him directly. It was unfortunate, she thought,
that Aunt Bella was out. Well, Susan would have to do as
a chaperone, she decided, ringing for her maid.

The Chevalier had taken a great deal of trouble over his appearance, Alex noticed, greeting him a few minutes later. His blond curls were arranged artfully over his noble brow, and the blue coat he wore was superbly cut to show off his broad shoulders and narrow waist. That the Chevalier had taken pains over his dress did not disturb her—most gentlemen did so if they wished to be among the leaders of the ton. What she disliked was his posturing. D'Orly stood as though waiting her admiration. Alex managed to give a creditable imitation of awed delight at his call, while wondering if it was the gentleman's vanity or something else in him that left her feeling cold.

"I hope I did not arrive too early, Miss Hilliard?" he asked, taking a seat on the sofa next to her, and much too close. "I found I could not wait to see you again."

"You could not come too early, sir," she assured him before rising abruptly. "But what am I thinking of? Surely, you have addled my wits, for I have offered you nothing to drink. What would you have, sir? Tea or coffee, or perhaps a glass of sherry?"

He had risen at once and managed to take her hand in his, drawing her back to the sofa. "Why, nothing, Miss Hilliard. I drink in your beauty and am replete. What more could a gentleman wish for?"

Heavens, thought Alex, managing to hide her laughter as she looked down in seeming confusion. "You put me to the blush, Chevalier. Tell me, are all gentlemen in France so . . . so poetic?"

"Any gentleman would be moved to poetry, my dear, when addressing so sweet a flower," he murmured, caressing her hand.

Susan coughed discreetly, and Alex managed to withdraw her hands from his, but tried to make it appear that she did so with reluctance. Still, it seemed little encouragement was needed to set the Chevalier to paying fulsome compliments, and she parried his extravagant praise as well as she could while trying not to completely discourage him. She learned quickly enough that it would take a great deal to discourage the Frenchman, and determinedly refused his plans for a clandestine meeting.

"Surely, sir, you would not wish me to compromise my good name?" she asked, turning her wide eyes on him in stunned surprise.

"Ah, but no one need know, my dear one," he whispered. "Meet me in the tea gardens at Bayswater and we can steal an hour or two alone. Here, I cannot say the things I wish to say to you. Here, I cannot take you in my arms as I so ardently wish to do."

"Chevalier!" she cried, and did not need to pretend the shock that showed on her face.

He retracted instantly, aware he had moved too fast. "Forgive me, say you forgive me. Of course, I should not ask such a thing of you, but I look into your eyes and forget myself. I am desolate to think I have offended you," he pleaded, reaching out for her hand again.

The door opened abruptly, and Alex looked up with enormous relief. "Jeremy! Oh, come in, dearest. The Chevalier called and he was just telling me of the most delightful place where we might all go for tea one afternoon."

Jeremy strode in, followed by Gillingham. The coolness of his greeting to d'Orly was not lost on the Chevalier, and after a few moments of stilted conversation, the Frenchman took his leave. Jeremy would say nothing to her in front of Gillingham, but the look of reproach he leveled at his sister was sufficient to bring a blush to her cheeks. She hastily excused herself and fled to the small salon.

The drizzle that was falling steadily matched the gloomy look on the Chevalier's face as he left Hanover Square. Frowning, he considered the uncomfortable notion that Miss Hilliard was making game of him. Her words and her manner towards him were those of a young lady who found him irresistible, but something nagged at him. Was it only his imagination, or had her eyes glinted with amusement when he was passionately suggesting a tryst? His intuition told him she was playing him false, but such a thing did not seem possible, and he decided she could have no possible reason.

The problem weighed heavily on his mind as he aimlessly tooled his carriage. If he were not successful in marrying a fortune in the very near future, he would be forced to flee the country. The rumour of an advantageous match would hold off his creditors for a little time yet, but he could ill-afford to make a mistake. To continue his pursuit of Miss Hilliard and not prove successful would be catastrophic. On the other hand, there were not many ladies who were proof against his charm. And Miss Hilliard was not only lovely, but had an air of elegance that a Frenchman could appreciate.

The problem was he was not entirely certain that he could bring her up to the mark. And if not Miss Hilliard, then who? The only other heiress in Town this Season was the shy Miss Calvert. A possibility, the Chevalier conceded, but difficult. Miss Calvert was heavily chaperoned by Lady Edenbough.

D'Orly brought his attention back to the present, slowing his horses as he turned into Bond Street. His attention was arrested by the sight of Miss Marietta Hilliard and Miss Comstock emerging from a select hat shop, their maid trailing behind. He effortlessly pulled his team over, and after greeting the young ladies, offered his assistance with the numerous parcels they were struggling to balance.

Marietta responded happily, elated to see him. "A true knight come to our rescue. If you would be so kind, good sir, to drive us a few blocks to where our carriage awaits us, I shall forever be in your debt."

The Chevalier descended and helped the ladies into the landau, arranging matters so the little maid sat in the back, her lap piled high with packages. Marietta maneuvered so that she was seated next to d'Orly, and turned her large blue eyes on him.

"I fear the shops in London have gone to my head, and I just want to buy everything I see. However do people manage who don't enjoy a large income? La, if Alexandria had my passion for shopping, she would be a pauper in no time. But my fortune is so large that I'm sure these few trifles will hardly make a difference." She slanted her eyes, peeping up at d'Orly to see how he was receiving this information.

"I am certain, Miss Marietta, that it is little wonder you are enticed into buying so many pretty bonnets and gowns. On you, anything must look enchanting. Most ladies are not so fortunate to have hair like spun gold."

"What a pretty compliment!" Marietta gushed, lowering her eyes and then looking up through her lashes. "I thought you did not even notice me. I was so disappointed when you did not ask me to stand up with you last night."

"Not because I did not wish to, little one, I assure you. But what chance did a poor Chevalier have when you were surrounded by so many young lords?"

Marietta lowered her eyes and smiled, well satisfied with her morning's work. Sara was staring at her in astonishment, and Marietta quickly directed the Chevalier to stop in front of a clothier's where their own carriage waited. She rushed Sara along, not giving her the opportunity to say anything, and then turned back to thank d'Orly.

He bowed low over her hand, daring to place the lightest of kisses on the inside of her wrist. "I promise, as soon as the opportunity presents itself, I will be first in line to claim this pretty hand."

"I shall hold you to that, sir," she replied breathlessly, batting her eyes and giving a fair imitation of a young lady in transports of ecstasy.

So intent were they that neither noticed the equipage of Lord Arlington as it passed. The Marquess, accompanied by his secretary, merely raised an eyebrow in surprise as he observed his ward and her companion.

Mr. Carstairs also noticed the couple, and watching the obsequiousness with which the Chevalier bent over the young lady's hand, enquired who the new heiress was. "She must be worth a small fortune for d'Orly to be so attentive."

"I don't believe you have had the pleasure of meeting my ward, Robert. The young lady is Miss Marietta Hilliard."

"Gad! What is she doing with the likes of the Chevalier? I know you will not countenance that misalliance," Carstairs said, turning back to stare at the couple.

The Marquess expertly maneuvered his carriage between two others before remarking calmly, "When last I saw Miss Marietta, she appeared much attracted to young Gillingham, an unexceptional match, and one which has my approval. I don't know what the child is playing at, Robert, but I'll wager any sum you please that she has no real interest in the Chevalier."

"I'd be careful if I were you, Phillip. D'Orly seems to have a way with the ladies. Your ward would not be the first to succumb to his lures. Why, only look at the Wendover girl. Her engagement to Farleigh was all but announced when d'Orly succeeded in attaching her affections. Rumour has it the girl even tried to elope with him, but old Wendover put a stop to that."

Arlington returned no answer, seemingly lost in thought, and they were almost at his town house before he commented. "It is ironical, is it not, that barely a week ago my ward assured me that she and her family would be no trouble to me. Since that memorable interview, I have had to pay a morning call on her sister, and I was compelled, for reasons I still do not quite comprehend, to escort them to the theatre. After that I encountered young Jeremy at White's, where a well-meaning friend invited him to play whist at my table. It took some expertise to manage to lose to him, I assure you. The boy's an abominable card player, and was four sheets to the wind besides. And now Marietta appears to be encouraging the advances of a sharp, and I fear, yes, I very much fear, I shall have to take a hand in this. Miss Hilliard also seems to have taken a liking to the fellow. Pray tell me, what have I done to deserve this?"

Robert grinned. It was so seldom one saw the Marquess moved to such extremes. "I hate to say it, but it appears you have a further treat in store. Is that not your sister's town carriage?"

Arlington nodded, having also recognized the Colburn crest on the carriage blocking his drive. He nobly resisted an urge to sweep his team past, and instead brought the pair of greys to a smooth standstill. A groom came running at once to take charge of the team, and the Marquess gave him explicit instructions on their care before leisurely strolling into the house beside Carstairs.

Hodges relieved him of his driving cape and gloves before informing him, in a voice notable for its complete lack of emotion, that Lady Colburn was in the drawing room, having insisted on waiting for his lordship's return.

"Thank you, Hodges. Robert, where are you going? You would not be so craven as to sneak off and leave me to my sister's mercies?"

Carstairs reluctantly turned back. "I assume Lady Colburn wishes to be private with you, Phillip. She won't welcome my presence."

"All the more reason you shall attend me. Perhaps she will not feel compelled to make a long visit."

They found Lady Colburn seated on the cream-coloured sofa, presiding over an ornate tea service. Her younger daughter sat beside her, nervously twitching the folds of her gown.

"Ah, Phillip. I knew you would have no objection to my ordering up tea while we waited for you. May I pour you a cup?" She glanced at Carstairs and pointedly did not offer him any refreshment.

"Thank you, Elizabeth. Robert, would you care for a cup of tea?"

His secretary discreetly declined, trying to efface himself into the background. Lady Colburn paid him no attention, but continued. With a wave of her hand she indicated the girl at her side. "This, in case you do not recollect, is your niece Deborah. Say hello to your Uncle Phillip, dear."

The girl raised her eyes briefly and managed to stammer a shy greeting before taking refuge again behind her teacup. Arlington took up a position by the fireplace, wondering how someone of his sister's aggressive and demanding nature had managed to beget such nonentities for offspring.

"I have a dinner appointment, Elizabeth. You may remain and enjoy your tea, but I warn you I must take my leave within a few minutes. Was there something you particularly wished to say?"

"Indeed there is. Mr. Carstairs, would you be so good as to show Deborah the gardens? It is too ridiculous, but she has never visited her uncle's home before." She waited composedly while Carstairs and her daughter both hastened to do her bidding, taking the opportunity to observe her brother. She judged her best avenue of approach to be directness and so came immediately to the point.

"Phillip, you did nothing to assist me when Deidre made her come out last Season, and I did not protest overly much, for I understood your reluctance to enter Society, however foolish I may have thought it. But now that you have taken an interest in the Hilliard girl, you must realize that to do less for Deborah would be . . ."

"Unforgivable? Reprehensible?"

"Yes! You do see, don't you, that people would think it most odd if you do not make an effort to see your own niece established, when you would do as much for a complete stranger."

"I see nothing of the sort. You managed to marry your other girl off without my assistance, and I am persuaded you will manage admirably with this one, too. She has you and Colburn to look after her, as well as her sister and a host of Colburn's relations. The Hilliard girl, on the other hand, has no parents or influential aunts and uncles."

"No, only a remarkably attractive sister! Is that why you are interested, Phillip? The *on-dit* is that you are much attracted."

"So I have heard. You should not listen to gossip, Lizzie. You may hear things you would rather not know."

"Such as your escorting your ward to the theatre, when you won't even acknowledge your own niece? It is mortifying. Phillip, I beg you to consider my feelings." She approached him, and with a softened voice and caressing hand on his arm pleaded, "It's such a little thing I ask of you, and yet, it could mean so much to Deborah. You did not used to be such a hard brother."

He looked down into her eyes, and memories came

flooding back of the little girl with whom he'd once shared a schoolroom. She had always entered into all his pranks and followed him around with childish adoration. If they had grown apart, he knew himself to be at fault, and was momentarily sorry for it. His sister was no worse than any other matchmaking mama, and perhaps better than most, and what she was asking was not so very much after all.

He relented, but not wishing to appear softhearted, told her abruptly, "Very well. If you promise to leave me in peace, and promise to have that girl looking halfway presentable, I'll undertake to escort you both to Almack's on Wednesday."

"Oh, Phillip! Thank you, best of brothers!" Before he could stop her, Elizabeth had thrown her arms around his neck and kissed him soundly. Carstairs returned just as he was rearranging his neckcloth, and just as speedily withdrew.

The Marquess hastily excused himself, wondering what the devil had possessed him to make such a commitment. The thought entered his mind that Miss Hilliard would also be at Almack's on Wednesday, but he banished it abruptly. Miss Hilliard, he rationalized, was on his mind only because he had decided he must speak to her about Marietta.

Arlington found Carstairs and tersely ordered him to send a message round to Edward Margate's. "Make up some excuse or other, Robert. I won't be able to keep our engagement this afternoon."

"Is there a problem, sir?" Carstairs asked with some concern. It was not like the Marquess to cancel plans with someone like Margate. However careless he might behave in polite society, he was scrupulous in his dealing with his personal friends.

"A problem, Robert? Yes, I rather believe there is," Arlington answered thoughtfully.

The Marquess arrived in Hanover Square just as Alexandria was setting out with her maid, and he quickly hailed her.

This time Alexandria did not have to feign delight, and

she smiled warmly up at Arlington. "Hello, sir. If you are looking for the twins, I fear you are too late. They are both out and we do not expect them to return before dinner this evening."

"It was you I wished to see, Miss Hilliard,"Arlington said, keeping a tight rein on his frisky greys while admiring the blue and black walking dress she was wearing. "Where are you off to? My carriage is at your disposal."

"Thank you, sir, but I was just taking a stroll. Now that the sun has come out, I found I could not bear to stay indoors." She was about to offer to return to the house with him when Arlington motioned to his tiger. Before she could protest, he had leaped down from the curricle and was walking beside her. "But your horses, my lord—"

"The boy will walk them," he said, placing her arm in the crook of his own. "Shall we?"

Alex looked around helplessly. Under other circumstances she would have been delighted to stroll with the Marquess, but if someone should see them together, it would only fuel the rumours.

"Are you worried about your reputation, Miss Hilliard?" Arlington asked, his eyes full of amusement as he glanced down at her. "You need not be, you know. It might even add to your consequence to be seen walking with me."

"Perhaps, sir, but I should not like it to be thought that I was 'setting my cap' for you," she answered honestly, recalling Mrs. Drummond's remark. The moment the words were said, she felt him stiffen and knew he had misunderstood her.

"I believe your credit will survive a stroll around the square, Miss Hilliard, and if someone should observe us, then you may tell them that I was merely discussing my ward with you."

"That is not what I—"

"Let us not quibble over it," Arlington interrupted curtly. "My time is limited and playing nursemaid to your family is not how I had envisioned spending it."

Alexandria flushed at the rebuke and her temper flared. "Certainly, there is no reason for you to do so. I have managed my family's affairs quite capably without your assistance and see no need for interference on your part!"

"No, Miss Hilliard?" he drawled, his own temper rising. "Are you aware that Marietta was seen flirting quite openly with the Chevalier d'Orly in the middle of Town? Or that your brother had the audacity to sit down at my table at White's? I was forced to either play cards with him or give him a set down in front of his friend. Then I had the task of losing to him, which, given his condition at the time, was damnably hard."

"And who introduced him to White's in the first place, my lord?" she snapped, while inwardly gratified to know he'd not tried to take advantage of her brother. "If you had not sponsored him—"

"For your information, Miss Hilliard, White's is the leading club in London. My sponsorship of your brother, however misguided, assured him acceptance by the ton. I could scarcely be expected to foresee that he would be foolish enough to drink himself under the table his first night there."

"Had you accepted your duties as his guardian and behaved properly, you might have known it," she whispered heatedly. "Jeremy is only a boy, and this is his first visit to Town, but perhaps you have forgot what that is like?"

He stopped abruptly and turned to face her, oblivious of the maid listening with opened-mouth astonishment, and knew an urge to shake her until she was willing to listen sensibly.

Alex tilted her head to look up at him, a quiver of fear running through her, but she met his eyes unflinchingly.

Arlington gazed into her eyes, pale green in the sunlight, and suddenly found himself wondering what it would be like to kiss those cool red lips that were opened so invitingly over her small, white teeth. He saw the pulse beating in her throat and the small hollow there that was made for a man's lips to taste.

"My lord . . ." Alex began hesitantly.

He turned away abruptly. God, what was the matter with

him? What was he thinking? His long legs covered the ground in huge strides that had Alexandria scurrying to keep up with him, though he was hardly aware of it until he heard her voice again.

"Lord Arlington, I am sorry if I . . ." Her words trailed off and she gestured helplessly, not knowing what it was she wished to apologize for. She only knew a longing to somehow comfort him and that, she told herself sternly, was absurd. Of all the people in London, surely the Marquess was in the least need of comforting.

Arlington saw with relief that they were nearing his carriage. He glanced down at her and, his emotions more or less under control, spoke more softly. "Let us both put Jeremy's problems aside for the moment. It was really Marietta that I came to speak with you about. Keep her away from the Chevalier, Miss Hilliard, that is all that I ask."

"Oh, is that all, my lord?" she said, her voice rising in spite of her good intentions. "And how do you suggest I accomplish that when he is received everywhere?"

"You might start by discouraging him yourself. I have already heard of the exhibition you made of yourself last night at Lady Comstock's. You set a poor example for your sister—Miss Hilliard, I have not finished!" But finished he had, for he was left talking to the wind. Alexandria had whirled away from him and was already walking in the opposite direction with her maid. Damnable girl, he thought, gesturing to his tiger.

A moment later he was driving his carriage out of the square, driving at a furious pace, cracking his whip over the heads of his horses, and he did not even glance at Miss Hilliard as he passed her.

Chapter 8

WHILE ALEXANDRIA WAS quarreling with the Marquess, Marietta was busy devising a plan to bring her sister and Lord Arlington together. She had already figured out a way to lure d'Orly from Alex's side, and believed she knew how she might manipulate the Marquess. All she needed was the right opportunity to put her plans into effect.

Marietta waited impatiently, but it was Wednesday before she had her chance. She was in high spirits as she dressed for the assembly at Almack's. So impatient was she that she rushed Alex and her aunt, only to have to wait for Jeremy to finish his toilet. Even so, their party arrived at the assembly rooms on King Street, St. James, at an unfashionably early hour. Marietta looked at the plain brick building with patent disappointment, for she had expected something much grander. The interior was little better, and after being admitted by Mr. Willis, they ascended the staircase to the large ballroom. It was a huge, spartan room, adorned only by six windows with rounded arches. Whatever the rooms may have lacked in grandeur, however, was compensated by the elegant throng strolling through them. Here was the cream of London Society.

Although the hour was early, several young gentlemen had witnessed their arrival and hurried forward to solicit a dance before Marietta's card was filled. She chatted gaily while her eyes scanned the room. With inward satisfaction, she saw the Chevalier making his way across the room towards her. Their eyes met above the crowd, and she gave him a sweet smile.

He looked exceedingly handsome in a tight-fitting,

110

double-breasted cutaway coat of dark blue, with a striped blue and white waistcoat over close-fitting pantaloons. Marietta watched complacently as he made his bow to Bella, extravagantly complimenting her aunt on her gown of rich burgundy.

Bella, who intended to find the means of depressing the Chevalier's pretensions, or at the least snubbing him, was at a loss. She had no opportunity to do more than utter a weak thank you before d'Orly turned to Alexandria. Bella watched warily as he executed a smooth bow and exclaimed how perfectly the ivory satin gown suited Alex. She was both surprised and relieved that he did not ask her older niece for a dance. Her relief was short-lived, however, and turned to opened-mouth astonishment when d'Orly focused his attention on Marietta and asked her to stand up with him instead.

Both Bella and Alex were left speechless as Marietta laughed and promised the Chevalier the opening minuet, blinking her huge eyes at him from behind her fan. Alex was shocked by her forward conduct and longed to snatch the fan from her sister's fingers and apply it to her bottom instead. Marietta ignored their looks and continued to flirt with d'Orly, who looked totally enthralled.

Alex was ready to take Marietta aside for a private scold when Lord Gillingham approached the group. After greetings were exchanged, he, too, solicited Marietta for the promise of a dance. Although she granted him a quadrille, she did so with such a languid air of unconcern that Gillingham studied her searchingly. The first set was forming, and Marietta excused herself, her tiny hand resting on the Chevalier's arm as she allowed him to lead her out.

Chagrined, Gillingham immediately requested Alex to stand up with him, and as they took their positions, he demanded to know what devilment Marietta was about.

Alex was unable to offer any enlightenment, and watched with growing concern as Marietta and d'Orly went through their steps—their eyes never leaving one another.

Gillingham observed them, also, his dark frown leaving no one in doubt that he was not enjoying his own dance. At

the end of the set, he escorted Alex back to her aunt and left
her with a curt bow. His dark eyes, usually so full of good
humour, were hard with anger.

Alex watched helplessly as he left the room with a
stiffened back and head held high. She noticed several of
the dowagers watching the scene with relish, and hastily
motioned to Marietta.

If her sister saw her gesture, she chose to ignore it, and
took her place in the new set forming with Lieutenant
Hastings. Frustrated, Alex scanned the room for Jeremy,
but he, too, was engaged for the set and was already leading
Sara Comstock out. Alex started to speak to her aunt, but
was forestalled by Lord Quarrels, who begged her to stand
up with him.

"Have something to say to you, my dear," he confided,
as he noted her hesitation. She gave him her hand and
allowed him to lead her out. Conversation was difficult as
the steps parted them frequently, but he managed to impart
that he had observed Marietta with the Chevalier.

"Won't do, my dear. Fellow's a cad."

At a loss for words, Alex was grateful the dance parted
them before she had the opportunity to reply.

"Know you are new in Town. Thought I'd best warn
you," he said as their hands touched once more.

She nodded, went gracefully down the line, and returned.
Lord Quarrels apparently had no further comment, and they
completed the rest of the set in silence. At the conclusion,
he bowed and was escorting her back to her aunt when a
loud murmur passed through the ballroom. They paused, as
did most couples, to see who was creating such a stir, but
the crowd blocked their view. A tall, young gentleman
directly in front of them, able to see over the heads of the
gathering, exclaimed in a loud whisper, "I vow it's Arlington. Never thought I'd live to see the Marquess here."

Alex felt faint. No doubt, she told herself, from the crush
in the overheated rooms, and compelled Lord Quarrels to
continue across the floor. He left her at Bella's side, where
she plied a fan to cool her flushed cheeks.

She could see the Marquess now. It was little wonder he

had created a sensation, for he looked magnificent in a well-cut black coat with long tails. He saw her at the same instant. Abandoning his sister and niece, he made his way across the room to her, as did Sally Jersey from the opposite side. They both reached Alex at the same moment, and Lady Jersey spoke teasingly to them.

"I see how the moth is drawn to the flame."

Arlington ignored her and directly addressed Alex, his voice warm with amusement. "If I do not ask you to stand up with me immediately, I fear we would disappoint a large number of people. Will you do me the honour, Miss Hilliard?"

"Thank you, sir, but it is a waltz, and I—"

"La, child, don't hesitate," Lady Jersey intervened, giving her the coveted sanction. "It will provide us all pleasure to see the Marquess waltz within these rooms once more."

Alex found herself on the dance floor, Arlington's arm lightly around her, and the slight pressure of his hand burning against her back. Although she had waltzed at Allenswood, she had never been so aware of the closeness of her partner. Conscious of watching eyes, she tried to concentrate on the music, and that failing, on the mother-of-pearl button just inches from her eyes.

Arlington looked down at the auburn curls beneath his chin. The lights from the candles made her hair seem alive with fire, in marked contrast to her ashen countenance. The desire she aroused in him made him feel foolish and he spoke abruptly, his voice sounding more sarcastic than he intended. "What? Have you nothing to say, Miss Hilliard? You surprise me."

"It is I who am left speechless with surprise, my lord. I did not expect to see you here."

"But surely, you have heard the rumours that I am enamoured of the enchanting Miss Hilliard. How could I have stayed away?" he said, meaning only to tease her, but the words came out wrong, and he silently cursed his tongue. Damn, it had sounded as though he cared about those ridiculous rumours.

Alexandria met his eyes then, her own a cool, silvery gray. "I do not know how such a thing got about, but you have only given the wags more cause to speculate by standing up with me!"

"Does that not meet with your approval? I would have thought it precisely what you desired. It will certainly lend you and your sister a certain cachet with the ton."

"I don't wish to sail under false colours, whatever you may think," she whispered furiously, her colour heightened. "I did what I could to scotch that rumour by encouraging d'Orly, and now you have undone all my efforts."

"Ah, that explains it," he said, executing a smooth turn. "I admit I was puzzled by your seeming affection for the Chevalier. But if you feel you must make yourself the subject of idle gossip, you would do much better to practice your smiles on me. I am, or so I've been told, a much better catch than d'Orly, and much more influential, you know."

"I know your audacity and conceit exceed all bounds," she whispered in a low, angry voice, her eyes flashing.

"Now that is more like you. I regret if I have offended you, but I really cannot allow your name, or that of your sister, to be linked with d'Orly's. It reflects poorly on me."

"I fail to see how it has anything to do with you, sir."

"Then allow me to elucidate. Marietta is my ward, little as either of us may like it. That fact is well known, and the Hilliard name is now associated with my own. I will not allow either of you to sully it by a dalliance with a creature like d'Orly." The words were quietly threatening, and wrapped in ice, but he continued to smile engagingly for the benefit of their audience.

"You are a guardian in name only, my lord," she said, barely managing a smile as they whirled past Lady Jersey. "You chose to ignore us for three years, and I see no reason for you to take a hand in our affairs now."

"Don't you, Miss Hilliard?" His features softened as he gazed into her eyes, and his arm tightened around her. He swept her into a series of rapid, graceful turns. The candles seemed to tilt above her, and she was left breathless and shaken as the music stopped. She found herself beside her aunt before she had time to compose her disordered senses, and barely heard Bella's words as Arlington walked away.

"Alexandria, do pay attention! You must do something about Marietta. She is behaving outrageously, flirting with that Frenchman, and I fear she has angered Gillingham. That child will ruin everything if you don't do something."

Feeling as though she had stepped out of a dream, Alex tried to focus her attention on her sister. "Where is she? When last I saw her, she was dancing with Lieutenant Hastings."

"Yes, and the whole time she was ogling the Chevalier, and he following her every movement with his eyes. Disgraceful. I sent Jeremy after her, and he has her in hand for the moment. They are over there talking with Countess Lieven, and I have been praying she won't utter anything to offend the Countess."

Had Bella been privileged to hear Marietta's conversation, she would have been able to relax a little, for her niece was on her best behaviour. Well aware of the power the Russian ambassador's wife wielded as one of the Patronesses, Marietta was angling for permission to waltz. Wisely, she allowed Jeremy to tell the Countess of how they had waltzed together at home, and presented the demeanour of a very modest young lady. The Countess, a thin, exotic beauty and an expert in dalliance herself, was not deceived. She had seen the child with d'Orly. Still, she found Marietta amusing and Jeremy a handsome, as well as personable, young man. She kindly accorded him permission to lead his twin out.

Alex and Bella watched as they took the floor, and both ladies felt a certain amount of pride in the young couple's appearance. The twins had practiced together so often that they danced as one, their movements perfectly matched, and with exquisite grace they circled the floor. It was a pleasure to watch them as they seemed to float across the room.

Lord Gillingham even forgot his anger with Marietta, only longing to be the next gentleman to waltz with her and feel the exhilaration of holding her so close. He was not alone in his feelings. The Chevalier was also waiting to solicit the next waltz. Both gentlemen edged around for position next to Miss Meersham, where Jeremy would bring Marietta at the close of the dance.

The Chevalier arrived first and bowed to Miss Meersham. He received a frosty reply before Bella presented him with her back. It did not matter. Marietta was approaching, and her eyes were on him. He held out his hand, and was instantly blocked by Gillingham stepping smoothly in front of him. The Viscount immediately requested the honour of the last waltz on the card. Before Marietta could answer, d'Orly brushed past Gillingham pleading for the same privilege.

Marietta looked from one to the other, and although she longed to experience the intimacy of the waltz with Gilly, she thought of her plan and turned instead to d'Orly. She allowed him to pencil in his name on her card. Her smile faltered as she felt Gillingham's anger, and from the corner of her eye she saw him turn his back on her and walk away.

Alexandria, witnessing the exchange in silent fury, stepped forward swiftly. Laying her arm about Marietta's shoulders, she begged the Chevalier to excuse them. "I need my sister's assistance with a torn flounce," she said with a smile, before compelling Marietta to follow her to a small anteroom where they could be private.

As soon as they were alone, Alex demanded, "What has gotten into you? You are behaving like a brazen doxy, and never have I been more embarrassed. How *could* you disgrace us all? And treating Gillingham the way you did was beyond anything. Honestly, Marietta, I am almost ashamed to call you sister."

Marietta shrugged, turning her face away. Alex's words hurt. She knew her sister could not understand her motives. Still, she could have at least asked her why she was behaving so badly, she thought. But no, Alex has already judged her. Marietta, her lips drawn into a pretty pout, returned a noncommittal reply.

"I am warning you—if you don't stop making sheep eyes at the Chevalier, I will take you home immediately. You are to have nothing more to do with him, Marietta, or by heavens I promise you we will return to Allenswood."

"You are only jealous because d'Orly prefers me!" Marietta retorted, wanting to hurt Alex as much as she had been hurt. She regretted the words instantly, and tears filled her eyes as she rushed from the room.

Alex gasped and stood staring after her in shocked disbelief. How could Marietta think such a thing? What was happening to them? Life had been so much simpler at home, and she considered that it might be wisest to keep her word and return to Allenswood. She left the room with a heavy heart, and found Lord Gillingham waiting for her.

She did not wish to speak to anyone just then. Her head was aching abominably and all she wanted was to go home. Only the look on Gillingham's face as he begged for a word in private halted her. Reluctantly, she allowed him to lead her to a secluded alcove at the end of the hall where they could talk quietly.

She sat down, waiting for the young man to speak, but he appeared at a loss for words, pacing back and forth in front of her.

"Is it Marietta you wish to discuss?" she asked helpfully, wishing he would come to the point.

"May I speak frankly," he asked, sitting beside her. His gloved hand raked through his hair as he tried to sort out his thoughts. "I fell in love with her the first time we met. I had thought she returned my . . . my regard. I was going to speak to Arlington and put forward an offer for her hand—"

"Arlington! Why would you— Yes, I see. He *is* her guardian. I'm sorry, sir. Do go on."

"I had intended to wait a little, to give her time to enjoy her Season. But now, well I confess I am at a loss to understand her. You know her better than I do, Miss Hilliard. Would you advise me? Tell me what you think I should do."

Alex searched for words to comfort him, her own distress forgotten for the moment. The earnest entreaty in his eyes moved her, and he looked desperately unhappy. "Don't lose heart, sir. I know Marietta is behaving strangely, and though I cannot pretend even to begin to guess at her reasons, I am convinced that she cares for you."

It was faint encouragement, but he looked heartened. "What should I do, then? She seems to ignore me whenever the Chevalier is about. I don't mind telling you, Miss Hilliard, that I am half green with jealousy. Seeing her with him, well it doesn't bear speaking of."

His words gave Alex an idea, and if she knew Marietta, it just might work. "Lord Gillingham, may I make a suggestion. If I were you, sir, I think I would turn the tables on my sister."

She had his attention, and he looked more hopeful, eagerly asking what she meant.

"Only consider this. Marietta has been rather spoiled. She is accustomed to having all her suitors at her beck and call. What do you suppose would happen if you should appear to lose interest? Perhaps appear to have formed another attachment?"

The gleam in his eyes answered hers, and they put their heads together, discussing the details. Alex felt a pang of guilt as she connived against her sister, but she reminded herself that it was for Marietta's own good. She returned to the ballroom with Gillingham, both feeling a little better, only to see Marietta with d'Orly again. He was leading her out for the final waltz. Alex quickly urged Gillingham to stand up with another young lady, and watched with satisfaction as he crossed the room and led out Miss Harrington.

Her moment of satisfaction was fleeting. Lord Arlington had seen Marietta, too, and he wasted precious little time in making his way to Alex's side. She saw the anger reflected in his eyes as he took her arm, drawing her aside.

The Marquess had been annoyed when Marietta took the floor with d'Orly, but his anger had risen unreasonably on seeing Alexandria enter from the small hall with Gillingham. He kept his voice low, his words clipped. "I observe I was correct in my estimation of you, Miss Hilliard. You appear incapable of chaperoning my ward. I thought I made it clear that I would not countenance—"

"You made your opinion odiously clear," she replied furiously, her words as hard and icy as his own. "But if you can think of a way to prevent Marietta from standing up with him without creating a scene, then I give you leave to do so."

"Might you manage to smile? People are beginning to stare, and however one may conduct one's self in the country, I assure you it is not the thing to engage in a public row at Almack's. Don't look now but Lady Jersey is approaching."

Much against her will, Alex smiled up at him, while muttering through clenched teeth, "You have the manners of a stableboy."

"We are agreed, then?" Arlington was improvising smoothly for Lady Jersey's benefit. "We'll go to the circus at Hadleigh on Monday. I am sure my ward will enjoy it excessively."

"I hope I'm not interrupting," Lady Jersey purred, with the cattish air of one who knows she is. "From across the room it almost looked as if you were coming to blows with our beloved Marquess."

"Oh, no. Do not say so when he has been so kind as to get up an expedition for my sister's amusement. I suppose I may have looked aghast, but it was only the thought of Lord Arlington's discomfort in chaperoning a group of youngsters to a circus. It's very *noble* of him, don't you agree?"

"Very obliging, to be sure," Lady Jersey replied suspiciously. "I'm surprised, Arlington, for you don't suit my notion of a chaperone. Almost, you tempt me to join you."

"You'd be most welcome, Sally. Shall I call for you? We leave at eleven Monday morning."

"Eleven? Don't be absurd, Arlington. You know I never rise before noon. No, I won't go, but you shall come and tell me about it—at a decent hour, mind you."

They were joined by the twins, and Lady Jersey sweetly told Marietta that her guardian had arranged a treat for her. "He proposes to take you to Hadleigh on Monday so you may enjoy the circus."

"Oh, famous!" Marietta cried, with a flashing smile for the Marquess. "I knew I was going to adore having a guardian. Please, sir, might Sara come with us?"

The Marquess looked from his ward's excited face to Alexandria, whose green eyes were suddenly alive with laughter. He replied dryly, "You shall have to beg permission from your sister. I won't undertake to chaperone more than one of you without assistance."

Marietta, her grievance momentarily forgotten, pleaded with Alex to join them. Jeremy, who might be thought too old for the circus, added his entreaties. He reminded Alex of the fun they had as children when their father had taken them to see a nearby circus.

Aware that Lady Jersey was still an avid listener, Alex reluctantly gave her consent to the scheme and then bid Marietta gather her things.

The Marquess bowed, wishing them a good evening, and Lady Jersey demanded his escort. He promised to see them all on Monday, and with one last, incomprehensible glance at Alex, strolled away, with Sally leaning on his arm.

Alex was still watching him when Gillingham came over to say good night. He had Miss Harrington on his arm, and Jeremy promptly began telling them of the proposed expedition. Cordelia wore such a wistful look that Alex felt constrained to invite both her and Gillingham to join the party.

Marietta, returning with her pelisse, was in time to hear their enthused acceptance. She sent one hurt, stricken look at Gillingham and then, before Alex could stop her, hurried off again. Alex watched helplessly as Marietta approached the Chevalier and gestured excitedly. The two stood together in animated conversation for several minutes, and then d'Orly took her arm as they made their way across the room again. Alex barely nodded to the Chevalier, and curtly told Marietta they must leave at once.

Marietta, with a guileless look, sweetly informed them that the Chevalier had agreed to join their party on Monday.

Alex saw no way to retract the invitation, and could just imagine what the Marquess would have to say to her. Barely restraining her anger, she propelled Marietta into the hall, where Bella was waiting with Jeremy. He had told her of the proposed expedition, and Bella was much impressed that Arlington would put himself out to such an extent, and happily congratulated Alex.

"You've not heard the whole of it yet," Alex replied ominously, with a dark look at her sister, and refused to comment further until they were in the privacy of their carriage.

"I don't know why you should be so vexed," Marietta pouted a few moments later, flouncing on the seat opposite Alex. "You invited Lord Gillingham and Cordelia Harrington, and Jeremy will keep Sara company. Why should I not be allowed to invite the Chevalier? Besides, I have already done so."

"You have done what?" Bella's voice rose dramatically, and the look she directed at Marietta was fierce enough to make her shrink back into the upholstered seat.

Alex laid a restraining hand on Bella's arm and spoke to her sister in chilling accents. "I may as well tell you that your guardian has twice taken me to task for allowing you to stand up with d'Orly. Arlington does not consider him fit company for you." She held up a hand as Marietta started to protest. "Save your explanations for the Marquess. He will undoubtedly have a great deal to say to you when he learns that you had the audacity to invite the Chevalier to a party not of your making."

"Well, no one told me Lord Arlington disliked d'Orly, and *you* said we should not snub him just because of idle gossip."

Jeremy snorted. "There's a vast difference between not snubbing him and standing up twice with the fellow, making a cake of yourself! I don't see how you can prefer a loose screw like him to Gillingham, anyway. I thought you had more sense. Gilly is worth ten of d'Orly, and you ignored him all night. I warn you, Mari, you'd best not be playing off your tricks on Gilly, or you will lose him."

Marietta was near tears. Nothing was going right. Accustomed to being the pampered darling of the family, she

was unused to such severe criticism, especially from her
twin. Jeremy had always been her champion. She suddenly
felt as if everyone was turning against her, and the mention
of Gillingham reminded her of the lavish attention she'd
seen him bestowing on Cordelia Harrington. She hadn't
believed Gilly would turn to someone else so readily. That
he had done so, she thought sadly, proved that he really did
not love her. A large teardrop rolled unchecked down her
cheek, and she turned her face to the window. She would
show him, she vowed. She would show them all.

The carriage rolled to a stop, and Alex let her go without
further words, having seen the tears in her eyes. Bella,
however, would not be denied, and followed Alex to her
bedchamber, demanding to know what had occurred between her and the Marquess. Alex reluctantly dismissed
Mary, and turned to her aunt with a tired sigh.

"Arlington asked me to waltz in order that he might rake
me down privately. He told me he would not allow either
Marietta or myself to sully his good name by a dalliance
with d'Orly. The Marquess feels it would reflect poorly on
him."

"Well, my dear, he does have some justification on his
side, and I think his concern for Marietta does him credit."

"Credit? Aunt, he is not concerned about Mari, only
about his name—as if his own reputation was spotless."
Alex seethed, yanking a dressing gown from her wardrobe.
"Then he had the unmitigated gall to ring a peal over my
head because Marietta stood up with d'Orly again. How I
was to prevent it has me at a loss, but Arlington seemed to
expect it. That's when Lady Jersey came up, and Arlington
started rattling off some nonsense about a trip to Hadleigh.
It is not the thing to engage in a row at Almack's, he told
me, which was quite unjust since he began it."

Bella regarded her with mingled astonishment and disappointment. "Then the trip to the circus was all a hum?"

"It was, but I don't see how he can cry off now. Marietta
asked him if Sara could join us, and then Gillingham and
Miss Harrington were invited. It's fixed for Monday unless

I can think of some pretext for canceling it or else postponing the date."

"I knew the Chevalier would cause trouble. Oh, how I wish you had never encouraged him, Alex."

"That does not signify now," Alex said, secretly wishing the same. "I must think of some means to prevent him from joining us on Monday. Perhaps I could pretend to be ill and cry off. Arlington said he would not go if I did not help him with the chaperoning."

"Well, sleep on it, my dear," Bella advised, kissing her good night. "It's amazing how frequently problems are solved while one is sleeping, don't you think?"

Alex watched her go, envying her aunt her composure. But it was not Bella who would be facing the Marquess' wrath on Monday. She suddenly felt her own anger toward Marietta flare. Why could not the child get herself engaged to Gillingham, as she was obviously meant to do? They were perfectly suited, and anyone with half an eye could see Gillingham worshiped her.

Marietta, the cause of Alex's indisposition, was equally miserable. Unable to sleep, half-blinded with jealousy, she let the tears fall as she sobbed into her pillow. He hadn't made the least push to win her from the Chevalier, which he most certainly would have done if he truly loved her, she reasoned. Well, she would show him. She'd marry d'Orly, and then they'd all be sorry. And then, only then, would she tell Alex of her sacrifice. Gillingham would eventually learn of her noble actions, and he would be heartbroken that he had so little understood her. She would show them, she muttered, drifting into a troubled sleep.

Chapter 9

ALEX HAD JUST sat down to breakfast with her aunt when Susan brought her the news that Marietta was requesting a tray in bed. After making certain that her younger sister was not seriously ill, but merely indulging in a fit of the sullens, Alex reluctantly granted permission. She cast an apologetic look at Bella. Trays were normally reserved for illnesses. Her mother had firmly believed that breakfast in bed was an unnecessary indulgence that encouraged idleness and ego.

"I know I should not allow it, but I *cannot* cope with a display of temper this morning. Marietta would enact us a Cheltenham tragedy and I should likely throttle her."

"If you ask me," Bella said, buttering a scone, "she should have her dinner there as well. There's something to be said for the days when a recalcitrant miss could be locked in her room till she came to her senses, and it is clear Marietta's mind is disordered if she prefers d'Orly over Gillingham. I had thought it was you he was after, and that was disturbing, but at least you were not giving up such an agreeable connection as the Viscount."

"I fear I was not infatuated enough to suit our Chevalier. He seemed to sense I would not lose my head over him enough to wed him out of hand, but now I am afraid he thinks Marietta will prove easier game."

"Alexandria! You don't mean to say you think he would actually try to elope with her?" Bella said, dropping the butter knife and clutching at her breast.

"I am very certain he would, given half the chance, but don't fret, Aunt Bella. Marietta might be spoiled and behaving somewhat rashly, but I very much doubt she could ever be brought to agree to an elopement. Why, she would have to be nearly desperate to even think of such a thing."

"You should forbid her to see him, Alex. Don't give him any further opportunity to work on her affections."

Alex sipped her tea and sighed. "I wish it were that easy. What do you propose I say to him when Marietta has already invited him to join us on Monday? I cannot retract the invitation now."

Jeremy strolled in, looking very dapper and sounding extremely cheerful as he wished them both a good morning. "Anything I can do for you while I am out? Gilly and I are going to a horse auction this morning. Where's Mari?"

"She's having breakfast in bed this morning," Alex answered before their aunt could express her views.

"Just as well. Gilly's calling for me here, and if Marietta treated him as rudely as she did last night, I think I'd box her ears. Honestly, Alex, he's the best of fellows and it really galls me that my own twin cannot see it."

"Please don't say anything to her, Jeremy. I know it is vexing, but you know how stubborn she can be. If we don't oppose her, perhaps she won't be so determined to encourage d'Orly."

Bella motioned to them to be quiet as she caught a glimpse of Marietta on the stairs, and she hastily changed the subject. "I have ordered the carriage brought around. Flora wants me to call this morning, and I know she'd be pleased if you joined us."

Marietta entered, glancing around defiantly. She murmured a sullen good morning as she sat down and helped herself to tea. Her head down, she seemed to be waiting for the storm to break. Jeremy busied himself at the sideboard, while Alex and Bella continued their conversation.

"Thank you, Aunt Bella, and I hope you will give Lady Fitzhugh my warmest regards, but I promised Mrs. Castlemain I would call today, and then I have another fitting. Marietta, if you are feeling better, would you like to bear me company?"

The young girl looked gratified by the invitation but shook her head. "I promised Sara I'd see her this morning, that is if you don't have any objection? Lady Comstock promised to send her carriage."

"No, that's fine," Alex said, giving her a smile as Dobbs entered. He informed Jeremy that Lord Gillingham was waiting in the drawing room. Alex saw the spark in her sister's eyes, and before Jeremy could speak, directed Dobbs to bring Gillingham to the breakfast room. She met Jeremy's eyes unblinkingly. "I am certain Lord Gillingham would appreciate a cup of tea before you leave."

Jeremy looked ready to argue, but Gillingham was already in the doorway, and Alex pressed him to sit down. The Viscount greeted them all, and if his eyes lingered for a moment longer on Marietta, it was not commented on. Pleasantries were exchanged, and then Bella excused herself. The gentlemen rose, and Alex laid her hand on her brother's arm.

"Would you delay your departure for just a few minutes? There's a matter that needs your attention in the library." Jeremy opened his mouth to object and received a pinch from his sister, who practically pulled him from the room.

Marietta, left alone with Gillingham, suddenly felt shy of him. She took refuge in pouring out his tea, and kept her eyes down as she passed him the cup.

Gillingham took a deep breath, and striving for nonchalance asked, "Shall I see you this evening at Lady Edenbough's?" He watched her sitting there, with the sun coming in the window behind her and lighting up her hair. He knew she was unaware of how beautiful she looked, and he owned himself to be forever lost. No matter what might happen, his heart would always belong to this diminutive lass setting before him, whether or not she wanted it.

Marietta, who could not bring herself to look at him, heard only the studied indifference in his voice. She sat, idly playing with a flower from the centerpiece, determined that he should not see how much his defection hurt her. "Oh, of course. Everyone will be there. The Chevalier told me he is attending, and can you imagine, he wanted me to promise him every dance on my card? Of course I refused, but only think of the talk it would have caused. He is so amusing."

"If you care for that sort of thing," Gillingham replied, trying hard to control his temper. "Personally, I would not subject a young lady I cared for to tattlemongers' gossip by asking her to stand up for more than two dances."

Hearing the anger and disapproval in his voice, Marietta stood abruptly, her blue eyes flashing. "No, I'm very sure *you* would never be so carried away with passion that you'd forget the conventions."

For an instant he was tempted to sweep her into his arms, as he'd been longing to do, and show her just how passionately he could put aside polite behaviour. He took a step towards her, but Jeremy's return held him in place, and he watched helplessly as she left the room without another word.

Jeremy, seeing the pain in his friend's face, considered going after his twin and talking some sense into her. But Alex was there, urging them to be on their way. She smiled warmly at Gillingham and reminded him that she was looking forward to seeing him at the ball.

Marietta, who had fled to her bedchamber, stood behind the heavily draped windows watching forlornly as Jeremy and Gillingham left. She saw Jeremy clasp his friend on the shoulder, and whatever he said elicited a laugh in response as they climbed into the curricle. Marietta would have given much to exchange places with her brother, but after seeing Gilly's lighthearted behaviour, she vowed he would never know how much she loved him. Or how deeply he had hurt her. She blinked back the tears resolutely, thinking of how he had toyed with her affections. She crossed to the wardrobe, determined to look her best that evening. Then, perhaps, Lord Gillingham would be just a trifle sorry he had lost her.

Marietta was undecided between a creamy ivory and a pale pink gown embroidered with tiny rosebuds, when Alex knocked on her door. She called for her to come in, and Alex entered, carrying a vase of fresh garden flowers.

Seeing the gowns spread out on the bed, Alex expressed

her preference for the pink, and wasn't at all surprised when Marietta immediately decided on the ivory. Alex only nodded and spent several minutes idly arranging the flowers before casually remarking that Lord Gillingham had seemed rather upset when he had left.

Marietta stood in front of the cheval glass, holding the ivory gown before her. She looked unconcerned, but her heart skipped a beat. Tilting her head as if concentrating on her gown, she replied casually, "Lord Gillingham's feelings are no concern of mine."

"Oh, have you had a change of heart, then? I recollect that a few days ago you thought Gillingham all perfection."

"That was before I learned his true nature. Last week he pretended an affection for me. Now it is Cordelia Harrington, and next week it will probably be Miss Colburn or even Sara. I have no use for such a fickle creature."

Alex could sense her unhappiness, and she placed a comforting arm around her shoulders, remarking gently, "The same might be said of you, Mari. Last week it appeared Gillingham was first oars with you, and now it seems he has been cut out by the Chevalier. I don't want to press you, but it is a dangerous game you're playing—"

"I don't have the least notion of what you are talking about," Marietta interrupted, pulling away. "And now, if you'll excuse me, Sara is waiting and I have to get dressed."

Alex was presented with Marietta's back, and she barely managed to restrain her urge to shake her sister. "Very well, but I'm warning you again. If you don't cease this foolishness, not only will you lose Gillingham, but I'll keep my promise to take you home. Send the Chevalier about his business, and mend your fences with Gillingham before it is too late. He's not the sort of man who will wait forever." Alexandria swept from the room, resisting a strong impulse to slam the door on her stubborn sister, vexed with herself for losing her temper.

Marietta, lacking any such control, hurled her hairbrush across the room, mimicking Alex as she angrily strode about. "He won't wait forever. Ha! He didn't even wait a day before making up to Cordelia." She yanked her pelisse from the wardrobe, and grabbing her reticule, rushed from the room, anxious to see Sara. At least there was one person in Town who still approved of her.

When the girls were settled in Sara's bedchamber, Marietta confided the distressing encounter she'd had with Gillingham that morning, and triumphantly recounted her parting shot. Sara gazed at her with admiration and awe.

"What did he do? What did he say?" she asked eagerly.

"Nothing," Marietta admitted despondently. "Jeremy and Alex came back just then, and I left the room. Alex told me he seemed upset when he left, but I do not believe it. I was watching from my window, and he and Jeremy were laughing. He cannot have been much distressed."

"Perhaps he was only putting on a brave front," Sara consoled her friend. "You know gentlemen don't like to display their emotions. I will wager anything that even if his heart was breaking, he would probably laugh just so no one would know."

"You have not heard the worst of my news. Alex has threatened to send me back to Allenswood!"

"Oh, no, Marietta! I could not bear it if you left. What has happened? What did she say?"

"She told me if I did not cut the Chevalier and mend my fences with Gillingham, she would take me home. I never knew Alex could be so unfeeling. And when I think that it was only for her benefit that I encouraged d'Orly in the first place, I could just cry. She has no notion of how my heart is breaking. None! *She* thinks I am only a heartless flirt. My own sister."

"Oh, how could she, when you've behaved so nobly?" Sara cried. She had just finished reading *The Mutual Attachment*, and saw her friend in the light of a heroine. "Forsaking your own love to save your sister from the Chevalier, and now she turns against you. Why, it is just like a play."

"Alex made it sound so simple: Send the Chevalier on his way and make it up with Gilly, she said. As if it were that simple. He's too interested in Cordelia now to pay me any

attention, and I shall probably be sent home in disgrace. I
would as lief marry d'Orly!"

"Marietta! You would not."

"Well, I don't particularly wish to, but if Gilly proposes
to Cordelia, it won't matter much who I marry, and perhaps
d'Orly would take me to Paris."

Sara grasped her hand. "Tell me you do not mean it. I
cannot bear to think of it."

"What else is there for me to do?"

Marietta sounded so pathetic that Sara ached to be of
assistance to her. She tried to think of what the heroine in
her book might do in such a situation, but the only idea that
came to mind was to speak to Lord Gillingham herself. The
notion filled her with terror, and she was not at all certain
that she would be able to summon up sufficient courage to
approach a gentleman like the Viscount and dare to discuss
his private life. She did not even mention the idea to
Marietta.

Sara allowed her friend to take her leave, promising only
to think of something to help her. She spent the remainder
of the afternoon lost in pleasant daydreams in which she
figured the heroine. In her imagination, both Gillingham
and Marietta announced their undying gratitude to her for
bringing them together, declaring their firstborn would be
called Sara. She giggled at the thought that the first child
might be a boy, and then turned her mind to the more
serious problem of what she would say to Lord Gillingham.

Alexandria saw Marietta return, but did not try to detain her
as she slipped up the stairs. After much deliberation, Alex
had penned a note to Lord Arlington, asking that he call on
a matter of some urgency. She had hoped the Marquess
would put in an appearance that afternoon so she could tell
him at once of Marietta's invitation to the Chevalier. After
all, she reasoned, he was her guardian, and the most proper
person to warn off the Chevalier. Unfortunately, there had
been no response from him, and she knew she must shortly
retire and dress for dinner. The sound of a carriage drew her

eagerly to the window, but to her disappointment, it was only her aunt returning from Lady Fitzhugh's.

Bella came in, full of excitement, and anxious to share her news. "You will never guess! Lady Fitzhugh had it straight from Harriet Edenbough this morning. Lord Barstow has proposed to Miss Calvert! I would never have believed Amelia would allow her only son to marry the daughter of a Cit, but there you are. And Lady Edenbough said the announcement will be made at the ball tonight. Oh, Alex, if only you had encouraged him a little, it could be your wedding being planned."

Alex laughed, but not unkindly. "I promise you, I am very happy for Miss Calvert. I am sure they will suit admirably. She has such an obliging nature, she should deal extremely well with Lady Barstow—much better than I would have done."

Bella gazed after Alex's departing figure thoughtfully. She had been keenly disheartened by the announcement at first. Then Flora had told her that she thought Alexandria would do much better than a mere Viscount. Although she could not be induced to say more, Bella took her to mean Lord Arlington, and she had explained at length how frequently he and Alex disagreed.

Flora had only shaken her head and smiled, remarking that a great many people would find it quite interesting to know why the Marquess had left town for a few days. It was beyond Bella's power of assimilation, and hearing the clocks chime the hour, she hurried to her bedchamber to change. She planned to wear her new lemon-yellow gown. The bodice was an intricate weave of yellow roses, and dear Flora had given her a matching turban covered with large gold beads.

If the stares Bella evoked later in the evening were any indication, her gown was a success, and this triumph effectively drove all other thoughts from her head. It was not until they had passed through the crush of the receiving line, and had a few minutes in which to observe the crowd in attendance, that Alex expressed her disappointment over Arlington's absence.

"Did I not tell you, dear? The Marquess left town for a few days. Flora told me he does not return until late Sunday evening. I thought I had mentioned it."

"No, Aunt, you did not, but at least that explains why he returned no answer to the message I sent him," Alex said, her expressive eyes registering her disappointment.

"You sent the Marquess a note?"

"I intended to let him deal with Marietta since, as he frequently points out, he is her guardian. I thought he might be induced to do something useful—like warning off the Chevalier," Alex said quietly. She turned with a smile as she observed Lady Barstow bearing down on them, her son and Miss Calvert in tow.

That Lady Barstow had last parted with Alexandria on less than amicable terms was not evident as she greeted her with gushing enthusiasm, lavishing praise on her gown. Then, with a gleam in her eye, she leaned close to confide her news. "Although it has not been formally announced, I can tell you both, our closest neighbours and dearest of friends, of our good fortune. Jonathan has asked Miss Calvert for her hand, and she has accepted him. I have told dear Caroline, a dozen times I am sure, that I could not wish for a better daughter." She drew the girl forward as she spoke, and Miss Calvert, well aware of her fiancé's prior partiality for Miss Hilliard, smiled uncertainly.

Alex did her best to set the girl at ease, expressing her sincere wishes for their future happiness, and then congratulated Lord Barstow on his excellent taste. Barstow looked much like a man in a daze, had little to say, and stood with a fatuous, self-satisfied smirk.

Bella, uncharitably reacting to the smug triumph of mother and son, was drawn to remark, "It is not official yet, but we shall also have some interesting news before the end of the Season." Leaving them all stunned, she turned and made her way across the room to Lady Edenbough's side. Alex watched, fascinated, as the bright yellow gown bobbed up and down, reminding her of a waddling duck.

Lady Barstow tapped her on the arm with her fan, demanding an explanation of Bella's enigmatic remark.

"Has Marietta brought Gillingham up to scratch, then? Or was Bella referring to you, my dear?"

"I assure you, Lady Barstow, that I have not the least notion of what my aunt meant. Would you excuse me, please? I must go to Marietta." She had seen her sister and Sara Comstock come out of one of the small salons. They were chatting now with Lady Comstock, Jeremy, Miss Harrington, and Lord Gillingham beneath the large arched window on the east side of the room. Alex was stopped several times by acquaintances, and by the time she finally neared the group, Jeremy was leading his sister out. Sara was standing just behind Gillingham, and Alex wondered if the girl was ill. She seemed to be swallowing convulsively, and her hand kept jerking towards Gillingham and then darting back.

Lady Comstock greeted Alex warmly, and after compliments were exchanged, she told her how pleased she was that the Hilliards had been so kind to their daughter. "Jeremy and Marietta have included her in all their activities, and she is like a different girl."

Alex could well believe that, looking at Sara. The girl was oblivious to their conversation, her eyes drilling into Gillingham's back. Alex returned a polite comment, watching fascinated as Sara's hand crept forward once more, this time tugging timidly on Gillingham's sleeve. He turned, surprised, and inclined his head as Sara whispered something to him. Alex could not hear what was said over the music, but it seemed of some importance. Gillingham immediately begged leave to be excused and made his way from the ballroom.

The twins joined them as the set ended, but Alex was frustrated in her attempts to get a private word with Marietta. No sooner had she returned than her hand was solicited for the next set. Jeremy looked around for Sara, intending to lead her out, but she had disappeared, and he politely asked Cordelia Harrington to stand up with him. Alex caught a glimpse of Sara slipping out the side doors in a furtive manner, and wondered what she was up to. If it was mischief, she had little doubt Marietta was behind it, and hastened after the girl.

Sara, who had taken advantage of her mother's distraction to slip away, found the small anteroom where she had asked Gillingham to meet her. He was waiting for her, but her whispered words that she must speak to him about Marietta had caused him considerable agitation. He greeted her gruffly, demanding to know what was wrong.

"I'm about to tell you, but first you must understand that Marietta is my dearest friend and confidante," she said, daring to lay her hand on his arm. "If I betray her confidence, which I feel I must, you must swear that what I say shall go no further." Sara was beginning to enjoy her role as heroine and spoke in dramatic accents—inciting in Gillingham a strong urge to shake her.

His fists clenched and unclenched, and he longed to put them around the girl's neck and wring the words from her. He stepped backwards, his hand at the door. "If you don't cut line, Sara, and tell me what is wrong, I'm going back to the ballroom."

"Have I your word of honour that this—" The ominous look in Gillingham's eyes, and the menacing step he took towards her, were not what she had envisioned, and she hurriedly changed tactics. "Marietta is only pretending to like the Chevalier— It is you she truly loves!"

Gillingham was as much stunned as Sara could possibly have wished. "Sara, for your own sake, I hope you are not making game of me. Are you saying Marietta confided in you? Why should she pretend an affection for that Frenchman?"

"I told you, Marietta is my dearest friend, and she would *kill* me if she knew I was telling you this! But I *cannot* allow her to ruin her life while I stand idly by."

"You still haven't explained anything, Sara," Gillingham said, unable to control the sudden surge of hope that lit his eyes.

"Marietta is sacrificing herself for the sake of her sister," she said dramatically, and when Gillingham still looked confused added, "You see, Marietta believes the Chevalier is only after Alexandria's fortune, and she was afraid Alex would make a terrible mistake and wed him. She was hoping her sister would make a match of it with Lord Arlington."

"With Arlington! But—well, never mind that now. What does that have to do with—"

"I am trying to tell you," Sara interrupted. "Marietta let d'Orly know that her fortune was even larger than Alex's. She encouraged him to dangle after her just so Alex would see what a cad he was. It was all going splendidly, only Marietta did not think your love was so lukewarm that you would turn to another so soon. Now she believes you love Cordelia, and if you marry her, then Marietta will wed d'Orly because she said it won't matter who she marries."

"Lord! The pair of you should be locked up until you develop some sense. Of all the bird-witted schemes. Come on, I'm taking you back to your mother before someone notices we are absent."

Sara hung back, distraught. "I was wrong," she moaned. "You do not love her."

"Of course I love her, and if it sets your mind to rest, I promise you I shall marry her. I shall have to, to keep her out of trouble. Now come on, and say nothing of this to anyone else."

This was better, but still not the undying gratitude Sara had pictured. She could not resist asking, "And will you name your firstborn after me?"

"What? My firstborn? If you do not come along at once I shall be more likely to turn you over my knee!" Not looking to see if she followed, he strode from the room, anxious now to find Marietta. He paused just inside the ballroom doors and scanned the room. He saw her at once, standing next to her aunt.

Marietta felt his presence before she saw him, and her eyes were drawn to the doorway where Gillingham stood. His head was thrown back, a look of fierce determination in his eyes, and she felt a shiver of anticipation snake down her back. There was a new forcefulness and vitality about him that held her still.

Marietta watched him cross the room, scarcely daring to breathe. A man laid a hand on his shoulder and was shrugged off. Marietta unconsciously straightened her shoulders. Whatever he had to say to her, she would face him.

Gillingham stood before her, holding out his hand, and Marietta unhesitantly placed her own small hand in his. Bella heard him softly ask Marietta if she would waltz with him, but Sara later swore that he did not say a word. He just swept her into his arms and circled the room with her, staring ever so romantically into her eyes.

While it may have looked romantic from Sara's viewpoint, Marietta was, in reality, receiving a thunderous scold. Gillingham *did* stare into her eyes, but he was telling her, in a stern voice, "If you ever again engage in such a harebrained scheme, I shall remove you to my country home and lock you in the North Tower until you come to your senses."

Hearing only the latter part of this enticing promise, she neglected to ask what scheme he was referring to. Lowering her eyes, she remarked to the third button on his coat that such an action might be construed as kidnapping.

"I believe there is a legal way around that, and I shall discuss it with your guardian as soon as he returns. To say more to you now would be most improper. And if you dare to tell me that it is a sign of passion to forget the tenets of polite behaviour, I shall . . . I shall kiss you passionately, here and now!"

Blue eyes looked up at him provocatively.

"And that's another thing! If you bat those pretty eyes in the direction of d'Orly once more, I swear I shall call him out."

"Oh, no! I promise I shall not only . . . the thing is I *did* invite him to make one of our party on Monday." He swore quietly, and she added hastily, "But only after *you* agreed to escort Cordelia Harrington."

"Ah, Cordelia. A lovely girl, don't you agree? It is too bad that she has her heart set on Hastings."

"Lieutenant Hastings? But I thought—"

"Yes, I know you did. You were meant to, and Cordelia thought a little jealousy might bring Mark up to scratch, too. What a devious set of people we seem to be."

Marietta giggled, but thoughts of the Chevalier intruded once more. Gillingham assured her she would not be left alone with d'Orly for an instant, and confided that he believed Arlington to have plans for ridding them of the Chevalier's tiresome presence. "Where is the fellow, by the way? I expected to find him languishing after you this evening."

"I don't know what occurred. He did plan to attend, but Miss Calvert told me he sent a note late this afternoon expressing his regrets."

Lord Gillingham bowed deeply to her as the waltz came to an end and escorted her back to her aunt, keeping a possessive hand on her arm.

Bella watched with beaming approval as the pair approached. It appeared one of her problems was resolved. Now, if only Alexandria would cooperate. She glanced round, suddenly realizing her elder niece was not in the room. She detached Jeremy from a giggling Sara long enough to ask if he had seen his sister, but he had no notion where she was. Nor had Sara seen her. Bella was about to send Marietta in search of her when Alex strolled into the ballroom from the hall.

If Bella had looked at her closely, she might have observed that Alex was a trifle pale and her gray eyes had an unnatural shine to them. Alex had followed Sara to the small anteroom and had overheard her conversation with Gillingham. She blamed herself for Marietta's foolishness and berated herself for the harsh words she'd spoken to her sister.

Marietta was not the spoiled, self-indulgent minx she had been imagining, but a kind and loving sister who had acted, however misguidedly, from the best of motives. And if Mari's behavior had been outrageous, well it was no worse than her own. Marietta had only followed Alex's example, playing a dangerous charade of hearts with d'Orly. Alex prayed no harm would come from the game, but she mistrusted the Chevalier and wished devoutly that the Marquess was in Town.

Alexandria stood among the chattering group of family and friends, scarcely aware of the conversation flowing around her. Lord Quarrels claimed the privilege of taking her into dinner, and Alex walked docilely beside him. Her mind was still on Marietta, now happily reunited with Gillingham. They shared a table with them at dinner, and Jeremy joined the group, with an adoring Sara beside him. The remaining two seats at their table were occupied by Lord and Lady Comstock.

Even distracted as she was, Alex could not help but note the fond looks the older couple cast at Jeremy. It appeared that Marietta would fulfill Bella's promise of an interesting announcement, but if she did not, then Jeremy might. He obviously met with the approval of the Comstocks, and love was definitely in the air. The thought depressed her, and she sternly told herself she should be happy for the twins. It was not as though she were really losing her family. Certainly, she would see them often.

Lord Quarrels, surprisingly perceptive, leaned over and patted her hand. "Almost enough to make one wish to become betrothed, is it not, and that is a state which has never held much appeal for me."

"And how is it, sir, that you have managed to elude the matrimonial nets all these years?" Alex asked with a soft smile as she determinedly turned her attention to the man.

"Very simple, my dear. I never found a woman who was enough of a lady to suit my extremely nice notions, or a lady who was enough of a woman to indulge in such a vulgar act as falling in love."

"Vulgar, my lord?"

"Indeed. The aristocracy marries for wealth and position, while the commoners succumb to the romantic idea of a love match. You must realize that it is only in the last decade or two that persons of our class have been permitted to marry where there was a degree of affection."

"You do not approve of a love match, then?" she asked, sampling the lobster pattie before her.

"Let us say, rather, that I believe love makes fools of gentlemen and turns otherwise sensible young ladies into quite unreasonable creatures. While it may add a great deal to an alliance, I do not believe it should be the criterion on which to base a marriage."

"Precisely what criterion do you suggest? Wealth? Position?"

"Not entirely. While breeding and background must be considered, I do feel one should have a certain amount of respect for one's future partner as well as compatibility regarding one's outlook on life. Take your brother, for example," he said, gesturing with his wineglass.

Alex turned to watch Jeremy across the table. His head was bent towards Sara as he made some teasing remark. She sat looking up at him, her features plainly showing her adoration.

"Lord and Lady Comstock are pleased to smile on him because he possesses the requisite breeding and a handsome fortune," Lord Quarrels spoke softly in her ear. "He is a personable young man, so Miss Sara looks up to him and will, no doubt, obey him. She is such a tiny thing and rather helpless, which will make your brother protective towards her. An ideal match, wouldn't you say? It is rather sad . . ."

"I'm afraid I don't understand you, sir," Alex said, wondering if he was quizzing her.

"It is sad, my dear, because she *loves* him, and he her. Instead of domestic harmony, there will be domestic disputes. Should he stay away from home for too long, or pay too much attention to a pretty lass, she will nag at him. On the other hand, if she cannot balance her household accounts, or run his home smoothly, he will not be able to discuss the matter in a reasonable manner. Passion will rule. Tears and recriminations will follow. Ah, poor fellow, he will never again know peace."

Alex could easily picture the scenes he had described, but she could not allow him to paint so cynical a portrait without rebuttal. "Perhaps there is some measure of truth in what you say, but my own parents married for love, and I am very sure they never regretted it. To the contrary, our home was filled with joy, and I cannot recollect ever hearing them disagree. Why if one of us did something wrong, Papa would tell us we were making Mama unhappy. Or she would tell us Papa would be sad to know how badly we were behaving."

He was fascinated by the play of emotion that kept changing the colour of her eyes, and provoked her further. "Perhaps they reserved their disagreements for the privacy of the bedchamber."

Alex shook her head. "In truth, I doubt they would have considered our feelings that much. Nothing mattered to them except each other. When Mama died, a part of Papa died with her. He still had all of us, but it was not enough. I never heard him laugh aloud after Mama died. He followed her two years later, and you may laugh, sir, but I still believe he died from a broken heart. He just did not care enough to live without her." Alex laughed herself, a trifle self-consciously. "I did not mean to ramble on like this, but when you have witnessed that kind of devotion, it makes a lasting impression."

Lord Quarrels had listened attentively, and she had spoken so earnestly that he found himself moved by her words. "That kind of love is rare, almost idealistic, one might say. If that is what you seek, I fear you may be disappointed. Shall you remain a spinster rather than compromise your standards?"

Alex laughed. "As no one has offered for me since I came to Town, it has not been a problem I have had to deal with." Then, aware she had been neglecting Lord Comstock, seated on her right, she turned to him with an innocuous remark.

"Hmmph," he grumbled. "I'll be glad to get back to the country. I've no patience with all this faradiddle, and balls and such. My lady insisted our little girl had to have her Season, and I will say that if she hooks up with that young brother of yours, it won't have been a complete waste!"

Alex knew not how to reply. Jeremy had given her no indication of his intentions, but everyone seemed to be taking it for granted that a match was in the making. She murmured tactfully, "Sara is a lovely girl, and I'm certain you and Lady Comstock must be very proud of her."

"Got her looks from her mother, but not a brain in her head. My girl needs a strong hand. Think that brother of yours will be able to control her?"

Alex looked at him helplessly, unable to think of any sort of answer. It was fortuitous that Lady Edenbough chose that moment to call for her guests' attention. Standing on a raised dais at the far end of the room with her niece, Caroline Calvert, Lady Barstow, and Lord Jonathan Barstow, she raised her champagne glass in the air. She asked her guests to join her in a toast to Caroline's future happiness on her betrothal to Lord Barstow. There was a smattering of applause, and several guests made their way forward to press best wishes on the bride-to-be.

Lord Quarrels whispered, "Must be something in the air highly contagious. I would not be at all surprised to hear several more announcements before the end of the week."

"Well, it is the reason so many young ladies are in Town."

"And you, Miss Hilliard? Are you intent on finding your ideal love in London?" He posed the question in a teasing voice, but his eyes studied her intently as he waited for her answer.

"Now, how shall I answer you?" she laughed as she rose from the table. "If I say yes, you will think me a hopeless romantic, and if I say no, I lend myself to your cynical point of view."

"You intrigue me, my dear. A lady who combines beauty with wit is almost as rare as this mythical love you seek. Given time, you might persuade me to alter my views."

"I hope you are not offering me Spanish coin, my lord?" she teased, accepting the arm he offered.

"No, Miss Hilliard, that I am not. The Season is far from over, but should you discover that your situation changes, and you find yourself willing to settle for less than perfect love, perhaps you will see your way clear to informing me."

Alex searched his kindly face for signs of mockery, but

he appeared to be in earnest. He regarded her with a benevolent air, and patted her hand. "If I have disconcerted you, I offer my humblest apologies. Do not try to answer me now, but remember, should you have need of me, I am at your service."

Chapter 10

ALEXANDRIA SAT AT the large oak desk in the library, penning the last of the invitations to the select dinner party she planned for the following Friday. The dinner would serve the dual purpose of returning some of the hospitality the Hilliards had enjoyed, as well as providing an appropriate time to announce the double wedding of Jeremy to Sara Comstock and Marietta to Lord George Octavius Luton, Viscount of Gillingham.

Although the formalities had been settled between Jeremy and the Comstocks, Sara had pleaded for the announcement not to be made public until her best friend, and soon to be sister-in-law, could announce her betrothal also. Marietta's engagement could not be officially proclaimed until Lord Arlington returned, gave his formal consent, and arranged the settlements with Gillingham.

Alexandria carefully sealed the last invitation and thought about the changes soon to be wrought at Allenswood. Marietta would be at their home for a few weeks before the wedding, and then would be off on her honeymoon trip. Gillingham planned to take his bride to Paris, and Alex smiled as she recalled his adamant refusal to share the trip with Jeremy and Sara. The twins would finally be going separate ways.

She did not believe Jeremy had decided on a destination for his own wedding trip yet, but it could not be long before he would return home, and she would hand over the household keys to Sara. Her fingers trembled slightly at the thought. It would be difficult for her to step aside. Yet Alex knew it would be better for everyone if she removed from her old home as soon as possible. Although she knew she would be welcome to stay at Allenswood for as long as she wished, she had no desire to become the helpful, live-in spinster aunt.

Jeremy had tried to convince her otherwise, but she would not allow him to persuade her. A household could have but one mistress. No, she would stay only long enough to show Sara how to go on and to introduce her to the tenants. Then she would arrange for suitable lodgings. The question was where? Alex had tried to discuss the matter with Bella a number of times, but her aunt was too full of wedding plans. Bella felt there would be ample time after the double wedding to arrange for their own accommodations.

Alex thought again of Lord Quarrels and his very tentative and surprising overture at Lady Edenbough's ball. Could she ever settle for anything less than a love match? Would a marriage of convenience be any more advantageous than her own comfortable little house with Aunt Bella as her companion? It was not as though she needed to consider the financial aspects, and as far as companionship was concerned, what she ached for was the warm and caring relationship her parents had shared.

Dobbs tapped lightly on the door and entered bearing a tea tray. He tactfully reminded her that she had guests expected at eleven, and it was already going on ten o'clock.

Alex thanked him, and as he was about to depart, enquired hopefully if it was raining.

"No, miss. It appears the sun is breaking through, and you should have a fine day for your outing."

Alexandria had prayed shamelessly for a heavy downpour, in the hope that inclement weather would prevent d'Orly from coming, as he proposed to make the trip on horseback. Although no one had seen the Chevalier since last Wednesday at Almack's, he had continued to send Marietta flowers each day. Yesterday's posy of carnations contained a card expressing his regrets for the unfortunate circumstances that compelled his continuing absence—and his assurances that he would not fail her today.

She had an uneasy premonition that d'Orly would not

take Marietta's defection lightly, and owned to herself that she would be glad of Arlington's presence. She placed her dependence on him to restrain the Chevalier from any display of temper. Of course, she reminded herself, Arlington was bound to be annoyed by Marietta's indiscretion in issuing d'Orly an invitation to begin with, but she felt sure this would be offset when he learned of her engagement to Gillingham.

Alex rehearsed what she would say to the Marquess as she dressed, and the clock was just chiming eleven when she descended the staircase. Arlington, she saw, was waiting in the hall below. She had chosen to wear her new dark green walking dress and a straw hat with a dashing ostrich plume. She knew she looked her best, and glanced hopefully down at Arlington, but there was not a trace of admiration in his stormy eyes.

Civility went by the wayside when, without any sort of greeting, he demanded to know what the devil all those people were doing gathered in the square in front of the house.

"Good morning, Lord Arlington," she greeted him, giving a creditable imitation of serenity. "I perceive you are one of those persons who cannot be civil until the noon hour has passed."

"My dear Miss Hilliard, until the precipitous advent of you and your siblings into my life, there was not the least necessity of my appearing before noon. My days were well ordered and conducted with a degree of politeness of which even you would have approved. Now I leave Town for a mere four days and return to find an *urgent* summons from you, demanding my presence. On my arrival here, I find a host of people bent on joining an expedition that was intended to be of a private nature."

"Well, if you will calm yourself for a moment, I shall explain it all. Come into the library where we may be private, unless you prefer to brangle here in the hall." She was quite prepared to find that, in his present mood, he would not oblige her but would insist on giving her a thunderous scold in front of the servants. She was more than a little surprised when he followed her into the library, and somewhat apprehensive as he carefully shut the heavy doors behind him.

Alex turned to face him. He really could look most formidable when crossed, she thought, and she hurried to explain. "You will recall that after proposing this expedition, you immediately left with Lady Jersey. Well, then Miss Harrington heard about it, and she looked so envious that there was really nothing I could do except invite her and Gillingham to join us. And Marietta, quite understandably, suffered from an attack of jealousy and rushed off and impulsively asked the Chevalier d'Orly to accompany us."

"Do you really wish me to believe that you found your sister's behaviour *understandable*?"

"Of course I did not at the time," she said, trying the effect of a smile on him. "I promise you I was quite vexed with her. In fact, I was feeling rather at wits' end and sent that note to you the following morning. I did not know what else to do, and I was afraid d'Orly might try to elope with her. You, of course, were not at home."

"Most inconsiderate of me, I agree. And if what I have learned about the Chevalier is true, you were right to be alarmed."

"Well, I was. Only now Marietta has made up her quarrel with Gillingham, and he called on me yesterday to ask my blessing. He plans to speak with you privately later today. *That* relieved my fears that Marietta might be induced to an elopement, but I confess I am worried about how the Chevalier will take the news. I cannot be easy that he will accept her engagement with good grace."

Arlington seemed to have lost some of his anger. At least his eyes no longer glowered at her, but his voice was still grave. "Given the fact that he is in a desperate situation, I think your fears are more than justified."

"Oh, I am so glad you agree. That is why I invited all those other people." At his puzzled look, she added, "Surely, he must behave himself in such a crowd."

"Let us hope so. I stopped at Bath on my way back to London and spoke with Wendover. He had d'Orly investigated, and as I suspected, your Chevalier fled France to avoid his creditors. He also has a rather unsavory reputation as a Captain Sharp. On his arrival in England, he spent a short period in Brighton and was called out by a certain Mr. Fairchild, who accused him of cheating at cards. The unfortunate Mr. Fairchild was killed by an unknown assailant the night before the duel."

"You don't think that d'Orly—"

"I do, and so does Bow Street. I spoke with the officer in charge, who has followed d'Orly to London. He located a witness to the assault and brought him along to see if he can identify the Chevalier. The only problem is that d'Orly has gone to ground and no one has seen him since last Wednesday."

"Arlington! He sent Marietta a card yesterday saying that *unfortunate circumstances* have compelled his absence but that he would not fail her today."

"Then I shall send a note round to Bow Street and inform Captain Morgan of our plans. Perhaps he can arrange to have his witness at Hadleigh." He strode to the desk and busied himself composing a note, oblivious to the look of outraged horror on Alex's face.

She followed him, watching over his shoulder as he penned the note. "You are not seriously proposing that we allow a . . . a felon to accompany us today?"

The Marquess looked up, surprised. "Certainly. If we warn him off, he may escape. Don't be concerned. There is nothing he can do amidst that crowd you invited."

"How can you expect me to face him knowing that he might well be a murderer?"

"Come now, Alexandria. There must be a few people among the ton that you don't care for but nevertheless manage to behave civilly to? Although now that I recall our first meeting . . ."

He rose, towering over her, and Alex felt herself blushing. He had called her Alexandria, she thought irreverently, and took a step away, trying to bring her thoughts back to order.

"My lord, there is a vast difference between a person one

unaccountably takes into dislike and someone who is a
murderer. You could be placing us all in danger."

The Marquess ignored her, calling for Dobbs, and when
that stalwart appeared, blithely instructed him to have his
note carried around to Bow Street at once. "Come along
now," he told Alex, placing a comforting arm about her
shoulders. "I saw Jeremy, Gillingham, Barstow, and Hastings out there. You cannot think d'Orly a match for all of
us?"

He held the door open for her, and as she reluctantly
passed through, remembered one other thing he wanted to
tell her. "Try to get Marietta alone and warn her not to let
d'Orly know of her engagement. I will take care of
Gillingham."

As he spoke, Marietta came in the front door to see what
was detaining them, and Alex hurried to her. "I cannot
explain now, but please, whatever you do, don't let d'Orly
know of your engagement. Please, Mari, just this once do
what I ask without arguing."

The door opened again to admit Lord Barstow with Miss
Calvert, and Marietta had no further opportunity to question
her sister. She cast a curious glance at Arlington as he
herded them all out the door and began sorting out the
traveling arrangements.

Alex saw the Chevalier at once, seated on his showy
black stallion, and he raised his riding crop in greeting.
Although he was smiling, she read a threat in the gesture
and moved closer to Marietta.

The Marquess arranged for Sara, Marietta, and Alex to
ride in his own carriage. Lord Barstow would follow in his
curricle with Caroline Calvert, and then Gillingham with
Cordelia Harrington in Gilly's pretty black and yellow
landau. Jeremy, Hastings, and d'Orly would all ride horseback.

It was a breezy drive to Hadleigh, and Arlington set a fast
pace. His passengers were impressed with the skill he
showed in passing a stagecoach on a narrow strip of road
with only inches to spare. Confident of his ability, they
settled back to enjoy the drive on the narrow, twisting lanes.

Alex, under pretext of observing the scenery, kept a wary eye on d'Orly as he occasionally brought his stallion alongside their carriage.

When Arlington finally brought his bay horses to a steaming stop, it was well after one o'clock and they found the enclosure was already filled with post chaises, tilburys, and curricles of every color and size. The postilions and ostlers were kept busy, but two, recognizing quality at a glance, jumped forward to assist the Marquess. Arlington led his party into a large tent set up for refreshments, and revived them with one of the specialties of Hadleigh—mugs of hot negus. It was made with wine, hot water, lemons, oranges, and sugar. Alex welcomed its warmth and sweet taste, as did the other ladies.

Most of the party was in high spirits and anxious to stroll about, surveying the caged lions and tigers. Barstow proposed a visit to the barns where the trained horses were stabled, and as they trod across the field, Alex remained firmly by her sister's side. With Arlington on her other side, d'Orly remained frustrated in his attempts to speak to Marietta privately.

An old gypsy woman, dressed in garish colours, and clutching a dirty shawl about her bony shoulders, called to them to come and have their fortunes told. Sara and Marietta pleaded for permission, and the Marquess, laughing at their excitement, obligingly placed some silver coins in the gnarled hand held out to him. Sara stepped forward first, timidly extending her palm. The old crone examined it carefully, a dark finger tracing the lifelines and turning it this way and that.

"You will travel some distance away from your home and wed a well-to-do young gentleman. Ah, you will be the mistress of a fine estate, and mother to several children. I can see the children playing happily beneath tall trees, and there is much joy."

It seemed to be the usual good fortune, and Alex was not overly impressed. She shared a smile with Arlington as Sara beamed at her intended.

Encouraged, Marietta stepped boldly forward, holding out

her hand. The gypsy pretended deep concentration as she
studied the tiny lines, and said nothing for several minutes.
At last she looked up and intoned in a deep voice, "I see
trouble in the near future, and one who cannot be trusted."
She paused dramatically, and stared into the bright blue
eyes before her. "Guard yourself, child, for danger is very
near."

Alex shivered at the old hag's intensity and involuntarily
looked at d'Orly. Marietta, too, seemed daunted by the
unhappy prophecy. Miss Calvert and Miss Harrington took
their turns, and the gloom was dispelled as they received
promises of good fortune and marriage to well-disposed
gentlemen. Alex refused to have her hand read, and none of
the gentlemen were willing to have their fortunes told.

Arlington suggested d'Orly might wish to do so. "Sometimes a warning, if heeded, serves well," he added enig-
matically.

The Chevalier eyed him warily but still declined, and the
ladies declared they were famished. The group set off in
search of refreshment, stopping only to reserve the sixpenny
seats set aside in a roped-off section for the gentry. They
ate, at Arlington's suggestion, another Hadleigh specialty.
Suckling pig roasted on a spit and served with warm
chestnuts. Caroline and Sara decided to try a glass of the
vaunted mineral water, but pulled such faces on tasting it
that no one else was tempted to sample it. Alex glanced
covertly around the huge enclosure, wondering if a Bow
Street runner had arrived. There were several characters
present who fit her notion of what a runner might look like,
but none of them seemed interested in their group.

After eating, and amid much confusion, the Marquess led
them to their seats in the big tent. The Chevalier was
incensed to find himself in a seat at the end of the row next
to Arlington. He was acute enough to realize that the
Marquess had arranged the seating deliberately, and sat
down with poor grace just as the circus act was about to
begin. As everyone's attention focused on the parade of
horses, elephants, and clowns, Arlington leaned forward
and whispered to d'Orly.

"I feel certain you will be interested to learn that I have just returned from a visit to Bath."

"Then your feelings have misled you. I have no interest in your jaunterings."

"How unfortunate, when Lord Wendover specifically bade me to convey his greetings to you. Wendover was quite interested in your whereabouts. In fact, he had your background investigated. Need I say more?"

The Chevalier remained silent, and sat with his jaw clenched, staring straight ahead. Arlington's message was perfectly clear, and he knew the Marquess would not allow him to continue his pursuit of Marietta. He could ill-afford to have the news of his background spread, and he silently cursed Arlington. D'Orly decided to play for time, remarking at last, "I shall be leaving Town in a few days. I trust that will meet with your approval."

"It does, so long as you don't find time for a visit with my ward," Arlington said, carefully adjusting the lace at his wrist. He watched d'Orly's profile for a moment before turning his attention to Alex.

She appeared enthralled with the high tight-rope act in the center ring. The young woman performing, scantily clad in spangles and feathers, was daringly making her way across the highwire. Alex, along with the rest of the crowd, gasped as the woman made a graceful leap and turn midway across. Unconsciously, Alex gripped his arm. Her fingers relaxed as the woman returned safely to the ground, only to tighten again as the lion tamer bravely placed his head inside a lion's gaping jaws.

The Marquess closed his hand over hers, and startled, Alex turned to him. He smiled and gestured to the ring. The clowns were out, dousing each other with pails of water, and eliciting a great deal of laughter as they tumbled over one another. Seals performed, bouncing rubber balls off their noses, and trained dogs were brought out to entertain them with their tricks.

It was an amusing performance, but Alex's attention was diverted. The warmth of Arlington's hand over her own drove all other thoughts from her head. She knew she should not allow such an intimacy, but was powerless to protest. In truth, she delighted in the sensations he was evoking and found herself wishing that they were not in the midst of a loud and noisy crowd. The thought of what might occur were they alone brought blushes to her cheeks, and she stole a look at Arlington. He appeared immersed in the performance, and she turned her eyes back to the ring.

The climax was met with enthusiastic applause from their party, and as they made their way back to the carriages, Alex turned to thank Arlington for such an enjoyable day. She intercepted a malevolent look from d'Orly, directed at the Marquess' back, and shivered in the cooling air. She judged Arlington must have spoken to d'Orly, but could not imagine what he'd said to engender such an evil look. Surely, he would not have told him Bow Street was on his heels! She decided she must warn Arlington at the first opportunity to beware.

Marietta and Sara chattered endlessly, discussing all the fascinating sights they'd seen. The girls giggled over the fortunes told by the old gypsy, and Marietta couldn't resist teasing her guardian as he expertly drove his team through the enclosure. "The gypsy warned me someone nearby would place me in danger. I wonder if she was casting aspersions on your driving, sir?"

"Mind you manners, girl, unless you wish to walk back to London," Arlington retorted, cracking his whip skillfully over the team's head.

There ensued a nonsensical debate regarding Lord Gillingham's actions should Arlington set Marietta down. Sara maintained that Gillingham would instantly oust Cordelia from his curricle and take up Marietta. Alex listened with growing impatience, and was ready to consign both girls to the nursery by the time they reached Hanover Square.

As they entered the drive, they saw Bella standing in the doorway, obviously on the lookout for them. She urged them all inside to partake of a buffet she had laid out. Alex ushered Marietta and Sara in before her, thankful to finally be at home.

Lord Barstow and Miss Calvert begged to be excused, as

they were expected at Lady Edenbough's. The Chevalier came as far as the steps, and found his way blocked by Arlington. He looked at the Marquess with marked contempt, barely controlling the rage that seethed within him.

"I trust you will allow me take my leave of Miss Marietta?"

"I think not. Rest assured that I will make your excuses for you. I know you are most anxious to be on your way."

Arlington drawled the words in a bored, casual voice, but d'Orly nonetheless felt the menace, and the implicit challenge that was issued. Furious, he turned on his heel and remounted, vowing silently that Arlington would have cause to regret his interference. The Marquess watched him depart and made certain d'Orly had left the Square before he entered the house. He found Marietta lingering in the hall.

"What did you say to d'Orly to make him so angry?" she asked with frank curiosity.

"I told him to 'never darken your door again,' " he said, smiling down into her large eyes.

"Well, I do think he might have put up more of an argument," she said before succumbing to an attack of giggles.

"Yes, I can see you are quite heartbroken. Try not to be so distressed, my dear. You still have Gillingham at your beck and call."

She nodded and appeared serious for a moment. "But it is lowering to think that one is wanted only for one's fortune."

"Mortifying," he agreed. "But if you are looking for a more tender emotion, I don't believe you have to seek very far. Gillingham has been giving an excellent rendition of a young man in the throes of love."

Dimples appeared again. "He will make me an excellent husband, don't you think?"

"I do, if he learns to turn you over his knee when you get up to your tricks—which, I warn you, I will do myself if you do not behave until you are safely wed."

"You would not dare!"

"Your sister informs me that my audacity exceeds all bounds. I don't advise you to put it to the test."

Marietta was left standing with large eyes and open mouth. Bella came to see what was keeping them, and with an admonishment to her niece for keeping the Marquess standing about when he must be fair starved, she urged them to join the others already filling their plates at the lavish buffet.

Arlington, with a plate piled high, made his way to Alexandria. He longed to ease the look of worry from her fine eyes, and answered her unspoken question with a smile. "The Chevalier asked me to convey his regrets. He leaves Town in a few days, and I have warned him not to attempt to see Marietta, so I think you may rest easy."

"I fear I shall not be able to until he either leaves London or has been arrested. I hope you will take care. When we were leaving the tent, I saw him watching you and I have never seen such a look of pure hatred. I know he means to do you harm, my lord."

"Lord Arlington is such a cumbersome title. Do you think you might contrive to address me as Phillip," he asked lightly, his spirits lifted at this evidence of her concern for him. Perhaps she was not as indifferent to him as he'd believed.

Before she could reply, Gillingham was at Arlington's shoulder. "Phillip, I must have a word in private with you."

"The devil! Can you not see that I am conversing with Miss Hilliard?"

"Oh, Alex won't mind. She must know it concerns Marietta."

"Very well," he conceded with poor grace, setting aside his plate. He rose, bowing to Alex. "Will you excuse me, and allow us the use of your library?"

She nodded her consent and watched him quietly lead the way out of the room, Gilly at his heels. They were closeted for some time, and Alex wondered what was taking them so long for what was, after all, a mere formality. Gillingham reappeared first, a tremendous scowl on his handsome features, and went straight to Marietta.

Puzzled, Alex slipped out of the room and found the Marquess still seated in the library, apparently lost in thought. He looked up as she entered, and then stood, his face unreadable. "Have you come to harass me, too?"

"Harass you? Certainly not. When you have been so kind to—"

"I asked Gillingham to postpone any announcement of their engagement, at least for a week or two."

His answer gave her pause, and she considered his words before asking, "But why? I know you approve of the match. Indeed, I understand it was your intention from the beginning that they should wed."

"I don't oppose it. I merely feel they should wait a week or two before making it official. Surely, if they are steadfast in their affections, a week or so cannot matter."

"I see," she said, taking the chair to his left. "Your sudden desire for a postponement would not have anything to do with d'Orly and the fact that you expect him to leave Town shortly, would it, my lord?"

He looked down at her with a smile. "Too smart by half, as Jeremy would say. I wish you were not quite so perceptive, my dear. It would spare you a great deal of worry. The truth is I believe d'Orly to be emotionally unstable, and I fear that if he learns of Marietta's engagement, on top of his other problems, he might try to wreak some sort of vengeance."

"That was the feeling I had this afternoon," she said uneasily. "And I can understand your reasoning. Did Gillingham object? Surely, if you explained the circumstances—"

"Impossible. The young fool would go off half-cocked to call d'Orly out on one pretext or the other. No, it's better he thinks I am merely being unreasonable in my role as guardian."

"Lord, what a coil! I cannot even confide in Marietta because she would, of course, immediately tell Gillingham. I am not at all sure you'll be able to—" She broke off her words as the door flew open.

Marietta stormed into the library, Gillingham right behind her. Without ceremony, she approached Arlington. "Why can we not announce our engagement? Why, we have already told half a dozen people. How will it look if no announcement is forthcoming?"

The Marquess looked helplessly at Alexandria, and she was about to intervene when Bella joined the party.

"Why are you all closeted in here? The Lieutenant and Miss Harrington are waiting to drink a toast to Marietta. Shall I bring them in here?"

Arlington looked at the persons arrayed in front of him, the triumph on Marietta's face, the determination on Gillingham's, and gave it up. "Very well, let us not keep them waiting. Miss Hilliard, will you join with me in making the announcement?"

Alex agreed, knowing Arlington had only capitulated because he realized there was no hope of keeping the betrothal a secret. It was with a heavy heart that she joined him and drank the traditional toast to the young couple. What should have been a joyous occasion was marred by the shadow of d'Orly. Her thoughts kept turning uneasily to him, and Alex wondered what his reaction would be when he leaned the news.

The Chevalier had spent the long ride back to his lodgings pondering ways and means by which he could destroy the Marquess. He was in a foul mood, and it was not improved when, turning his horse into the alley running alongside his new lodgings, he spied two suspicious-looking men. They were clearly watching the cheap hostelry where he had put up. Cursing, he backed the stallion and turned east.

He had already been forced to remove from the Captain's Inn, where he had enjoyed decent accommodations, to this rundown, seedy hostelry in Half-Moon Street. Now it looked as though his creditors had sniffed him out again. Fortunately, there was not much in the room he had need of. If he could only find a place to put up safely for a few days, then he would stay in England only long enough to teach the arrogant Marquess a lesson.

He passed Curzon Street and was nearing the center of Town when the crowd emerging from Covent Gardens put him in mind of Cecily Fanchon. She would help him, he thought gleefully. D'Orly had encountered the actress just after Arlington had given her her *congé*, and she had been full of venom towards the Marquess. Cecily, he was sure, would relish helping him teach Arlington a much-needed lesson, and perhaps earn them both a handsome profit in the bargain.

D'Orly could not chance being seen with her. He reversed direction again, deciding to await the arrival of the actress at her lodgings. Hopefully, she would be alone. The last he'd heard, she was still searching for a new protector. With Arlington's defection, Cecily had lost much of her popularity, and her greedy demands were too high a price for the younger bucks to pay.

He found her lodgings without difficulty. There were candles lighting the lower windows, but from all appearances she had not yet returned home. He tethered Diablo to the oak tree in the back of the house, and settled down to wait. The evening air had a sharp bite to it, and pulling his cape closer about him, he tried to warm himself with thoughts of Arlington's humiliation at his hands.

The Chevalier had almost dozed off when the sound of a carriage and his own horse's soft nickering alerted him. Luck was in. Cecily Fanchon stepped out of the carriage with only her dresser in attendance. He waited in the shadows until her coachman drove the carriage off towards the stables, and then hailed the actress.

Cecily turned, startled, and saw a dark figure emerging from the shrubbery. With a shriek, she clutched at her dresser. D'Orly hastened forward to identify himself before she alerted the watch. Relieved that it was only d'Orly, Cecily released her hold on the frightened maid and sent her on ahead.

"La, Chevalier, what a fright you gave me! Whatever are you doing lurking in the bushes?"

"I wanted to see you privately, Cecily. I have a scheme in mind that I think you will find most interesting—and rewarding."

"Then come upstairs where we can be comfortable, and you may tell me about it." Seeing his nervous look around, she reassured him. "No one else is here except my dresser and maid. And they are both quite discreet."

D'Orly followed her up the narrow stairs that gave out into a warm, intimate room. Her maid had lit the fire and laid out an inviting supper, which he eyed hungrily. Cecily invited him to make himself comfortable. She removed her pelisse, dropping it carelessly over a chair, and moved to the sideboard to pour liberal drinks for both of them.

The warmth of the brandy shot through d'Orly, warming him and reviving his confidence. He settled back against the satin cushions, caressing the brandy glass between his hands.

"Before I reveal this plan I have, I must ask you a question, *mon chéri*. Have your feelings towards Arlington undergone any change since the last time we talked? Or do you still feel . . . how did you put it? Oh, yes. You'd like to cut out his heart and eat it for breakfast?"

Cecily let loose a string of French profanity worthy of a sailor, likening Arlington's antecedents to a pack of wild dogs, among other things.

"Good. Very good." D'Orly encouraged her. "You see, I have it in mind to marry his little ward, Marietta Hilliard."

"Bah! He will never allow it. If that is your plan, you are wasting your time, my friend."

"I don't intend to ask his permission, Cecily. If all goes well, he will know nothing until the deed is done." D'Orly took a sip of the brandy, smiling wickedly.

"Do not tell me that one is willing to fly with you? Gossip has it that she will wed Gillingham."

"Whoever said she was willing? I do not intend to ask her! I plan to force her to travel with me to France. I know a sea captain who, for the right price, will take us safely across, and no questions asked. Once in France, if she agrees to marry me, then I shall have her entire fortune at my disposal. Perhaps I shall settle her somewhere in the country, and I will be free to travel with someone more suited to my tastes." He reached for her hand, and brought it lovingly to his lips. "Do you care for travel, Cecily?"

She returned his smile, beginning to see some merit in his

plan. "But if she refuses to marry you, what then? It is no longer so easy to force a girl against her will."

He gave a shrug of his shoulders. "Then our friend Arlington will pay through the nose for her safe return."

Cecily recalled how Arlington had dropped her when the Hilliards had arrived in Town. She felt her anger flame again, and hoped d'Orly's little scheme would work. "How will you get her away?"

"Ah, that is where you come in. Now listen carefully."

Chapter 11

ALEXANDRIA AWOKE THURSDAY morning with a tightness in her chest—and an inexplicable feeling of impending disaster. For the last three days, the house had been in a constant state of chaos as Bella and Lady Fitzhugh busied themselves with the coordination of Marietta's bride clothes. Lady Fitzhugh had insisted that the trousseau was to be her gift to the bride, which, of course, entitled her to an active role in its selection. The result was an endless parade of seamstresses and milliners through the house.

In addition to the tradespeople, they had been inundated with morning callers, persons supposedly anxious to convey their wishes to the future bride. In reality, most were only seeking to discover a hint of scandal. Marietta's sudden engagement to Gillingham, after her public infatuation with d'Orly, had set tongues wagging. The disappearance of the Chevalier stoked the fires.

As the morning advanced, Alex knew there would be no respite. She saw Mrs. St. John and her daughter to the door, assuring her once more that she did not believe the Chevalier had been driven to suicide. "He was in excellent spirits when he left us on Monday, and spoke of returning to France. Perhaps he has already done so."

"But, my dear, I cannot believe he would just leave without bidding his friends farewell. He was always such a courteous young man. Oh, I do hope nothing has happened to him."

Dobbs stood, holding the door open for the ladies, and at last they took the hint. Alex thankfully watched their departure, wistfully sniffing the fresh air. It was such a

160

beautiful day, warm and breezy, with the sun casting shadows across the street. Impulsively, she instructed Dobbs to have the carriage brought around, and mentally justified her escape by rationalizing that a drive through the park would clear her head. Hurrying up the stairs to change, she called for Susan to accompany her. The carriage was waiting when she returned, and she blissfully settled back against the seat cushions. She spoke only to ask John Coachman to drive them through Hyde Park.

The park was not the peaceful retreat she had anticipated. Alex had neglected to consider the number of people they would encounter at this hour of the afternoon, and her carriage was stopped repeatedly as members of the ton hailed her. She countered their questions as best she could, agreeing to convey their wishes to Marietta and congratulations to her brother. She smiled continuously. Smiled until she felt her teeth aching with the effort. Her enjoyment of the day ruined, she gave orders to return home. Old John had just turned towards the gates when Lord Arlington, driving his curricle, brought his team to a stop opposite them.

"Hello! I have just come from calling on you. Dobbs told me you'd driven out for a breath of air." His eyes traveled over her, noting her rigid posture and the strain about her eyes. "It seems not to have done you much good. Might I tempt you to join me for tea? I can promise you peace and quiet, at least."

Alex declined, but only halfheartedly, and she found it ridiculously easy to allow him to overrule her. The truth was she had missed seeing him during the last few days and had wondered why he had not called when all the rest of London seemed to converge on her doorstep.

Arlington arranged matters to his own satisfaction. In a matter of moments, he had transferred Alexandria to his curricle and sent Susan home with a message for Bella.

Before she quite knew how, Alex found herself seated comfortably in a handsome drawing room. While the Marquess issued orders for tea, she admired the decor. The room was furnished with quiet good taste and provided a tranquil haven. The soft, muted colors blended unobtrusively with highly polished wood and some very fine oil paintings. It suited him, she decided.

Arlington returned, bearing a glass of sherry, and urged her to drink it while they waited for tea. Alex sipped at it cautiously and felt some of the tension leaving her. She felt him regarding her, and glanced up to see him looking unusually concerned.

"Drink the rest of the sherry, Alexandria. You look as though you need it," he ordered.

"Thank you, my lord," she said, smiling shakily. "Do I look a basket case? I never thought that planning two weddings would be so fatiguing. I don't believe I have enjoyed a moment's peace since the announcements were made, and I am sorely tempted to follow your example and cast off all my relatives."

"An admirable thought, but I fear you have not the temperament to carry it off." He smiled, sitting down opposite her. "Now, what is all this faradiddle about wedding plans? Surely, your aunt and Lady Fitzhugh are overseeing all that?"

"Well, yes. But they still wish for my opinion on gowns, hats, chemises, and such, and I declare they change their minds every hour. And when they cannot agree, which is frequently, I am caught in the middle. They each demand I tell the other her taste is outrageous, until I feel pulled in two. And then there are all the callers—more than you would imagine. One would think it was the Prince Regent getting wed, with all the attention we are receiving."

"And are all your callers subjecting you to an inquisition? I gather that d'Orly's sudden disappearance has given rise to some speculative talk."

"That, my dear sir, is a gross understatement. Mrs. St. John called only this morning and would have it d'Orly was driven to suicide. I had not realized the Chevalier was so popular, or that so many people would concern themselves with his absence. How are you handling the questions?"

Arlington frowned at her in his most haughty manner. "You do not suppose anyone would have the impertinence to question me?" He smiled then, his brown eyes suddenly looking boyish and full of mischief. "Have you ever seen a toad, my dear? An encroaching toad that is so bold as to come right up to you?"

Alex drew back, horrified.

"That's it," he said, encouraging her with a laugh. "You must practice looking just so at anyone who has the brass to question you. Picture the toad and you will have it." He demonstrated again, looking down his nose with a haughty air until Alex laughed.

Hodges entered, carrying a lavish tea tray, and beamed upon her. Arlington's staff was well trained and would never betray their surprise, not by so much as a raised eyebrow, if the Master chose to entertain a young lady of quality. But Hodges had been with him for too long, and could not quite contain the pleasure he felt at seeing the Marquess behaving like his old self. He placed the tray in front of them, and enquired in properly stoic tones if there would be anything else.

Alex caught the look of warm approval in his eyes, and saw the corners of his mouth lift in a smile.

The Marquess dismissed the butler without comment, asking Alex to pour the tea. He watched the graceful movement of her hands, feeling a measure of contentment, and mused how pleasant it was to sit here in her company.

Alex, reading something in his countenance, was reminded of the impropriety of having tea alone with him, and anxiously turned the conversation back to the weddings.

He read the uneasiness in her eyes and responded lightly. "I have been thinking of journeying to Allenswood for the weddings. Is there an inn where I could put up?"

"What nonsense is this, sir? You will, of course, stay at Allenswood. We have numerous guest rooms, you know, and . . . and Jeremy would not hear of you putting up at the inn. I believe Marietta plans to ask you to give her away in place of her father. I hope you will agree."

"I can think of little that would give me more pleasure than giving that minx into the care of another. I only pray Gillingham will be capable of handling her."

"I know she has not presented the picture of a compliant young lady, but generally she is very sweet, and she wants nothing so much as to please Gillingham."

He nodded, setting down his cup. "And what of you, Alexandria? What shall you do once you have seen the twins safely wed?"

"I have been trying to persuade Aunt Bella to let a cottage with me, perhaps in Bath. Unfortunately, my aunt is so involved with the weddings, she will not even discuss it."

"Have you ever stayed in Bath?" he asked, with the lift of a brow. "It will be rather dull after the excitement of a Season in London."

"Will it? Excellent. Dull and peaceful is just what I desire most, at least for a time. I fear I am not a social person, and a constant diet of balls and parties does not suit me. A provincial at heart, I suppose."

"I think not. The social whirl of London palls on everyone after a time. But have you considered traveling? There is a vast world beyond England."

Alex laughed, her eyes light with amusement. "You do not know the trouble I had in convincing Bella to even visit London. She prophesied all manner of disasters. I fear I shall have to be content to do my traveling through books, though I would dearly love to see Rome and Paris."

"Perhaps you should have wed poor Barstow. At least then you would have been free to travel wherever you desired."

"Thank you, no," she said, making a face, and then a distant look shadowed her eyes. "I can remember Mama and Papa discussing the many trips they enjoyed together. I think what they liked best was sharing their pleasure with each other. After Mama died, Papa never wished to go anywhere. I believe I am much like him. Without someone with whom I could share the excitement and discoveries, I would as lief stay in the country."

The clock chimed, interrupting their tête-à-tête and reminding Alex of the lateness of the hour. "Goodness, Aunt Bella will wonder what is keeping me. Will you arrange for a carriage to take me home?"

"I shall drive you there myself. Finish your tea while I have the carriage brought around."

During the drive back to Hanover Square, Arlington referred again to d'Orly's strange disappearance. "This morning I spoke with Beckett, the officer in charge at Bow Street. He is convinced that d'Orly is still in London but has gone to ground. Beckett believes our Chevalier is in hiding from his creditors and doesn't have the least notion Bow Street is seeking him on suspicion of murder."

"Then we have no reason to be concerned. Surely, d'Orly will be too occupied with returning safely to France to . . . to bother about anything else?" Alex asked, obviously hoping for reassurance.

Arlington hesitated. He hated to disillusion her. He suspected the strain he'd noted in her eyes was due to worry over d'Orly and not, as she had suggested, from bothersome wedding plans. Still, he thought, it was better that she be on her guard.

"It's difficult to judge what he might do. Merely as a precaution, Beckett has stationed a guard to keep an eye on Marietta, and another near my own house. I don't believe there's any real danger, but there's no sense in running needless risks."

The only sign of dismay his words evoked was a widening of her eyes, silvery green in the afternoon sun, and a tiny sigh that escaped her lips. Arlington was surprised, and pleased, that she did not react with what he considered typical female hysteria.

He brought the carriage to a halt and assisted her down, standing for a minute with her hand in his. "Alexandria, try not to worry. Bow Street is on hand, and I, too, will try to be nearby should you need me. Now go and enjoy your evening."

She left him with a smile, feeling strangely comforted. Dobbs opened the door for her, and she was halfway up the stairs before it occurred to her that the Marquess had used her given name again. Had, in fact, been doing so for some time. It would amuse him, she thought, to know that with the distressing news of d'Orly, her mind centered on the use

of her name. The Marquess had a devastating charm—when
he chose to employ it.

He continued to occupy her thoughts later that evening as
she stood in the receiving line and surveyed the crowded
ballroom. She was inclined to believe that Lady Fitzhugh
had invited most of London to the party honouring Marietta.
She looked at their sponsor in vexation, wondering how
much longer she would have to stand there.

Lady Fitzhugh presented an imposing figure. She was
swathed in yards of her favourite shade of purple satin, a
large and glittering tiara perched precariously on her head.
Alex idly speculated on the worth of the diamond tiara, if
the stones were genuine. If it was real, it represented a
tremendous fortune, one in danger of tumbling to the floor
every time Lady Fitzhugh nodded her head.

Alex had learned from Bella that the dowager favoured
purple because she believed it to be a regal colour. She saw
the tiara tremble as Lady Fitzhugh turned and nodded her
head, indicating they could abandon the receiving line.
Alex and Marietta entered the lavishly decorated ballroom
with relief, and in need of refreshments. A few minutes
later, Alex thankfully sipped the lemonade Gillingham had
managed to produce for them.

She watched her future brother-in-law lead out Marietta
for the first set, wondering where her sister found the
energy. Alex was just planning to join Bella in the alcove
where she could rest for a few minutes when the butler
announced a late arrival. She turned, catching Arlington's
eye from across the room, and felt the tiredness leave her.
Suddenly, she felt like dancing, and when the Marquess
made his way to her side, she happily gave him her hand.

It was impossible not to be aware of the staring eyes of
the crowd as they took their places in the set. The Marquess
created a stir wherever he went, and Alex tried to ignore the
looks directed at them.

"This is a pleasant surprise, my lord. I had not expected
to see you here this evening."

"Lady Fitzhugh and I are old friends. She's been trying to
get me to attend one of her affairs for years. Until now, I

never had any desire to do so." He smiled at her in a way that lent veracity to the rumours of his accomplishments as a lover, and she looked away in confusion.

He felt her tremble slightly, and noted the blush suffusing her lovely cheeks. "Have I tipped you a leveler?" he teased softly. "Then, we are even, my dear, for you handed me one the first time I laid eyes on you."

Her heart was beating rapidly, and she seemed to be having difficulty catching her breath. It was an effort as she replied lightly, "I wish I might know how I contrived to do so! As I recall, we disagreed on every subject, and I had the distinct impression you wished me at Jericho."

"No—not Jericho. I will admit you put me off-balance. It is unnerving to suddenly find a woman like you. I did not believe such a creature existed. After all these years, I—"

Arlington broke off as the music stopped, and Jeremy was suddenly there beside them, with Sara in hand. Alex was torn by conflicting emotions. She did not know if she was more relieved or disappointed at the abrupt ending to their conversation. It had seemed as though Arlington was about to make her an offer, and she could not even decide if she found the idea appalling or appealing. She found herself standing next to her aunt without any awareness of how she got there, and had to beg pardon when Bella put a question to her.

Alex had received several proposals in the past, but none which had imbued her with any desire to change her way of life, and she had more or less resigned herself to remaining a spinster. Now Arlington had cast her into an agony of confusion, and it was impossible to consider his offer with any degree of rationality. If, indeed, he even meant to make her an offer, she thought. She absently refused a request to join a set for the quadrille, her eyes focused on Arlington's graceful figure maneuvering through the crowd. He exited through the double set of French doors, and she indignantly exclaimed aloud, "He cannot be leaving!"

Bella looked at her, perplexed. "Alexandria, whatever ails you? You were almost rude to Exeter when he asked you to stand up with him, and now you are talking to yourself. Do try for a little composure."

Alex blushed, making an effort to appear complacent. She would have felt considerably better if she had known that the Marquess was experiencing his own share of turbulent thoughts.

Arlington had not intended to make an impromptu proposal in the middle of a crowded ballroom, nor anywhere else for that matter. At least not until this business with the Chevalier was taken care of and the twins safely wed, he emended. Although the notion of making Alexandria his wife had been in his mind for some time, he was not entirely certain of his own feelings, or of hers. He had meant to wait, give them both more time to know each other, but Alexandria had looked so enticing that his tongue had betrayed him.

He shook his head at his own rashness, but after the initial shock, he was feeling strangely elated and still inclined to put his luck to the touch at once. He would have asked Alex to step out on one of the balconies were it not for his tiresome ward.

When Jeremy had interrupted them, Arlington had been facing the entrance to the ballroom. From that vantage point, he was the only one to observe Marietta, after a furtive glance around, slipping into the hall. Her stealthy behaviour forced him to put all other thoughts out of his mind, and making his excuses, he tried to follow his ward.

When he entered the long hall, there was no sign of Marietta. He studied the numerous doors leading to private rooms, and considered the grand staircase at the north end of the hall, before deciding to investigate the servants' stairwell at the south end. Arlington found himself in a small hallway that apparently led to the kitchens and the staff's quarters. A young serving girl appeared in the doorway and eyed him with considerable surprise. Members of the nobility did not frequent this region of the house. Not unless they were up to no good.

Hesitantly, she asked if she could be of help, and watched suspiciously as the gentleman looked about. When he asked if a pretty young girl had come this way, she relaxed, deciding it was only a clandestine meeting. Regretfully, she shook her head no.

By the time Arlington found his way through the maze of passages to the foot of the grand staircase, there was no sign of Marietta, and fearing the worse, he hastened back to the ballroom. He was brought up short as his astonished gaze took in Marietta, chatting in idle innocence with Gillingham. He watched her for a moment before strolling over to join them.

Marietta saw her guardian approaching, and eyed him with trepidation. She did not think he could possibly know of the missive she had just received from Cecily Fanchon, which was now tucked securely in the bodice of her gown. Still, she did not like the speculative look in his eyes.

"Ah, there you are, Marietta. Alexandria was wondering where you were, and I thought I saw you leave the ballroom."

She looked up at him, widening her eyes in her best imitation of pure innocence. "The most vexing thing, I had to go pin up my flounce. Gilly is such a clumsy brute, no doubt he stepped on it."

Gillingham protested the injustice of this, while Arlington merely continued to stare at her. Marietta turned nervously to Gillingham and asked him to escort her to her sister. She dared not look down, certain the note in her bodice must be obvious to Arlington's penetrating gaze, and was anxious to escape him.

She strolled across the room with Gilly, praying all the while that the Marquess had not seen the maid who, under the pretext of pointing out her torn ruffle, had passed the message that a fine lady was waiting to speak with her downstairs "private like." She was sure Miss Fanchon had bribed the girl heavily, but she would not place any dependence on the maid's silence if Lord Arlington chose to question her.

Marietta had been astonished when, after following the girl to a small drawing room on the first floor, she found the famous actress waiting for a word with her. Miss Fanchon hurriedly introduced herself, although there was no need. Marietta recognized her instantly, and was delighted with the chance to speak with her. There were hundreds of questions she would have liked to asked.

The actress, however, stressed the need for urgency. She pleaded with Marietta to take the billet she handed her. "Hide it until you have the opportunity to read it in private."

Marietta took the note curiously and started to unfold it.

"No, no," Cecily said, laying a hand on hers. "You have not the time to read it now. We may be interrupted any moment."

"But who—"

"It is from the Chevalier. Your guardian has forced him to flee the country, and he leaves tomorrow evening. He knows of your engagement, but begs you will grant him a last farewell. I pray you will not fail, for it means so much to him. The Chevalier, ah, he breaks his heart for you."

The actress was gone before Marietta could reply. She stared after her, fingering the note in her hand. Hearing voices in the hall, she had hastily tucked the note in the bodice of her gown. It nestled there now, rather uncomfortably, and Marietta was, for once, anxious for a ball to end.

Alex felt the same way. She saw her sister approaching with Gillingham, and the Marquess directly behind them. Where moments before she had been aggravated by his abrupt departure, she now wished he would disappear. Her senses were too disordered for her to think rationally, and she prayed he would not resume their conversation. She need not have worried.

The Marquess was preoccupied with his ward's behaviour, and as soon as that young lady took the floor with Gillingham, he expressed some of his concern. "I fear Marietta is up to mischief. She slipped out of the room while we were talking, and her manner was so secretive . . . see if she will confide in you later this evening. If not, try to stay near her for the next few days. Don't let her out of your sight."

Alex was disconcerted. This was certainly not the declaration she had expected. Her senses were reeling, and she had to make a concentrated effort to focus on his words. "Do you think she met with d'Orly? I cannot believe it of her!"

Arlington was watching Marietta. "She was absent very briefly, and if it were not for the manner in which she left, I would not be so suspicious. I don't think d'Orly would be foolhardy enough to show his face here, but I fear he sent her some sort of message. Perhaps for an assignation."

"I realize we've spoiled her, and she doesn't always behave as she ought, but I cannot credit that she would do anything so improper as to meet him clandestinely. Not now. Not when everything is settled with Lord Gillingham."

"Your sister, my dear, is a beautiful pea-brain. You must know she has not an ounce of sense. What she does have is an exceedingly kind heart, and if d'Orly is shrewd enough to play on her emotions . . ."

Alex acknowledged there was some truth in his words and turned to watch her sister. Marietta was dancing innocently with Gillingham, looking very sweet as she gracefully executed the steps. Alex was almost certain that Arlington was mistaken, but she recalled the numerous occasions when her sister had looked just as angelic—the pose but a prelude to some outrageous piece of misconduct. Reluctantly, she promised to heed his warning and keep Marietta close by.

"Good," he said quietly. He was standing slightly behind her and spoke softly into her ear. She could feel his warm breath on her neck and was afraid to move. His next words, however, were like a splash of cold water. "Now, if you will give me leave, I want to have a word with Beckett and find out if Bow Street has made any progress. I promise I shall call on you early tomorrow and keep you informed."

She turned then, about to utter some retort. His smile and the warmth in his eyes stopped her.

"I have not forgot our earlier conversation, Alexandria. Perhaps, we can . . . pursue it tomorrow." His gloved finger lightly touched her cheek, and then he was gone.

The rest of the evening passed in a blur, and Alex, with
so much to consider, was more than ready for her bed. She
had tried, futilely, to induce Marietta to confide in her. The
only information she'd received was a detailed catalogue of
the bridal clothes and a lengthy list of Gillingham's excellent qualities. Convinced anew that Arlington was mistaken, she bid her sister good night and retired to her own
bedchamber. She was so tired, she was sure she would
immediately fall into a deep sleep. Thus, she was considerably vexed to find herself tossing restlessly as thoughts of
the Marquess kept intruding.

She turned over, trying to find a more comfortable
position. What would it be like to share a bed with
Arlington? The thought popped into her mind unbidden,
and she blushed in the darkness. She had never encountered
anyone who held such sway over her emotion. There were
times when she liked him intensely, and his presence set her
heart racing. There were other times when she felt almost as
if she hated him, and wished him to the devil.

None of her other suitors had ever troubled her thoughts
to such a degree, and not one of them had caused her to
wonder what it would be like to nestle in his strong arms or
to be passionately kissed. He would be an accomplished
lover, she thought, neither clumsy nor awkward. A rake
would have to be. And that was another thing. He had any
number of lightskirts in keeping, and *she* had no desire to
marry a rake. Did she? Annoyed with her own thoughts, she
punched the pillow and resolutely settled herself for sleep.

While Alex was wrestling with her thoughts, Marietta
waited impatiently for the house to settle. When, at last, she
was sure everyone was asleep, she crept out of bed and lit
a taper. She searched through her reticule, where she had
secreted d'Orly's note, and carried it back to bed with her.
The lines were closely written, and she almost burned the
note as she held it close to the candle flame.

"My little angel, your guardian has used his power to
force me to leave the country, and I return to France
tomorrow. I have learned of your engagement, mon

petite, and I felicitate you. Lord Gillingham is a gentleman almost worthy of you, unlike my poor self. Although circumstances forbid that I could ever wed you, I shall hold your memory etched in my heart forever. Never will I love again as I love my little angel. Fate has been unkind, and I leave England with a heavy heart. I ask only for one last look at you, one moment of your time that I might say adieu. One little memory to warm me on cold and lonely nights. I pray you will come to bid me farewell tomorrow morning, at Madame Fanchon's lodgings. She is an old friend who can be trusted. I beg of you not to fail me, for your memory is all that I have left to cherish."

There followed a crudely drawn map with Madame Fanchon's direction, and a last impassioned plea that she come alone, telling no one of their tryst least she be prevented. As she read the words, her blue eyes glistened with unshed tears. Marietta, so completely happy in her engagement to Gillingham, felt immeasurably sorry for the poor Chevalier. Forced by Arlington to flee the country, alone and penniless, he was still noble enough to be glad for her.

She pictured the scene. D'Orly kneeling before her, memorizing every line of her face, while she stood—the grand and gracious lady. Of course she would not refuse such a simple request. It was the least she could do after leading him on.

Marietta blew out the candle and settled down to consider how she might contrive to slip away. She knew she would have to confide, at least a little, in Sara. They had planned to visit a manteau-maker's shop in the morning, and if Sara could be brought to assist her, she was certain she could get away then. Surely, it would not take more than an hour to bid the Chevalier good-bye. No one would be the wiser, and d'Orly would have his fond memory of England to take away with him. She fell asleep with visions of the scene she would enact.

She did not know that as she lay dreaming, the Chevalier was near the house. Seated on his black stallion, he had

watched the upper windows, unsure which was Marietta's.
He had seen the candlelight flicker in one window, and was
certain it was Marietta reading his note. He prayed the little
fool would be gullible enough to meet him alone. Diablo
snorted in the cool air, and d'Orly reached a hand down to
soothe him. "Soon, my friend, soon. We shall teach these
English a lesson they will never forget." He cantered off,
barely giving a thought to the burly figure sleeping heavily
against a tree opposite the house.

Marietta dressed with special care the next morning. If the
Chevalier was going to carry an image of her in his heart
forever, she wanted to be certain it was one in which she
looked her best. It was not so much that she was vain;
rather, she had been so frequently complimented on her
beauty that she had come to take it for granted. Numerous
young men had written lengthy sonnets addressed to the
perfection of her angelic looks, starry eyes, or rosebud
complexion. So many gentlemen had languished about the
halls of Allenswood that one tripped over them much like
stray cats and dogs. They fell in love with her with such
regularity that she accepted it as a rule of nature, and so
never questioned d'Orly's declaration of undying devotion.
She merely felt a faint stirring of compassion for him.
    If the truth could be told, Marietta thought it was all
rather romantic, and could hardly wait to share his letter
with Sara. However, she intuitively knew that none of her
family was likely to view the matter in the same light, and
might even prevent her from granting d'Orly his one small
request. She felt justified in not mentioning the matter when
Alex questioned her about her plans for the day.
    Alex did not see how any harm could come to her sister
if she allowed her to go shopping with Sara. The Comstocks' maid would accompany the girls, as well as the
coachman and at least one footman. Surely, Arlington
would not object to so innocent an expedition. A small
doubt assailed her, and she considered, briefly, going with
Marietta. However, the thought of enduring the nonstop
conversation of two young ladies, both anxious to exchange

all the details of their respective weddings, effectively deterred her. That, and Arlington's promise to pay her a morning call. She saw Marietta off with mixed emotions, and extracted a promise that she would return early.

Marietta was hard put to control her desire to confide in Sara during the carriage drive, but the servants' presence forced her to keep her lips buttoned until they were safely inside Madame Lapides' shop. She quickly drew her friend into one of the small private fitting rooms.

"Sara, I need your help. The Chevalier is leaving tonight for France, and he has sent me a message. Miss Fanchon passed it to me last night—"

"Cecily Fanchon? The actress? Why, I did not see her there!"

"No, of course not. She bribed a maid to find me, and I slipped downstairs to meet her. Here, read this." Marietta produced the much-folded note and passed it to Sara, who stood reading it, wide-eyed.

"Oh, Marietta," she breathed. "How very much he must love you! What are you going to do?"

Marietta took the note back and returned it to her reticule. "I am going to grant his wish, of course. It is the least I can do, but I need your help. Now, Sara, I want you to stay here. Delay over your fittings as long as possible. Try on every chemise in the shop if you have to, but whatever you do, stay here until I return. I am going to leave by the side door and hire a carriage to take me to Madame Fanchon's. I'll be as quick as I can, probably no more than an hour. Then, when I slip back in, we will leave together and no one shall ever know."

"Marietta, do you think you should? I would not dare. Only think of what Jeremy would say, or Gillingham."

"It hardly matters since we are not going to tell them. Now, don't be a goose. Just delay as much as possible and try to pass by the front windows now and then so your maid may see you. She will think we are both in here and won't worry." With a last adjustment to her hat, and a kiss on the cheek for Sara, Marietta stepped out of the room and disappeared before her friend could think of anything to say to stop her.

She walked jauntily through the side door and hurried down the cobblestone alley in search of a hackney coach. She found one right away, and fortunately the driver was familiar with the direction she indicated. He promised to have her there in a trice, and she wedged herself into a corner, carefully shielding her face from view.

The coach stopped in front of a small cottage, which appeared to be almost deserted. She questioned the driver, but he assured her this was the address she had given. Marietta found her courage waning as she stepped down and somewhat hesitantly asked the driver if he would wait.

"I can't do that, miss, but I'll be back this way in a bit, and I'll keep my orbs peeled for you."

She nodded, told herself she was being foolish, and bravely approached the entrance.

Cecily and d'Orly had been on the lookout for her, and Cecily opened the door before she had a chance to raise the knocker.

"Chéri, come in. I am so glad you found the courage to come. This way, *s'il vous plait*." The actress led the way up a flight of narrow steps to the sitting room and then discreetly retired. Marietta saw d'Orly immediately, looking very handsome in black riding attire, his Hessian boots gleaming in the light from the fire. He crossed the room to meet her, bowing gallantly and kissing her gloved hand.

"You did not fail me! How beautiful you are, my angel," he said, his eyes roving over her figure. "I shall treasure this moment always. I should have left some time ago, but the thought that you might come kept me waiting, and now I am rewarded. But I must make haste, or I shall miss my ship."

Marietta withdrew her hand, glancing around nervously. "It is just as well, for I cannot stay above a moment or two. I left Sara at Madame Lapides' and must hurry back before my absence is discovered."

She didn't see the rage that distorted his features for an instant. He controlled his fury, questioning her softly.

"Sara? Do you mean Miss Comstock? Surely, you did not tell her of our meeting?"

"I had to," she answered defensively, sensing his anger. "I could not have gotten away without her help. You have no idea how I am hemmed in by maids and footmen always, but Sara will not betray us. It is only that I do not wish her to become anxious."

D'Orly, aware that he should not have allowed her to see his alarm, changed tactics. Slipping a gentle arm about her shoulders, he propelled her towards the stairs. "I have a carriage waiting, little one. Come with me, and I shall have the driver return you to your friend before taking me to my ship."

Marietta hesitated. She was uncomfortable and enormously aware of the awkward position she had placed herself in. The tryst was not as she imagined it would be, and all she wanted now was to get back to Sara. Her eyes searched the lane as they left the cottage, but she saw no sign of the coach she'd hired. Reluctantly, she allowed the Chevalier to seat her in his carriage, which he had waiting behind the house.

They were off almost before the door was shut, and d'Orly seemed a little apprehensive, looking out both windows before settling back and reaching for her hand.

He gazed soulfully into her eyes. "Are you sure, my little angel, that it is Gillingham you wish to wed? Would you not rather fly with me to France? We could, I think, be very happy together. I know how to please a woman." His hand came up, his fingers gently stroking her cheek, and then holding her head still, he brushed her lips with his own. Marietta struggled to turn her head, and angrily pushed him away.

"Stop that! Are you mad? I demand you stop this carriage immediately and set me down." This was not the charming Chevalier she had dallied with.

He laughed harshly, capturing her hands in his. "I think not. I have booked passage for two on the ship, and you, my little one, are coming with me to France."

"You *are* mad! Let go of me at once. When Gilly finds

you, he will cut your heart out!" She struggled furiously to
free her hands, and turning her head, yelled for the driver to
stop at once. She managed to free one hand and rapped hard
against the window.

He let her go, knowing her struggles were useless. The
driver was in his pay and would not stop the carriage until
they reached the first posting house outside of London. He
searched in the valise at his feet and withdrew a heavily
folded cloth and a small green bottle. Marietta did not see
him uncap the vial, but she smelt the sickening sweet odor
as he doused the cloth. She turned then, horror in her eyes.

Her hands came up to ward him off, but she was no match
for his wiry strength. She bit him once, and he cursed
loudly before grabbing the back of her neck.

D'Orly forced her face into the chloroformed cloth and
held her there until her struggles began to lessen. Marietta
felt lightheaded, and the carriage seemed to spin around her.
She was powerless to prevent her eyes from closing, her
head from falling back. The last thing she saw was the sneer
on d'Orly's face, his eyes blazing with anger.

When he was sure she was unconscious, he removed the
cloth from her face, arranging her so she appeared to be
sitting up in the carriage. He lifted a limp wrist to his
mouth, and drawing back her glove, kissed her soft white
skin. "It is too bad, little one, that you are so unwilling, but
I shall have my way with you yet. You won't be so reluctant
when you find yourself alone and penniless in a strange
country."

Chapter 12

ALEXANDRIA, ANXIOUSLY WAITING for the Marquess to arrive, situated herself in the book room. She did not wish to give the appearance of being on the lookout for him, and the library also had the added advantage of allowing a more private meeting than if the Marquess were shown to the upper drawing room. She studiously pored over her account books, but as her attempt to total a column of figures had resulted in three different sums, it was only a token effort. Her mind refused to banish the Marquess from her thoughts, and she jumped every time she heard a carriage approaching.

Hearing male voices in the hall, she tidied her hair and looked up in expectation. She tried to hide her disappointment as Jeremy entered, with Gillingham on his heels. Both young men were in high spirits and had come in search of Sara and Marietta. Gillingham, it was explained, had purchased a pair of roans for his curricle and was eager to try them against Jeremy's greys.

"They're complete to a shade," he enthused. "Light necks, broad chests, and their quarters so well let down. I never saw such a well-matched pair, but Jeremy will have it that his is the better team."

"We intend to find out, and thought we'd drive the girls to Richmond," her brother added. "Where did Marietta say they were going? What the deuce is that?"

A loud commotion in the hall had drawn this last exclamation from him, and he strode towards the door. It opened before he could reach it, and Sara Comstock burst into the room. Her hat was sadly askew and tears streamed down her face.

"Oh, Jeremy," she cried, casting herself into his arms. "Thank heavens you are here! The most dreadful thing has happened!" An eruption of sobs prevented further disclosures.

Alexandria rose and reached the girl in two steps, pulling at her shoulder. The fear pervading her caused her to snap at the girl. "Where is Marietta? What has happened, Sara?"

"I . . . I don't know. She never . . . never came back," the girl wailed, drawing back into the shelter of Jeremy's arms.

He patted his intended on the shoulder somewhat helplessly, trying to stop the flow of tears, while Gillingham longed to wrench her from his arms and shake her until she made some sense. Alex hurried to the sideboard and came back with a small glass of brandy.

More calmly than she felt, she directed Jeremy to sit Sara in the large wing chair. Handing her a handkerchief, she urged her to dry her eyes and drink some of the brandy. Alex made a supreme effort to keep her voice soothing and gentle, but she waited impatiently for the girl to gain a measure of composure and the sobs to lessen.

The brandy had a calming effect, and grasping Jeremy's hand tightly, Sara managed to utter only enough to alarm them. "I knew I should not let her go alone, but she insisted, and how was I to stop her? She promised to be back within an hour, but it has been over two!" She sobbed into the handkerchief again, while her listeners tried to make sense out of her disjointed words.

Alex knelt in front of her, taking hold of her hand. "Now, Sara, no one is blaming you, but you must tell us what has happened. Where did Marietta say she was going?"

"To him! He only wanted to see her one last time, and he wrote her such a beautiful letter."

"Who, Sara? Who did she go see?" Alex prodded, and with a sinking feeling in her stomach added, "Was it d'Orly?"

Sara could only nod, her sobs turning into hiccups.

"Good God! I thought he had left Town," Jeremy said, looking in apprehension at Gillingham.

"The cur! If he has hurt one hair on her head—" Gillingham stood in front of Sara, looking thunderous and ready to commit mayhem. She grasped Jeremy's hand tighter, cowering against the back of the chair.

"He said . . . he said he was glad she was marrying someone worthy of her. He only wanted to say good-bye. It . . . it seemed so harmless . . ."

Alex brushed this aside. "Do you know where she was planning to meet him, Sara?"

"At Madam Fanchon's . . . she is a friend of his."

"The actress? Good Lord! Gillingham—" Alex turned, intending to ask if he knew the woman's direction, but Gilly was halfway to the door.

"Come on, we will follow in my carriage," Jeremy said, abruptly pulling Sara to her feet. "Try not to worry, Alex. We'll find her."

They were gone before Alex could think, and she collapsed into the chair Sara had vacated, momentarily stunned. She tried not to think of Marietta in d'Orly's vindictive hands, and absently sipped the brandy she was still holding. Its warmth restored her somewhat, and she pulled the bell rope for Dobbs before hurrying to her desk. The note she penned was not in her usual elegant script, but she had no time to waste.

"You rang, miss?" Dobbs said, appearing in the doorway. His face was as impassive as ever, but she knew he must be curious about the haste in which the others had left.

"Have one of the footmen take this note around to Lord Arlington at once. It is extremely urgent."

The butler bowed and left without comment. Alex sat at the desk wondering if there was anything else she could do, wishing fretfully that Arlington would arrive. As if in answer to her prayers, he appeared in the doorway.

"Whatever is amiss, Alexandria? Your front door is standing open to the world, and Dobbs seems to have disappeared."

"Arlington! Oh, thank God you have come!" Never had

he looked more wonderful to her, and even in her distraught state, one corner of her mind registered how broad his shoulders looked in an exquisitely cut coat. She rose and crossed to him, allowing him to take both her hands. "It's as you feared—d'Orly has Marietta!"

She relayed the scant information they had extracted from Sara, and somehow felt comforted for telling him. "Jeremy and Gillingham are already headed for that woman's house, but I cannot think how that will help since he is sure to have fled from there by now."

"Can you be ready to travel in five minutes? There's no time to be lost. Get your wrap while I leave a message for your brother in case he returns here."

She nodded, thankful to be doing something, and was at the door only moments later. Arlington had his phaeton in the drive, and they were off at a spanking pace before she had time to collect her breath. She sat silently for several miles, praying they would find Marietta before any harm had been done to her. She stole a look at Arlington's profile. The stone cast of his features boded ill for d'Orly, and she wondered if he were equally furious with her. She deserved that he should be. She finally summoned the courage to speak.

"You must think me foolish beyond belief. I never should have allowed Marietta to go with Sara this morning—not after you warned me something like this might occur."

"I did not intend that you constitute yourself a body-guard, if that's what you're thinking. I am to blame if anyone is. I should have warned your sister that d'Orly might try something like this." His voice was full of anger, and she flinched.

"Where . . . where are we going?"

"I suspect d'Orly means to return to France, and the easiest route would be from Brighton. He's probably hired a ship to take him across the Channel. But it's a hard drive. We might pick up a trace of him at one of the posting houses."

"You don't think it would help to question Madame Fanchon? She seems to have been in league with him."

"I doubt he would have confided his true direction to her. We will leave her to your brother and Gillingham. They will discover whatever she knows."

Although the day was sunny, the air was chilly, and she pulled her pelisse around her, wondering if Marietta was dressed warmly. Arlington told her there was a fur rug beneath her feet, and she pulled it up over her legs thankfully. As the miles flew past, her fears increased.

"Will he . . . hurt her, do you think?"

The Marquess took his eyes off the road for an instant and glanced down at her. She looked so vulnerable huddled beneath the rug, and he knew how desperately worried she was. He also knew an urge to stop the carriage and comfort her in his arms, but realized they could not afford to lose any time. "No doubt revenge is part of his motive, but d'Orly probably plans to force her into marriage. That failing, he may try to ransom her. Either way, it's not likely he would offer her physical harm."

Alex shivered again, although not from the cold. She asked no more questions, and sat watching the road while she prayed silently. She hoped Jeremy and Gilly would have some success with Cecily Fanchon.

Madame Fanchon, who had not anticipated that anyone would know of her involvement in d'Orly's little scheme, was surprised when she saw two carriages pull into her drive. Peering from behind the curtains, she saw Lord Gillingham leap down, the violence of his movements frightening her. She hurriedly instructed her maid to deny her presence, but it was too late. Gillingham had wrenched open the door, and was taking the stairs two at a time. The maid, on her way down, was pushed out of the way. Jeremy and Sara followed close behind him.

Cecily decided to brazen it out. She turned to greet Gillingham as though she was in the custom of receiving impetuous young men as morning callers.

"Really, Lord Gillingham, you must learn to control your passion. I am always delighted to receive you, but you might at least allow yourself to be announced—you and your friends."

Gillingham ignored her. "Where's d'Orly? What has he done with Marietta?"

"I haven't the least idea of what you are talking about," she said, pretending an inordinate interest in her ring. "Pray do not shout so. If you have come here merely to abuse me, for reasons I cannot comprehend, I shall have Maria show you the door."

"You do know," Sara cried out passionately, stepping forward to face the actress. "I saw the letter d'Orly wrote her, and he asked Marietta to meet him here!"

"Indeed? Perhaps then he merely used my address as a convenient meeting place." Her training as an actress came to her aid, and she appeared totally calm and only bored by their accusations. She picked up a tiny snuffbox, and only Jeremy noticed the trembling fingers.

He took the box from her hand. "You are most foolish to try to protect him, madam, but as you will. If you don't wish to speak to us, I shall call in Bow Street. I'm sure the officers would be interested to know that you have been harbouring a fugitive, and, possibly, you might even be considered an accessory to kidnapping."

"And I'll tell them Marietta told me *you* gave her the letter from d'Orly at Lady Fitzhugh's ball last night," Sara added, full of fury.

"What nonsense! I was not invited to any ball at Lady Fitzhugh's. I doubt the lady even knows I exist."

"Perhaps not," Gillingham said, and making a shrewd guess continued, "But I am perfectly sure her maid would recognize you. The one you bribed to slip Marietta the note."

It was obvious the actress was shaken. She paled considerably and sat down on the sofa. "Very well. I admit I gave Miss Hilliard a note from the Chevalier . . . but I had nothing to do with any kidnapping. He said he only wanted to wish her farewell in private. I saw nothing wrong with that! When a young couple is in love—"

Gillingham broke in angrily, "Was she here this morning? With d'Orly? When did they leave? Where was he taking her?"

"She was here," Fanchon admitted petulantly, "but only for a matter of minutes, and really, I did not eavesdrop. The Chevalier said he had to hurry to catch a ship, and I thought he was driving her back to the modiste."

Jeremy was impatient to be off again. Gillingham restrained him for a moment, putting a last question. "How long ago was this? What time did they leave?"

She shrugged. "An hour or two since, I suppose."

The trio left as abruptly as they had arrived, conferring briefly in the courtyard before setting off again. Jeremy wanted Sara to go back to Hanover Square, but she staunchly refused.

"Marietta will have need of me if . . . when we catch up with them. I am coming with you."

There was nothing Jeremy could do except warn her that they would be traveling fast. Between them, the young men had decided that if d'Orly was fleeing the country, his likely course would be from Brighton. The two curricles set forth on the London Road, not realizing Arlington was almost an hour before them.

When Marietta awoke, for a moment she could not fathom where she was or why she was unable to move her arms. Memory flooded back as she realized she was in a closed carriage, moving rapidly, and that her arms were bound behind her. They must have changed carriages while she was unconscious. She struggled uselessly against the cords binding her hands until her wrists began to chafe. She settled back resolutely, deciding to conserve her strength for when the carriage halted. Perhaps then she would have a chance at escaping. She thought of Sara waiting for her at Madame Lapides', and wondered how long her friend would delay before sounding the alarm.

Marietta felt the carriage slowing and braced herself to face d'Orly. She pretended to be unconscious as he entered the carriage, and there was a stretch of silence. She could sense that he was watching her, and she tried to be still.

Then she felt his breath near her face, and her eyes flew open.

"You beast! Coward! Untie my hands at once!"

"With pleasure, my dear," he replied smoothly and turned her so he could see the knots. She really was lovely, he thought, as he removed the cords and sat back in the carriage. Eyeing her appreciatively, his glance fell on her bruised wrists. He leaned forward, running a gloved finger over the bruise. "You must accept my apologies, little one. I never intended to hurt you."

Her hands flew up. "Do not touch me!"

He sat back again, nonchalantly. "I had hoped you would welcome my touch more warmly. Especially as I intend to make you my wife."

"Your wife? You're ridiculous. I would never wed you," she said, turning her head away defiantly.

"How unfortunate you feel that way. But perhaps you shall change your mind. Yes, I believe so—when you find yourself alone and penniless in France. I shall be your only protector, my little one. I think you shall be very glad to marry me in the end."

His words chilled her and she looked wildly about. Striving to keep the terror she felt from her voice, Marietta asked if they were still in England.

"For a while longer, my angel. We are at a posting house waiting for a change of horses. Are you impatient to be with me? Do not fret, we shall soon be off."

"It is merely that I am famished," she said, glaring at him. "Do you plan to starve me on this journey? Or are you afraid my brother and Gillingham will be after you?" She saw the anger flare in his eyes and provoked him further. "Too afraid to even stop for meals, Chevalier?"

"*I* do not fear any man! Besides, I believe your friend Sara will delay as long as possible before betraying your clandestine meeting, eh? And while you were sleeping so peacefully, we made quite excellent time. Why, we must be hours ahead of any pursuit—even if anyone had a suspicion where to look for you. No, my dear, I do not fear your brother or even the gallant Gillingham."

Her spirits sunk immeasurably with his words, and it took every ounce of her willpower to answer him calmly. "Then surely there is no reason why we cannot order a meal here, is there?"

"I am, I admit, reluctant to trust you in the posting house."

She looked at him defiantly, determined not to reveal the terror she was feeling. "What is it you fear I might do? Disarm you?"

"You have courage enough, little one, even for that—but I would not advise it. I warn you . . . one sign of defiance and you shall be put to sleep immediately." He allowed her to see the cloth doused with chloroform shoved in the pocket of his greatcoat, and she knew he would not hesitate to use it. "Now, I have arranged for a private sitting room and a small repast for myself and my *sister*. If you will give me your promise to behave, you shall have your dinner."

At her nod, he assisted her from the carriage, across the drive, and into the private room. Her legs were so weak she could barely walk, much less make a bolt for it even had she the chance. D'Orly gave her no opportunity. He kept a strong grip on her arm before making a show of seating her tenderly. Then he stood behind her chair, his hands gripping her shoulders. Not until the serving maid had withdrawn did he take his own seat.

He is mad, she thought, sipping the wine set before her. She ate as slowly as possible, trying desperately to think of some means of escape. Nothing occurred to her, and she wondered if she could reason with him. "Please, let me go. If you truly loved me, or ever cared for me at all, you would heed my wishes. I beg you not to do this."

D'Orly smiled. The girl had never looked more enchanting. Unshed tears made her large eyes glisten, and the red-blond hair fell in disheveled curls around her face. He replied, almost apologetically, "I fear I have no choice. Had your guardian allowed me to court you in a more acceptable manner—"

"It would not have made any difference! Don't you see that it is Lord Gillingham I love?"

"How very unfortunate. And yet, I was led to believe you were not indifferent to me, *n'est-ce pas*?" He rose, coming to stand behind her again, his hand caressing her hair. "You did not eat much, my dear. Finish your peach, and then we shall be on our way."

An ostler tapped at the door politely before poking his head in. "Beggin' your lordship's pardon, but your team's been changed, and they said as 'ow you was wishful to know."

"Come, my dear, our carriage is ready," d'Orly said, pulling her chair back, his hand tightening on her arm. Marietta made as if to rise, and then let her legs buckle beneath her, feigning a faint. The ostler rushed forward to assist her as d'Orly cursed under his breath. He was sure the little vixen was faking, but was forced to maintain the appearance of a concerned brother.

The ostler's shout drew the landlord. Seeing the young lady stretched out on the parlour floor, he yelled for his wife to come. Mrs. Broome, a large, buxom woman with an air of command about her, bustled in and ordered the men to stand back.

"Lord! What a beautiful young lady. Like a princess she looks," she cooed as she knelt beside Marietta, administering a vinaigrette beneath her nose.

The strong aroma was too much for Marietta's self-control. She allowed her eyes to flutter open and turned her head, moaning in her best theatrical manner. Her gaze took in the interested crowd standing around her, and she gave a small, satisfied sigh.

"There, she's coming around," Mrs. Broome declared. "You, Joe, help lift her to the sofa."

The Chevalier moved to shoulder the landlady aside. "Thank you for your help, madam, but I shall take care of my sister now. We have a ship to catch and must leave at once."

Marietta let her head fall back against the ample bosom of the landlady.

"Good God! She's gone off again. Your sister, sir, is in no state to travel—ship or no ship." Ignoring d'Orly's outraged protests, she moved the girl, assisted by her husband and the ostler. There were a number of people standing about, gawking at the beautiful young miss who looked so helpless. D'Orly fumed with impotence. Mrs. Broome recommended the doctor be sent for, and offered to send one of the stable lads.

"It is not necessary, madam. My sister has always suffered from these nervous attacks. If you would just clear the room, she will be better directly."

Marietta judged it time. Opening her eyes, she gave a cry of fright, and clung to Mrs. Broome's arm. "Please, don't leave me with him. He is not my brother! He is trying to kidnap me and force me into marriage with him! Oh, please, don't let him take me."

Mrs. Broome, who was not overly impressed with the Chevalier, turned a steely eye upon him. Her massive bosom heaving, she warned him, "We'll just be seeing about this."

"This is outrageous. My sister is cutting a sham, and I demand you cease this infernal interference in matters which don't concern you, or you shall have cause to regret your impertinence!" d'Orly ranted with a haughty air, snapping his riding crop against his boots. The landlord, having no desire to go against the gentry, looked beseechingly to his wife.

Mrs. Broome was made of sterner stuff. "Whether or no she's your sister, and we'll see about that, she's in no way fit to travel. You best be leaving her here to rest a bit."

"My good woman, I *told* you we have a ship to catch. She may rest in the carriage."

"I fear you are mistaken, d'Orly." Arlington's voice rang out from the back of the room, deadly in its calm, and the crowd parted to let him through. Alexandria followed him in, and seeing Marietta stretched out on the sofa, rushed to her with a sinking heart.

Mrs. Broome, recognizing what she called true quality, nudged her husband. "Now we'll see."

If the Chevalier was surprised by the appearance of the Marquess, he hid it well, drawling insolently, "I see I underestimated you, Arlington. You English have an annoying habit of intruding into my affairs."

"I believe I warned you not to attempt to see my ward," the Marquess said, drawing off his gloves.

"Bah! It is you who will pay for your curst meddling," d'Orly said, his hand clasped on his sword hilt.

Two of the ostlers stepped forward, but Arlington waved them back. "I'll brook no interference. Clear the room. The Chevalier and I will settle this between us."

Alexandria and Marietta watched breathlessly as the tables were pushed aside and both men divested themselves of their coats and boots. Alex knew there was nothing she could say to prevent the duel, but she had to bite down on her gloved finger to keep from crying out.

"*En garde*," d'Orly cried, and steel rang against steel. After the first clash of swords, they circled each other cautiously in the hushed room. Then d'Orly lunged. Arlington countered and delivered a lightning riposte. D'Orly parried the move gracefully, and circled again.

Eyes wide, biting her lip, Alex watched each lunge, wincing as the blades clashed. Marietta hid her head against her sister's shoulder until the sounds of striking metal drew her eyes again. A dozen times Alex closed her own eyes, thinking that first Arlington, and then d'Orly, must be run through. A dozen times she opened her eyes to the sight of the blades clashing furiously.

Unable to bear the suspense, she turned her head away, expecting to hear the thud of a falling body, and praying desperately that it would not be Arlington's. She heard only the clang of metal against metal and an occasional gasp from the men watching. When she found the courage to look again, Arlington seemed to have d'Orly on the ropes. The Frenchman backed towards the open door, relentlessly pressed by the Marquess. D'Orly fell back another pace, parrying in *quarte* as Arlington, with an incredible twist of his wrist, lunged forward. The sleeve was cut from d'Orly's shoulder and a vivid red splash stained his shirt.

Arlington lowered his sword, and d'Orly, with the frightened look of a cornered animal, dropped his own sword and ran for his carriage. A round of applause and cheers went up from the men.

Alex felt too queasy to utter a word and wondered if she was going to faint.

Arlington saw how pale she was, but before he could reach her, a commotion erupted in the courtyard. A moment later, Jeremy and Gillingham appeared in the open doorway, dragging a struggling d'Orly between them.

"Arlington! I thought I recognized your team. We caught this blackguard trying to make good his escape," Gillingham said, shoving d'Orly forward.

"For God's sake, what possessed you to stop him? Let him go at once!"

"What? Have you run daft? Let him go after what he did to Marietta? I'll be damned if I will."

"You will listen to reason, you young hothead—unless, of course, you would prefer to have the tale of this day's work bandied about Town? Marietta's name on everyone's lips as they discuss the latest *on-dit*? No? I thought not. Then I strongly advise you to allow the Chevalier to take his leave. I fancy we shall never again see his face in England."

Arlington had pulled on his boots, and with unruffled calm carefully replaced his coat. He bent a contemptuous look hard on d'Orly. "Bow Street is fast on your heels. I suggest you make your exit at once, or find yourself held on suspicion of murder."

The Chevalier, with an insolent air, retrieved his coat and boots, and with a last look at Marietta, who would not face him, gave a jaunty salute before strolling from the room.

"Well! I never did!" exclaimed Mrs. Broome, apparently the only one to find her tongue, and marched from the room, nearly colliding with Sara Comstock.

Jeremy had adjured her to wait in the carriage, but she had seen d'Orly leave and came now, timidly peeking into the parlour. Seeing Marietta on the sofa, she let out a most unladylike whoop and flew across the room. Confidences and explanations had to be exchanged, and Arlington stepped aside to confer quietly with the landlord, assuring the man he would be recompensed for any damage.

"I wasn't worryin', my lord. Anyone with half an eye could see you was a right one. Even if you was to leave without paying your shot, well I reckon it'd be worth it. It was a fair pleasure to watch you send that Frenchie right about. Never did I see such fancy footwork!"

Arlington managed to stem the flood of praise, remarking he was very sure his party was hungry. The slight hint was enough to set the landlord bustling. The room was rapidly cleared and, in due course, a table set—to the loud approval of both Jeremy and Gillingham.

It was a gleeful group that sat down to dinner, and Mrs. Broome condescended to wait upon them herself, casting an occasional concerned look at Alexandria, who merely picked at her food. Gilly and Jeremy both ate ravenously and were taking turns making boisterous toasts. Their respective brides giggled appreciatively and excitedly talked over their adventures. Arlington watched them tolerantly.

Only Alex was quiet. The truth was she was in a near state of shock, realizing how close Marietta had come to being ruined, if not actually physically harmed. If it were not for Arlington . . . she shuddered, unable to contemplate the thought. Her eyes rested on the Marquess, leaning back in his chair and smiling indulgently at Jeremy.

Alex was aware she owed him an enormous debt, and she blushingly recalled their first meeting when she had chided him for his lack of concern for his wards. How presumptuous she'd been, declaring she had no need of his assistance or advice. Yet, she had turned to him and met only with kindness. He had not uttered even one word of censure, although she had ignored his warning and placed her sister in danger.

She glanced at Marietta sitting safely next to Gillingham, and then back at Arlington. He looked so calm, and yet only a short time before he had risked his life. A shiver shook her slender body as she thought of d'Orly's rage and the savage way he had attacked Arlington. She could not have borne it if anything had happened to the Marquess. Any doubts she'd harboured were cast aside. She loved this arrogant, haughty, egotistical, and proud man. She loved the other side of him, too. The amusing, thoughtful, kind, and considerate Arlington, who cared about others in spite of himself.

Gillingham, who saw the way she gazed at Arlington, leaned forward and spoke quietly in his ear. "Don't you think it's time you put your luck to the touch? We could make it a triple wedding."

"If she would have me! I cannot be certain she even likes me above half," Arlington retorted, his eyes drawn to Alex.

"Like you? Are you blind, then? Why, you are her knight-errant. A veritable hero."

"It may be beyond your comprehension, Gillingham, but I would not have the lady's hand out of mere gratitude." He spoke at his haughtiest, and the discussion was clearly closed to further argument. Gillingham could not believe how obtuse Phillip could be, but then he did not know that Arlington was quietly fingering the ring in his pocket. The ring he'd been carrying about with him since his return to London. During his recent absence, he had visited his country seat and removed the diamond and emerald ring from the strongbox. It once belonged to his mother, and he had taken it with him, toying even then with the idea of presenting it to Alexandria.

He looked at her again, sitting composed, content to watch her sister as Marietta regaled them with the horrors she had endured, lavishly embellishing her tale with every detail she could conjure up. There were still signs of strain about Alex's fine eyes, and he realized she must be exhausted. The Marquess called a halt to the festivities, reminding them they must speed back to London before a hue and cry was raised.

It took a little time to settle their shot, with both Jeremy and Alexandria protesting as the Marquess paid. She told him, with a trace of her old spirit, "We are already too much beholden to you, my lord. There is no reason for you to assume this added expense."

He ignored her, pressing a roll of the ready on Mr. Broome, and finally assuring her he would settle the reckoning with Jeremy. She was left with nothing to say, and allowed him to shepherd her out to his waiting phaeton.

Jeremy took Sara up with him, and Gillingham tenderly handed Marietta into his own curricle. With the resilient spirits of youth, Jeremy tossed a wager to Gilly, and the curricles moved off in a wild race to London.

Arlington watched them leave with a chuckle. "I sincerely hope we have not gone to all this trouble to rescue your sister only to have that young fool overturn her."

Alex, aware of the dusk settling about them and the closeness of the Marquess beside her, did not seem to hear. She was still dwelling on the debt she owed him, and made another attempt to thank him. "I can never repay you for all you have done for us. If it were not for you, I don't know what would have happened to Marietta."

"Nonsense! Don't talk fustian. Marietta is an enterprising minx and she would have come about. I understand she already had Mrs. Broome defending her when we arrived, and I'd not wager a groat against d'Orly overcoming that lady!"

Alex smiled slightly. "But it need never have come to that if I had only heeded your warning."

"Then in the future, I suggest you listen to me." He brought his team to a slow trot, and then to a complete stop before turning to her. "Now, I have a piece of advice for you. This notion of living with your aunt in a cottage would not suit you at all. I suggest instead a delightful house in Somerset, not twelve miles from Bath. I think it would meet with your approval."

"Are you describing Arlington Park? Your country seat? I certainly could not impose on you to that extent!"

"Listen to me, my dear. You promised to, you know," he said, gently lifting her chin up and looking into her eyes. "It would not be an imposition, Alexandria . . . not if you would consider marrying me." The words were spoken quietly, and she could not know his heart was in his mouth.

Her green eyes turned to silvery gray in the dusky light, and she seemed to be considering his words.

"I'm making a mull of this and deserve you never speak

to me again. The thing is, I'm not in the habit of proposing . . ."

"I should think you'd be very good at making pretty
speeches, if half the rumours I have heard are true," she
said softly, lowering her eyes.

"That's another matter entirely. Words come easily when
one's heart is not engaged. When your entire future is in the
hands of the one woman you have discovered you cannot
bear to live without, it's not so easy . . . but if you want
a pretty speech, I will try."

He took both her hands in his and waited patiently until
she looked up again. He leaned towards her, lightly kissing
her lips.

"Arlington! What are you doing? Have you forgotten
we're on the London road? Suppose someone drives by?"

"Will I never convince you to call me Phillip?" he teased
before kissing her more passionately. The warm response of
her lips encouraged him, and he drew back slightly. "I love
you, Alexandria, more than I ever thought possible," he
murmured, gazing into her eyes. They were a soft green
now, full of warmth, and he raised one hand to caress her
cheek. "I do beg you to do one thing for me . . ."

"Yes, Phillip?"

"Remove that cursed bonnet so I may kiss you properly."
He helped her undo the strings and let his hands stray
through her curls. It was some time before he remembered
the ring in his pocket and withdrew it, placing it reverently
on her finger. "It was my mother's. One of the reasons I left
London was to stop at Arlington Park and remove it from
storage. It's lain there for years, waiting for you."

"You were sure even then?" she asked huskily, gazing at
the ring.

"Not entirely, no, but I think I knew the first time I saw
you. There I was, expecting a dried-up old spinster and you
walked into the room. Red hair and emerald eyes are a
deadly combination, my dear." He proved it, kissing her
again.

"Phillip," she managed to gasp, "I hear a carriage."

He glanced down the road briefly. "It's only the mail coach. Pay it no mind," he advised, kissing her eyes.

"I did promise to follow your advice . . ." she whispered, giving herself up to his delightful embrace. It's doubtful that either of them heard the coach rumbling past or the lusty cheers of the men riding on top.

It would be a triple wedding after all.

From the *New York Times* bestselling author
of Forgiving and Bygones

LaVyrle Spencer

One of today's best-loved authors of bittersweet
human drama and captivating romance.

___	THE ENDEARMENT	0-515-10396-9/$5.99
___	SPRING FANCY	0-515-10122-2/$5.99
___	YEARS	0-515-08489-1/$5.99
___	SEPARATE BEDS	0-515-09037-9/$5.99
___	HUMMINGBIRD	0-515-09160-X/$5.50
___	A HEART SPEAKS	0-515-09039-5/$5.99
___	THE GAMBLE	0-515-08901-X/$5.99
___	VOWS	0-515-09477-3/$5.99
___	THE HELLION	0-515-09951-1/$5.99
___	TWICE LOVED	0-515-09065-4/$5.99
___	MORNING GLORY	0-515-10263-6/$5.99
___	BITTER SWEET	0-515-10521-X/$5.99
___	FORGIVING	0-515-10803-0/$5.99